SYLYTH

The Argentia Dasani Adventures

The Shadow Gate Trilogy
Lady Dasani's Debt
The Gathering
The Dragonfire Destiny

The Reaches of Vengeance Duology
The Crown of the Revenant King
The Guildmaster's Gauntlet

The Tokens of Power Trilogy
Mouradian
Sylyth
*Bazu**

---

* Forthcoming

SYLYTH

An Argentia Dasani Adventure

C. JUSTIN ROMANO

SYLYTH
AN ARGENTIA DASANI ADVENTURE

iUniverse books may be ordered through booksellers or by contacting:

iUniverse
1663 Liberty Drive
Bloomington, IN 47403
www.iuniverse.com
1-800-Authors (1-800-288-4677)

ISBN: 978-1-5320-7811-8 (sc)
ISBN: 978-1-5320-7813-2 (hc)
ISBN: 978-1-5320-7812-5 (e)

Library of Congress Control Number: 2019909495

Print information available on the last page.

iUniverse rev. date: 08/30/2019

For Solace — this tale to call your own...

Acknowledgements

My thanks to all the usual suspects: the iUniverse team & Zach Turner for their publishing and creative magic; my family for their constant encouragement; and everyone who's followed Argentia thus far. Whether by campfire or digibook, stories are made to be shared. Enjoy this latest installment…

Prologue

The burned woman stood before the sea.

Though the air was bitter with late winter upon the coast of Teranor, she wore no cloak against the elements. The wind blew cold through her coarse sailor's shirt and sailcloth pants, molding the loose-fitting garments to the tall, slender form they covered, flying the black scarves that masked her horrific face out behind her like shadowy banners.

The burned woman did not feel this wind any more than she felt the chill splash of surf as it frothed over her bare feet, sinking them into clammy sand, scraping them with chips of shells dragged in with the tide. Her eyes—an icy cobalt that was strikingly incongruous with the dark wraps covering her face—stared unblinkingly out at the sea.

The tracks she had made coming from docks of Harrowgate to this stretch of beach south of the port were smoothed and filled by the scouring wind before she finally took her gaze from the water. The beach was mostly deserted: a few fishermen with their poles jammed into the sand and their lines stretched hopefully into the waves; a few hollow men digging for clams; a mongrel wandering aimlessly, barking at the gulls that swooped to peck and torment it.

I had a dog.... That pang of her past almost brought her to tears. Shadow was lost to her. *Like everything else....*

The falling sun turned the sea into shimmering flames, searing her with memories. The crash of the waves on the shore was mocking laughter: *Who are you now? What are you now?*

She had no answer; the glass of her reflection was distorted. No longer did she see the beautiful, red-haired form that she had owned for thirty-two winters. That body was mostly gone, burned by dragonfire beyond the grace of any magic known to wizards or clerics to heal. Her existence had become a nightmarish torment from which there was no waking, no escape except death.

She had tried to accept her fate. Tried to rationalize what had happened in terms of survival. She should be glad simply to be alive after what she had faced. But she could not hold to that. Could not look at this charred and monstrous shape and see herself in aught but its eyes, and in those there was only anguish: a hurt so deep that it had led her to flee the very friends who had risked so much to rescue her. To hide away in wretched alleys behind wretched buildings, her hours passed in gloom and grime and misery. To come every evening to this place and hear the call of the sea—once her greatest solace—beckon her to oblivion.

For the first time in her life she was broken in spirit. Lost in a starless night through which she could find no hope to light her way.

She reached up, closing her hand around the mithryl dragon's tooth that hung from a chain about her neck. *Please, help me....*

But the token remained dark.

PART I

Dark Desires

Pandaros Krite waited for the girl to follow him into the alley so he could take her.

The apprentice magus shivered; it was much colder in this dim space alongside the Laughing Tortoise than it had been inside the crowded tavern. He should have worn a cloak, but he had left in haste. The fool knight would be home tomorrow. Pandaros intended to be long gone with his prize before the sun rose on Artelo Sterling's return.

To do that, he had to have the girl. Without her, Sylyth would remain but a shadow. Without Sylyth, all was lost.

So Pandaros waited in the alley, shuffling his feet on the dirty crust of last night's snow, muttering out plumes of frosty breath. Minutes passed. It was too long. Something was wrong. She should have been here by now. She—

—stepped around the corner, turning her head from side to side like a wary animal that senses it is about to step into a trap yet is compelled by the bait to go forward.

This bait was magic, and its lure was potent.

What am I doing? Nema Drianni wondered. She had seen Pandaros Krite in Thackery from time to time over the past few months, but he scarcely merited attention. The fine, almost effete lines of his pale face beneath his silky tumble of black hair had always seemed plain, even weak-looking to her: not the rugged, hirsute woodsman looks she favored. She was not drunk—not *that* drunk, at least—so why was she out here in the cold and dark, eager to take him to her bed?

She stopped walking, confused. Before she could change her mind completely the medallion hanging over Pandaros' chest—a rune-etched golden circle surrounding an iron eye—began to glow. "Come closer," Pandaros commanded.

Nema obeyed without hesitation. She took Pandaros' extended hand. The world collapsed in a flash of gilded light.

⁓⊰┼┼┼⊱⁓

Nema sat up in the snow bank, shocked back to her senses by icy wetness. She scrambled to her feet but a wave of vertigo dropped her to her knees again. She gasped at the bitter cold on her bare legs. It was so dark: darker than it ever was in Thackery, where lamps burned the night through on their posts along the central street. Huge, humped shadows rose up to her left, blacker than their surroundings, threatening the starlit sky. She had no idea where she was, only that the village was nowhere in sight.

For the first time, Nema felt the terrifying immensity of the night. She hitched in a breath to scream.

"Calmly," Pandaros chuckled. The scream died in Nema's throat.

Recovered from the momentary daze of walking the aether, Pandaros straightened and stepped toward Nema. He heard the rustle of his robes as he moved. It was a sound that never failed to thrill him with a sense of power.

Since being cast from the service of Promitius of Valon, Pandaros had worn the habit of his art all too infrequently. It was not easy to tend sheep in a wizard's robes.

Spreading his arms like the wings of some great grackle, Pandaros closed his eyes and summoned the magic, murmuring the words Sylyth

2

had taught him. The medallion on his chest began to glow again, its golden light bathing Nema as she cringed in the snow.

Moments later, the medallion's garish glare faded to a more subdued glimmer. Pandaros raised Nema to her feet. She stepped close, running her palm down his chest, her eyes full of hot desire as she leaned in to kiss him. Pandaros shook his head. "Not here. Come on." With his free hand, he conjured a luminous globe to lead them up the hillside. Above, the cottage slept in darkness. The barn waited in shadow.

Trudging along as quickly as the snow would allow, Pandaros reflected that he hated this place. He had come here six months ago, seeking another waystation on his flight from Promitius. His plan had been to get as far as possible from Valon in case Promitius did link him to the theft of the medallion (though he feared that if Promitius was determined to find him, no place in Teranor was truly far enough or safe enough). Over weeks of almost ceaseless travel, he had come nearly a thousand leagues westward from the coastal city. He was exhausted, but he had never intended to stay in this pathetic shepherd's hovel more than a day or two.

Until he had seen Brittyn.

How clearly he remembered that summer night, as he made his way hopefully up this hill and saw her holding the gate as her six sheep filed into their pen. He had been so struck by her beauty that he was barely able to utter his plea for room and board. He could sense Fortune smiling upon him at last, as if all his travails after leaving Promitius had been designed to bring him to this place and this girl.

The moment was dispelled when a man emerged from the barn, wiping his brow with a rag held in his one remaining hand. Brittyn had hurried over to her husband, and even as he devoured the glimpses of her tanned legs beneath the flare of her skirt, Pandaros felt the first hatred for Artelo Sterling rise like bile in his throat.

Still, he managed to swallow his envy enough to make his manners to the couple and was rewarded with the invitation he had hoped for. After the meal, while Brittyn bathed Aura (whom the apprentice found instantly annoying), Pandaros confessed to Artelo that he had a small problem.

He was traveling to Byrtnoth, he said—making certain Brittyn was in earshot—on the highest recommendation of his master to study the deepest secrets of the aether with the wizards of the Stelspire. He was not expected until after Yuletide and had taken the months at his disposal to see something of the crowndom. But he was running short of coin and the cities were not kind to young, itinerant wizards. Unless you had a shop and a shingle, people thought you were a fraud. If they wouldn't mind, could he possibly help them out around the farm—he would take whatever they could pay him—at least through the harvest?

Artelo, who had been thinking of hiring some day labor from Thackery, agreed to a trial week. Pandaros worked harder in that seven-day than he had in many winters, performing tasks of physical labor strange and odious to his bookish nature. Every night he would drop into exhausted slumber in the hay-stinking loft of the horse-stinking barn and dream of Brittyn.

In those dreams the seeds of the present darkness were planted.

2

"Now what in Aeton's good name's he want foolin with *that* slutty bit?" Brittyn Sterling muttered.

The shepherdess was standing by the window of her cottage, watching through the partly opened shutters as Pandaros led Nema Drianni across the yard toward the barn. She had awakened from a thin, uneasy sleep in the twisted sheets of a bed that felt too large and empty without Artelo, uncertain if the noise she believed she had heard had been a cry in the night or her own scream of denial in a dream that her husband had abandoned her to return to his first love.

Sitting up in bed, she ran a hand through her thick blonde hair, brushing it out of her face. *Aura?* She wondered if her daughter had called for her, but the cottage was quiet and dark. Still, she would check.

As she rose, her bare feet touching the cold wooden floor of her bedchamber, she saw the light outside. *What?* An instant's confusion ended with her heart leaping up. *Artelo!*

She rushed through the cottage, almost bursting outside in her haste and eagerness to see her husband safely returned to her. At the last moment, some instinct checked her. She was a woman alone in the night in a place which, while far from an ungoverned wilderness, was not always safe.

Instead of the door, she went to the window. Drawing the curtains apart, she unfastened the shutter and cracked it open. The night air's chill rushed in, biting her fully awake.

The light was coming up the hillside. She could barely breathe. Anticipation vied with fear: was this Artelo returning or some danger come upon her and her daughter? She had been threatened in her home once before, by Gasten Crond and his thugs. Crond was gone, but the others still lived in Thackery. What if they had learned Artelo was away and had come back to finish what he had stopped them from doing on that fateful day three years earlier?

I'll fight them. I won't let them hurt Aura.... Brittyn waited. The light grew. The fear grew. The poker was across the room, propped beside the hearth. If she saw trouble coming, she could reach it before anyone could get to the cottage.

The light crested the terrace where Brittyn's father had built their cottage, barn, and sheep pens. Brittyn gasped to see the glow came from no torch, but a floating ball of luminescence. *Pandaros!* She recognized him in the wizard-light. Though her hope that it was Artelo was dashed, she felt a queasy relief that it was not a gang of bandits like the Crimson Palm or goblins marauding down from the not-so-distant Gelidian Spur. *What's he doing?*

Then she saw the other figure and understood exactly what Pandaros was doing.

In their maiden days, Brittyn and Nema Drianni had thrown hisses at each other over several of Thackery's eligible men. Time and wedlock had done little to dull Brittyn's dislike of the seamstress. On many a trip to the village she had seen the pig-lust in Nema's gaze when it fell on Artelo, and more than once she had thought to march up and beat the whorish smile right off Nema's face.

Brittyn was certain Pandaros did not know the reputation of the woman he had brought back or the trouble he was opening himself to. Part of her wanted to run outside and expose his folly before it was too late. Another part, a part with a stronger voice, told her she should be glad that Pandaros had found someone—even Nema Drianni—to occupy an eye that for six months had too oft been fixed on her.

At first, Brittyn had paid these attentions little mind. She was pretty, she knew, and she had been the object of ogling since her figure began to round itself toward womanhood. "Boys'll be boys," her father had told her, tousling her golden curls with his rough hand, and though Derwin Mayfair would have taken his cudgel to any boy who did more than just glance at his daughter, his good-natured dismissal of their behavior had shaped Brittyn's own view that by and large such looks were harmless.

The leers she could handle. It was the dreams that disturbed her.

How many times had she started from sleep, her mind confused, her body sweaty with the residue of a vision in which Pandaros had done things to her that she had never done with Artelo. Dirty things. Things that she had never even imagined...yet she had done them willingly, even eagerly in those dreams, and she had enjoyed them. Craved them.

The dreams confused Brittyn. With her confusion came guilt. She loved Artelo. She was happy with him in every way. Why then did she dream of Pandaros, who (and in this she agreed with Nema Drianni) was hardly the type of man she found attractive? What did it mean? What was wrong with her?

She did not know, so she tried to think on those dreams as little as possible. Still, sometimes, as she worked about the house or in the yard, Pandaros' dream-voice would flash wickedly across her mind and she would flush with a shocking but undeniable heat.

Those occasions were rare, however, and rarer still were the times (only vaguely remembered) she had actually risen from her bed, half-asleep, drawn to fulfill those dark desires. Fortune had protected her each time—she would bark her shin on the bed, Aura would stir and wake, an owl would split the night with its hooting chide—and she had never made it from her cottage to the barn.

She had never mentioned any of this to Artelo. Though she was unschooled, Brittyn was no fool. She knew some things in a marriage were best left unsaid.

Besides, Pandaros was a great help to Artelo, allowing him more time to be with her and with Aura. *Aye,* Brittyn thought bitterly. *If he were here at all....*

Six weeks earlier, Artelo—despite his renunciation of his knighthood in favor of a simple life with Brittyn—had left to answer the call of the Crown in her need. His departure had awakened Brittyn's deepest dread, provoking a moon and more of poorly slept nights and fretful days. Whatever questionable fantasies her subconscious might be indulging about Pandaros, Brittyn knew Artelo and Solsta Ly'Ancoeur had a history together that was very much too real for her liking.

He'll come back. Ye know it. He'll be true. He's gone t' do a good thing, and gone t' do it with your own blessing so don't begrudge him....

That was so. When Ralak the Red, Archamagus of Teranor, had arrived with a summons to help rescue Argentia Dasani, Artelo had turned the wizard aside with a flat refusal. It had been at Brittyn's bidding that he had gone, for she knew he was denying his impulse to aid his friend only to appease her and she could not hold him so.

But as the weeks passed without his return, her dread that she would lose him to some senseless death in the name of honor and duty—or worse, to the lure of the Crown (whom she had never met, yet who lingered in her nightmares as some seductive demoness)—increased. Instead of dreams of Pandaros Krite, Brittyn dreamed of Artelo and Solsta.

"Stop it," she murmured. "He's not even with her. He's looking for Argentia." That knowledge did not make her miss Artelo any less, however, and she felt a pang of loneliness as she watched Pandaros and Nema and the globe of light disappear into the barn.

Brittyn sighed. Her excited hope that Artelo was returning and her quick fear that bandits or raiders had targeted the cottage had both subsided. She stifled a yawn as she reached to pull the shutter closed again. Perhaps in the morning she would give Pandaros a bit of advice about Nema Drianni and—

Footsteps behind her.

3

Brittyn gasped and turned sharply.

"Mama?" Aurora Sterling said.

"Oh, pumpkin! Ye shouldn't be awake now." Brittyn hurried over and scooped her daughter up. It was like hugging a miniature version of herself: golden curls, dove-gray eyes, round face, dimpled cheeks, and a sparkling smile. Artelo often joked that he had contributed nothing at all to their daughter and he was glad of it.

Brittyn carried Aura away from the window, inhaling her powder-clean scent. She loved her so much that sometimes she would just look at her while she was playing in the yard or sitting at the table or sleeping in her small bed and almost choke with tears of joy.

"Dark time, Mama," Aura said.

"Mama knows, sweet. Come on. Back to sleep." She laid Aura down in her low bed, the down-filled mattress still warm from the impression of her body, and pulled the covers up over her.

"Was sleep...." Aura yawned. Her eyes were already slipping closed again.

Brittyn sat beside her on the edge of the bed and stroked her soft hair. "Sleep, pumpkin," she whispered. Then, in a gentle voice, she began to sing.

Hush-a-bye, my little one,
Day is done and night has come.
Don't ye cry, close your eyes
And dream of all nice sweet things.
When ye wake, 'twill be day,
And ye can play 'til day is done.
Night arrives, and seraphs come,
So hush-a-bye, my precious love.
Don't be scared, for I am here,
And I will always care for ye,
'Cause my babe I love ye so -
Now hush-a-bye, my little one,
My little one....

When Brittyn had cooed the last words of the lullaby, which she had learned from her mother and now had passed to her daughter in a chain of song that might outlast time, she rose carefully and slipped through the moonlit shadows of the cottage back to her own bed. *Nema and Pandaros*, she thought, chuckling as she settled onto her pillow. *Wait 'til I tell Artelo....*

The loft was an occult nightmare.

In the six months he had made his home here, Pandaros had clandestinely acquired the things he required to work his art. Some were commonplace items: black candles and cloths, plates and pestles, iron chains, bowls and cups, knives and spoons. Others were rarer species: phials and philters of strange powders, scrolls and books, censers that burned exotic incense, skulls, rune stones, and glyph etchers. Some had come from Devlin, the doddering old fool of an apothecary in Thackery. A few he had brought in his pack. Most he had purchased on a series of secret trips to Hamlyn, the next village down the North Pass and the farthest reach of his ability to walk the aether. Duralyn was just three days to the east, a much shorter aetherwalk, but the Ralak the Red dwelt there and Pandaros feared to go anywhere near the Crown City lest the Archamagus should somehow sense the medallion of summoning that had once belonged to Promitius of Valon.

He feared no discovery by Brittyn or Artelo. They knew he was a wizard already and had no idea what things were and were not appropriate to his art, so the array of arcana was revealed and ready when Nema mounted to the loft.

She froze at the strange sight. "What—"

Pandaros, coming quickly up the ladder behind Nema, shoved her onto the blanket-covered hay bales that served as his bed. He raised the medallion over her again, bathing her in its sinister light.

Nema moaned. "Shut up, you silly bitch," Pandaros snapped.

"But I need it...." Nema hoisted up her skirt and began to stroke herself furiously. Pandaros watched this display for a moment, amazed by the power of the medallion, which had wrested Nema utterly from her senses. He closed his hand about the token, feeling the throbbing heat in its golden round. Sylyth had instructed him in the spell and how to use the medallion to channel it. If Nema's response was any indication, once Sylyth was incarnate and her full strength returned to her, Pandaros could not fail to claim Brittyn Sterling for his own.

Almost since he had first laid eyes on Brittyn, the apprentice had tried to win over the shepherdess. For a while it had been important to him that she came of her own volition, acknowledging him as the superior choice to her doltish husband. When she did not invite him to her bed, he tried to seduce her with his magic, invading her dreams, plying her with rapturous fantasies. But his craft was imperfect (though he would never acknowledge this) and it faltered against the simple, pure flame of Brittyn's love for Artelo.

Pandaros had entertained many bloody fantasies of killing Artelo, but cowardice and pragmatism prevented him from trying. His aethereal mastery did not extend to spells of attack powerful enough to kill. Even if he stunned Artelo, he feared he would not be quick or strong enough to finish him with a knife or a club.

Fortunately, he had other weapons at his disposal: powers a simple shepherd like Artelo could not even conceive of. A tragic accident on the road to Thackery or in the grove of trees crowning the hill above the cottage where they went to chop wood would do—or so Pandaros had thought.

He waited for the perfect opportunity.

The Archamagus of Teranor arrived first.

When Ralak the Red paid his call to the Sterlings, Pandaros had been down at the well drawing water for their luncheon. He missed the entire encounter other than the flash of aetherlight that marked the exit of the Archamagus. When he found out about their visitor he nearly panicked, certain Ralak had come for him and the stolen medallion.

Though that proved to be untrue, the near disaster reminded Pandaros just how vulnerable he was. It also reminded him of the medallion, which he had not used since stuffing it into his pack. Now he wondered if it could serve him in his need to have Brittyn.

The medallion was a token of power that would it open a window into the aether and draw the thing the wizard wished to address to it like iron filings to a lodestone. Promitius used it to summon shades and query them for knowledge beyond the ken of mortals. Pandaros was usually permitted to assist his Master at these summonings, except when one particular scroll was used. On those days, Promitius would enter the conjuring chamber alone and emerge hours later looking very pale and exhausted.

Once, curious about what might have weakened so powerful a wizard, Pandaros had opened the chest where the summoning scrolls and medallion were kept. He found the scroll he sought but before he had time to do more than glance at the arcane words written thereon, Promitius had clamped a hand on his shoulder. "Your curiosity will be your undoing, boy," the wizard said. His brown eyes gleamed. "Heed me."

"Yes, Master," Pandaros said. He hastily furled the scroll and replaced it in the chest, but not before two words scrawled in the margin by Promitius burned themselves upon his mind: *Sylyth — Powerful....*

When his ineptitude ultimately led to his banishment from his apprenticeship, Pandaros stole the things he could lay hands to that he believed would be most painful for his former master to lose. Chief among those items were the medallion of summoning and the scroll. Though he had not taken them for any purpose other than spite, he decided now that he would use the medallion's magic just as Promitius had. The dead saw far; compelled by the medallion, the shade would tell him of secret things in Brittyn's heart that he might use to strengthen the wooing hold of his spells over her. He would make her forget Artelo and her child. Then he would take her and flee this place, settling in some city where she could serve him as he continued toward his destiny of becoming the next Archamagus.

So he had inscribed his pentagram in goat's blood upon the floor of the loft and called upon the power of the medallion.

What he summoned was no shade.

5

"Sylyth!"

Pandaros knelt in the pentagram. The glyphs and symbols had long since dried to a maroon so deep it was nearly black in the light of the many candles. Not by nature cautious, Pandaros was also not stupid. He had set the candles on plates and had swept away as much of the scattered hay from the vicinity as he could.

For a similar reason, he had been spying on the Gap Road every night since Artelo's departure.

Ralak's business, it turned out, had not been with Pandaros at all. Artelo Sterling was apparently no village bumpkin, but a former knight of the Crown whom Ralak had come to summon back into service. With the knight off on some mad quest to save an old friend, Pandaros had one less barrier between him and Brittyn.

The question was how long Artelo would remain gone.

When Pandaros had first summoned Sylyth, she had told him more than he had dared to hope. The way to his every desire was open and clear before him. There were certain requisites, but those could be accomplished. He only needed time.

So as not to be caught unawares by Artelo's return, Pandaros set a watch. The road from Duralyn to the Gap Outpost went past the

Sterling's cottage. It was, in fact, the only road that went past, which suited Pandaros well. It meant he had only one place to scrye.

Working in secret, Pandaros gathered the items Sylyth told him he would need. Some were easily had, others more difficult to come by, but eventually he secured them all. He was ready for the dark of the moon, which Sylyth said was most fortuitous time for the casting.

He counted the days.

Ran out of time.

Night after night, the scrying sphere had showed nothing but the woods and the Gap Road. Pandaros fervently hoped the view would never change; that Artelo would be cut down by whatever foes he was fighting. The more time that passed, the more possible that outcome seemed to be.

This evening, that illusion had been shattered.

The mists in the oculyr cleared to reveal a solitary campfire with a horse Pandaros did not recognize and a man he surely did. The camp was a day away. If Artelo rode the distance hard, as he no doubt would, he would arrive tomorrow.

Stunned disbelief was followed by frantic preparation. Pandaros could wait no longer, no matter what Sylyth said.

Dark of the moon or not, he had to take Brittyn tonight.

After arranging Nema, Pandaros checked the pentagram one last time. Shades were no physical danger to the conjuror but they could possess minds unprotected by the warding of the pentagram.

Even so, Pandaros did not doubt that he was master of this situation. Just the thought of what he had accomplished in this last month—summoning a shade and bending it to his will—sent a thrill through him. *Cast me away, would you, Promitius? You were jealous. Afraid of what I would become....* "You were right to fear, old man," Pandaros whispered. "You called me too rash to wield power, but you have no idea what real power is. It is mine, and tonight I will use it to claim what I deserve!"

Thrusting his hand forward, Pandaros summoned the medallion's magic and opened a swirling window into the aether. He spoke Sylyth's name. The candles around the pentagram dimmed suddenly. The medallion around his neck grew hotter.

"*Al t'Ei!* Sylyth, *al t'Ei!*" Pandaros commanded, rolling the last syllables of the spell with authority off his tongue, gesturing violently at the swirling gate.

Thunder rolled in the Fel Pits.

The succubus came unto Acrevast.

6

Sylyth appeared as she had always appeared to Pandaros: a lushly curved woman's shape wreathed in flickering shadow.

The apprentice wondered what she must have looked like in life to own so splendid a shade after her death. Sometimes he thought he could see some other shape within the shadows—a darker thing of swarming tentacles—but that was surely a trick of the guttering light or the swirling glare of the aether.

"Say she is mine!" Sylyth hissed.

"I did not bid you to speak, shade," Pandaros snapped back. The greed in Sylyth's voice was a thing new and frightening. *Control her. She can't harm you as long as you control her....* "Remember who is master here."

Below the loft, the carthorse whinnied and tramped in its stall, as it had done each time Pandaros had summoned Sylyth, maddened by what it sensed had entered the barn.

"I must have her," Sylyth whined, switching tactics with seamless fluidity. Even as she played the slave, the dark pits of her eyes—charcoal smears in a face that showed only rudimentary, shimmering features— grew for an instant more dangerously black than a storm over the Hills of Dusk. "I must, or I cannot help you." She bent her arms toward him in supplication.

Unwitting thrall that he was, Pandaros never stopped to think why all this was necessary any more than he pondered his vague suspicions about Sylyth's shape or why she had been able to come through the aethereal window when none of the shades he had seen Promitius summon had done more than hover on the far side of the rift in reality.

He never had a chance to.

Deep in cunning, the succubus had read the apprentice like an open tome. She worked her will upon him in their first encounter. With subtle manipulation, she tricked Pandaros into serving her own needs by making them seem requisites of her fulfilling his own desires. His mind clouded, he had never questioned anything—even the price she named for her services.

Sylyth demanded a host.

Pandaros had brought Nema Drianni.

"Take her," he said, lifting a magnanimous hand.

Sylyth flew to the hay-bale bed.

Nema's arms were stretched above her head, bound to the wall by shackles clamped to her wrists. This was some sort of bondage game, and not the first she had been involved in. So while it might have been surprising when Pandaros pulled her hands up from their unfinished business between her legs to clap them in chains, it was not really frightening. All Nema felt as she lay on the uncomfortable bed, hay poking and scratching at her through the grimy blanket, was impatience.

Her body was burning with carnal need. She did not understand why Pandaros kept delaying—she had begged him to take her so many times—but she was sure that the moment he did touch her she would climax uncontrollably. *Maybe sooner*, she thought, wriggling her bare bottom against the chafing blanket, reveling in the delicious friction. *If he doesn't hurry....*

But Pandaros showed no inclination to hurry. If she turned her head, Nema could see him, still kneeling on the floor, reading off a parchment. There were black candles all around him and they were flickering madly, as if caught in some storm wind that Nema could not feel.

Suddenly the whole loft darkened. Nema heard Pandaros speaking loudly. Smoke swirled before him: it appeared to have the shape of a woman in one instant, and in the next, of some horrific thing that was unspeakably inhuman.

What? Nema began to struggle against the chains. Suddenly she was sure something was very wrong—

The smoke-thing was above her.

Then it was atop her.

Nema jerked and gasped, inhaling the hot, syrupy sweetness of its rapturous scent as the smoke slid down her body, pouring itself fully between her legs. "Uhhhhhh!" she grunted, the climax she had anticipated blasting through her, making her feet beat a senseless tattoo on the hay. In all her many encounters she had never felt anything like that before, but oh she wanted it to happen again—and best of all, it was going to. She could feel the smoke driving deeper still, gorging itself on her flesh, invading every fiber of her trembling body, lifting her toward delirious heights of wanton, unimagined release.

Please.... It was coming. Surging. Rushing like an avalanche: almost terrifying in its inexorable force. *Oh Aeton yes!* She could not stand this pleasure. Screamed out—

—in agony.

Pandaros almost jerked to his feet as Nema's moan turned into a howl. Cold sweat burst on his brow. Everything human in him rebelled against what he was seeing on the bed.

But he did nothing.

Nema screamed again, her back arching. Pandaros could see the long muscles in her thighs shivering like the strings of a harp. Her eyes had rolled back, but instead of white cornea, he saw smoky darkness. Her mouth fell open, bloody spittle spraying as her head whipped back and forth.

Stop it! You have to stop it! a voice in Pandaros' mind cried out.

Still he did nothing.

Then the true horror began.

Nema's body rattled like a lone leaf clinging to its branch against an autumn storm. Blood ruptured from her eyes and ears, spewed from her mouth, flooded from her crotch, sprayed from her very pores in a red cloud, spattering Pandaros' face like hot rain.

He fell forward, throwing up his shaking hands if to ward off a gorgon. He knew Sylyth had demanded a host, but he had never imagined this. He heard the snapping of bones and the mangled, ripping noise: a visceral, savage rending of flesh much such as when Artelo had gutted the carcass of a sheep.

Below, the carthorse battered its hooves against the door of its confinement. Wood splintered, and with a crash the berserk animal burst free and fled the barn.

Silence filled the loft.

No. Not quite silence. There was a single sound that Pandaros finally recognized as coming from himself: a haggard gasping as he fought to keep from vomiting.

And then, a voice.

"Yesssssssss...."

Slowly, Pandaros raised his head, compelled to see despite his terror.

The loft looked as if a mad artist had flung buckets of crimson paint in a fury at everything he could reach. On the blood-blanketed hay bed, Nema's broken legs were thrust impossibly wide. Between them was a great, gaping wound from vagina to sternum where she had been split apart in some monstrous birthing. Pandaros could see the jags of her shattered ribs poking like atolls through the sea of ruined flesh. A loop of her entrails had slipped free. It was grayish and serpentine; for some strange reason (perhaps so he would be spared looking on the death-mask of Nema's face) it held Pandaros' attention until another form interposed itself between him and the massacred girl.

It was a woman's shape, naked and slick with blood and black fluid that clung to its limbs and torso and dripped from its head in a caul. It reached a hand up—Pandaros saw that its fingers were tipped with talons—and peeled the clinging slime away. Eyes that were really just black pits burned down at the apprentice from a face that was startlingly like that of Nema Drianni.

"What are you?" Pandaros whispered.

"Yours," Sylyth said. "Command me."

8

The succubus entered the cottage.

It was dark, which pleased Sylyth very much. She found the black of the night rapturous. The cold air, clean of the fumes and blistering smoke of her infernal home, was so unlike anything she had known that the very act of breathing was an intoxication. But the pinpricks of diamond light scarring the velvet sky burned hatefully at her eyes, and the pale silver of the moon glaring off the crust of white earth was more of a torment than the frigid ground that yielded beneath the hot press of her bare feet.

Inside—the simple latch on the door had fallen to her will when she took hold of the handle—there was relief from this bright pain. Sylyth moved silently through the cottage. Her eyes, accustomed to the perpetual gloom of the Fel Pits, could see quite well in this darkness. She did not stumble on the woven rug or bump against the chair beside the table as she prowled through the cottage, smooth and silent and lethal as a shadow cat.

The apprentice craved the woman who dwelt in this hovel. Even though his lust had made him easy prey for Sylyth's devices, the succubus was still bound to the magic of the medallion that had drawn her into this world. If she was to escape those chains she needed to complete her bargain.

What she required was in the room beyond this one. Sylyth moved toward that threshold. Stopped. There was something else here. Something she could scarcely believe.

The succubus crouched above the small, low bed where the child slept. *Bhael-ur is with me,* she thought. A child was the key to all her plans. Here was one ripe to be claimed.

She reached forward and caressed the child's soft curls, her talons leaving smears of blood in the blonde silk. The child stirred, whimpering and tossing in distress. "Sleep," Sylyth whispered. Her pitch-black eyes flashed with weird green light. The child calmed immediately.

You are mine, Sylyth promised. Grinning like a gargoyle, she rose and turned from the child's bed back to her original purpose.

9

Pandaros waited in the loft.

He was still kneeling in the confines of the pentagram. He had no intention of moving until Sylyth had returned to the aether—after which he would burn the scroll that had called her and cast away the stolen medallion.

His encounter with the shade—or whatever Sylyth truly was, for now he very much doubted she was merely the spirit of some long-dead woman—had unnerved him. In his mind, he could still see her before him: a gory specter that both terrified and aroused him. A thing of flesh and blood and terrible dark power.

Again and again that voice had shouted up in his mind to dispel her, but he knew he could not do that. He needed her power.

Besides, he told himself, it was too late to turn back now even if he wanted to. Nema was dead. Nothing could restore her. He could have stopped it (he believed) but he had not done so, and though the bloody horror of her death had shocked him, it did not change the essential fact that Nema meant nothing to him, while Brittyn meant everything.

For you. All for you....

If that meant he was a murderer, or an accomplice to murder, so be it. As soon as Sylyth was done her work, he and Brittyn could flee this place. The kidnapping, the conjuring, and the killing would all be a secret of the past, known only to him, locked forever away in the cisterns of his mind.

He glanced at the broken form on the bed. Moonbeams filtering through the seams in the barn's roof fell in bright slivers upon the slaughter. In their pale light, the spilt blood was very red. Pandaros knew he should throw a drape over the corpse, but he feared to leave the protection of the circle while Sylyth was abroad. If she should return and catch him out, he would have only the medallion to protect him. After seeing what she had done to Nema, he was not at all sure that would be enough.

"Never mind that," he muttered to himself. "Never mind. Can't be undone. Just don't let her sacrifice be for naught."

He would not. He would take Brittyn far from here and make his mark as a magus and raise her up into luxury, giving her all the treasures and riches her beauty deserved. She would love him and all would see and envy Pandaros Krite both his wife and his power.

If the vileness of his deed followed him in nightmares—for Pandaros had already felt the first whippings of his conscience and in sleep he would have no defense against its scourging—still those would be nightmares from which he woke beside Brittyn, and she would give him all the comfort he would ever—

Creeeak....

Pandaros raised his head like a startled weasel. He knew that noise well: he had stepped on the second rung of the ladder to the loft hundreds of times.

What was making that ascent now?

Terror seized him as he listened to the scuffing of someone—or something—climbing. He needed to keep calm, to maintain control. He was dealing with a very dangerous entity. He could not falter. He was safe in his circle, but that knowledge did not stop his heart from knocking too fast against his ribs. *Please Aeton, give me strength*, he begged, clutching the medallion. If her work was done, he would dismiss Sylyth. Once she was safely gone he would swear off all such conjuring for the rest of his days, no matter how mighty he became. *Yes, yes, I prom—*

A hand grasped the wooden post above the final rung of the ladder.

10

Brittyn climbed into the loft.

Her feet were bare and wet from the snow. A cloak was wrapped around her body, but the hood was down, and her sweet, winsome face looked earnestly at Pandaros. Her golden hair was mussed from sleep. Her eyes bore that just-wakened puffiness, a touch of confusion in their dark depths.

Pandaros thought she had never been more beautiful.

"Brittyn?"

"Aye." She came closer. Pandaros half raised a hand, ready to shout for her to stop, fearing she would see the mutilated horror on the bed, but she had eyes only for him and did not spare so much as a glance at the rest of the loft.

She stopped at the edge of the pentagram. Tugged the fastening of her cloak. It spilled off her shoulders, puddling behind her like a lump of shadow. She stood naked before him.

"Take me," she whispered, and stepped across the pentagram.

Whatever sudden fears Pandaros had felt vanished. She had passed over the barrier of the pentagram—a thing no creature of the aether could do. She was real. Flesh. Blood. Brittyn.

She was his.

Triumph swelled in him. Sylth was forgotten as Brittyn knelt before him. "Oh Brittyn! Finally, my love!" He clutched at her, kissing her mouth, her throat, squeezing the heavy globes of her breasts. Her flesh was hot, almost feverish beneath his lips and hands. She forced him onto his back. He closed his eyes as she wrenched his belt open, then grabbed his robes and ripped them violently apart.

Somewhere in the back of his mind, Pandaros he knew it was dangerous to do this here and now, but he had waited and wanted for too long to resist. Surely they could steal the time before dawn, perhaps even longer. It would take him only an instant to conjure an aethergate that took them far away. Artelo could be in the loft and still be too late to—

Her hand folded around him and all thought stopped. He had never known a more delicious pleasure than her touch—until she settled atop him. "Oh God," he groaned. "Oh Brittyn!" Her hot muscles clamped once and he lost all control, too delirious to be embarrassed as he jetted wildly into her.

"Yessssssss!"

Pandaros heard that hiss and knew he was betrayed. His eyes flew open.

The thing that gloated above him still looked like Brittyn, but the voice that had made that sound did not belong to the shepherdess, and the black, pupilless eyes that stared demonically down at him had no place in any creature born on Acrevast.

"The pentagram," he gasped in utter confusion. The wards should have protected him. How had they failed?

Spurred by sudden desperation, Pandaros fought to rise. Sylyth sank her claws into his shoulders, pinning him like a bug. He felt blood running from those wounds. Remembered how Nema had been torn apart. At least his death would be swift.

But that was not his fate.

Still pinning him with her inhumanly strong grasp, Sylyth began to slide back and forth atop him. Her eyes stayed open and blank as voids. Though Pandaros struggled to look away, he could not...nor could he stop the reaction he was having to her stimulation.

He realized then what he had conjured. What Sylyth truly was. All too late.

Pandaros Krite, who dreamed of one day being Archamagus, became instead a slave of the succubus.

11

Brittyn was at the window again.

This time it was neither hope nor fear that moved her, but confusion. *What in bebother?*

Their carthorse was standing in the yard.

Shaking her aching head—she had not had a good night's sleep at all—Brittyn set down the jar of jam she had just opened, dug a few cubes from the sugar bowl, wrapped her cloak around her shoulders, stepped into her wool boots, and went outside. She was careful to close the door behind her. Aura was sleeping, but as a rule there were no late-risers in the Sterling cottage. Brittyn did not want a three-year-old who was curious about everything roaming outside while she was in the barn.

The wind blew fresh and cold into Brittyn's face, though not as cold as when she had spied Pandaros and Nema Drianni last night. *Did they have something to do with this?* she wondered as she tromped through the snow. Releasing a horse to run free was just the sort of spiteful trick a girl like Nema would play, but she could not imagine Pandaros would go along with such a thing.

Depends on what she was offerin him to go along, don't it now? "Aye," Brittyn said. The carthorse—named Orsey by Aura—looked up, blinking his big, long-lashed eyes at Brittyn. "Come here, ye goose." She palmed some sugar and placed her hand beneath his muzzle, letting him munch while she stroked his strong neck, looking him over to make certain he was not hurt. "What're ye doin out here, then?" The horse flicked his thick tail and licked her hand. "All right, that's enough. Let's go. I've chores you're keepin me from."

Brittyn took the horse's lead and started walking back toward the barn. Mulling the mystery of how Orsey had gotten out in the first place, she did not see the crimson spatters and smudges on the snow or the bloody prints that marked the place where a thing of darkness had paused to look upon the night and learned to hate the stars.

Orsey followed obediently until Brittyn crossed the threshold of the barn. Then he stopped. "Come on." Brittyn tugged on the lead. Orsey snorted frosty plumes, lowered his head, flattened his ears, and stubbornly refused to go forward.

What is it? Brittyn wondered. *Somethin in the barn?* She let the lead fall, trusting Orsey to stay, and went into the barn. The new-risen sun was behind her and there was ample light. She knew animals could sense danger, but she also knew they could be skittish for no good reason. That must have been the case here, for she could see nothing amiss save the wide-flung gate to Orsey's stall.

Returning, she picked up the lead. The horse still would not budge. "Come on!" Frustrated, her head throbbing, Brittyn turned and swatted the horse across the nose. Orsey flinched and made a surprised whicker, but did not move. "Fine, then. Ye can stay here." She fastened the tether to a post and was about to head back to the cottage when it occurred to her to check the stall itself. Perhaps some other animal had gotten in and died there, spooking the horse.

She went back into the barn, past the hulk of the wagon and the pile of stones Artelo had gathered to build a terrace. "Oh for Aeton's sake!" Nothing was dead within the stall, but the door was badly broken. Orsey must have kicked his way free. The wood surrounding the latch was mangled and the metal hasp itself lay in the dirt nearby. She stooped to retrieve it—

Heard the noise from above: a protracted groan followed by a series of grunting gasps.

Brittyn froze for an instant, and then clapped a hand to her mouth to catch her laughter. She had forgotten all about Pandaros and Nema. *Ugh! I hope Artelo and I don't sound like that!* The noises coming from the loft were bestial, like rutting animals.

I'll come back later, she thought. Backing out of the barn, she bumped into Orsey. "No wonder ye fled, if ye were hearin them noises all the night."

This time she could not stop the laughter. She staggered her way back to the cottage with tears in her eyes. She could not wait to tell Artelo. They would laugh together at this strangest of coincidences even harder than she was laughing now.

Ye will, if he ever comes home, a rude voice intruded.

That thought sobered her. She stopped walking and peered at the road below, which led south past Thackery and then turned toward Duralyn in the east. Where Artelo had gone beyond the Crown City she did not know. It had taken a great act of courage for Brittyn to let Artelo go at all, and these six weeks had been the hardest of her life; harder even than when Artelo had abandoned her to fight for the Crown against the demons at the Battle of Hidden Vale. Then, he had left without giving her a choice in the matter. This time—having come to the hard acceptance that her husband could not deny his impulse to do good and still be true to himself—she had sent him forth. If he did not return she had no one to blame but herself. *But he'll be home again,* she assured herself. And in an added prayer: *Bring him home....*

With a last, lingering look down the empty, snow-covered road, Brittyn went back inside. She would make some tea, have breakfast with Aura, feed the sheep, and get to work cleaning—

"Oh Aura! Not the jam!"

Aura had awakened in Brittyn's absence. Spying the jam jar on the table, she had clambered up onto a chair and helped herself to a favorite treat. She now had duskberry preserves on her hands, her face, her nightclothes, and even in her hair. "Jam," she said, before shoving her fingers in her mouth again.

"Oh, ye— What am I going to do with ye?" Brittyn could not be angry with her. She picked her up and sat her on the table. "Here, ye missed a spot." Dipping a finger in the jam, she painted a stroke onto Aura's pert nose.

Aura giggled. "Ye promise Mama ye'll not go in the jam without askin na'more," Brittyn said, looking at Aura's spattered nightclothes. *I'll never get these clean....*

"Pwomise," Aura said. She looked so somber and sincere that Brittyn pulled her close and kissed her.

"All's well, then. Let's go get cleaned up."

12

Sylyth sighed contentedly.

The succubus lay on her back, staring at the trail of smoke rising to the cobwebby, wooden-beamed ceiling of the loft as the sweat cooled and evaporated from her body. The smoke came from the scroll that she was burning with one of the black candles. In a few moments, the parchment containing the secret of her name was reduced to ash.

Sylyth could not be dismissed from this world.

Sighing again, Sylyth closed her eyes. Her hand made small, circular stroking motions across her belly, caressing the life already quickening in her vile womb.

Twisting over, Sylyth plucked the medallion of summoning from Pandaros' stalk of a neck and placed it about her own. The tarnished circle hung between her breasts. She could feel the power of the token: power that had called her and bound her to this plane, as it could call and bind anything of the aether, good or ill.

Power that she would gift to her spawn.

Part human, part demon, her fell offspring's dual nature would grant it authority over the magic of the token that no Pit-bred demon could ever have. With the medallion, the spawn would be able to defy the barrier of the Shadow Gate and call forth fiends.

Call them he would. Sylyth knew so. It was his destiny.

He would be a prince among demons. Sylyth would be a queen.

But that was far ahead. First the spawn had to be formed, and it would take many more men than Pandaros to sustain its life. After crossing the pentagram, whose glyphs of warding were not nearly as perfect as Pandaros had believed, Sylyth had used him all through the night and morning, until he was utterly spent and withered. The apprentice had begun the work of feeding the spawn; it would be for others to finish.

When it was done, when she was heavy with her offspring, Sylyth would make for a shimmyr, a place of darkness, for only in such an unhallowed space could she give birth. Then would come the final measure, the one of utmost import. In the moments immediately following its birth, the spawn was most vulnerable. It could not yet survive in this world. Like Sylyth, it owned no true form, so it required a vessel.

A vessel like the one Bhael-ur had seen fit to provide.

A vessel Sylyth now rose to claim.

13

Morning wore toward noon with no sign of Pandaros.

At first, Brittyn was too busy to notice his absence. She gave Aura a bath and they shared a proper breakfast, after which she brought in the basin and washboard to tend the jam-soiled clothes. While the clothes soaked, Brittyn straightened up, then bundled her daughter in a scarf, hooded cloak, wool mittens and boots, and took her outside to build a snow creature.

They toiled joyfully beneath a winter-blue sky, sculpting two great snowballs for a body and a smaller one for a head. Aura clapped in delight after setting a black stone for the creature's single eye. "I swear ye've your da's sense of humor already," Brittyn said.

"Where da?" Aura asked.

"Off 'n away," Brittyn said. "But back soon, don't ye fret." She said this as much to herself as to Aura, glancing down the road again as she did. "Come on, inside now."

"Hungy," Aura said when they were once more in the cottage.

"All right," Brittyn said, struggling to divest Aura of all the fleecy layers she had wrapped her in. "But stop fidgetin or I'll never get ye out of these wet things."

Brittyn made Aura a bowl of porridge and sat with her while she ate. It was only after that, when Aura was down for a nap and Brittyn went back to the washbasin, that she realized she had not seen Pandaros all morning.

That's odd.... Pandaros almost never missed breakfast. On those rare occasions he did oversleep, he was certainly about the farmstead by the time the bells in Thackery tolled eight. Today they had counted eleven already. *He can't still be up there....*

Given what she had heard earlier, she could not completely discount that possibility. More likely, however, Pandaros had decided to escort Nema back to Thackery. *He could have at least said he was goin. There's bread and such he might've brought back....*

Annoyed, Brittyn decided to find out exactly what her wayward boarder was about. *High time he stopped his screwin and started workin. Plenty to be done, and he's wasted half the day already with that silly slut....*

On her way to fetch her boots and cloak, she detoured to check on Aura, who was sleeping with her thumb tucked in her mouth and her favorite blanket nestled beneath her chin. Brittyn kissed her gently. As she straightened, the feeling that she was being watched made the hair on her nape rise like a wolf's hackles. She turned quickly, thinking it was Pandaros and prepared to give him a taste of her tongue. He was hired help, not the lord of the manor to be coming and going whenever he pleased.

Someone was staring in through the cottage window. It was not Pandaros.

Brittyn's mind reeled. "What?" she gasped.

The face outside the window was her own.

Sylyth regarded the woman whose shape she had stolen to seduce Pandaros. Her other powers were still waking—she would need more men before she could draw on all the formidable strength at her disposal—but shape-changing was easy magic for the succubus. Though the imitation was not perfect, looking at the woman before her was almost like looking in a mirror. The chief difference was the trapped-animal fear rampant in the woman's pale gray eyes.

That fear made the succubus smile, revealing a set of tiny, serrated fangs better suited to some predatory fish. She extended a clawed hand toward the woman.

"Give me the child and I will spare your life," Sylyth said.

14

Brittyn's first thought was that she had been struck mad. She could not possibly be facing what she seemed to see. It was some phantasm. A fever of her mind.

Then the woman spoke in her grave-gravel voice. The words (child...give me the child...the child....)
bludgeoned through Brittyn's head. *Aura...* "No!" With terrific bravery, Brittyn grabbed the shutters, slammed them closed, and jammed the latch home, locking the woman out.

That's no woman, some remarkably detached part of her mind said. She had seen its eyes: those black, emotionless eyes that might have served for a doll or a cobra, but not for a woman. Nothing human could own such eyes.

Run, ye fool! This new voice was not so calm as the other, but it was the one Brittyn heeded—because it did not truly matter what the thing was or where it had come from. All that mattered was what it meant to do.

Brittyn snatched Aura up from her bed, covers and all. Aura woke with a startled cry. "Ow! Mama!"

Brittyn wheeled about. Panic had taken her. She would have screamed for help, but no one would hear her. She was alone here in the hills. She did not know what to do, where to go, only that she had to protect her child.

Get out! Brittyn took a step toward the door. *Not that way! It's out there! Use the back!*

Brittyn spun around again. Ran into the kitchen.

The front door to the cottage ruptured, broken by some monstrous force.

No! Brittyn dumped Aura down. "Under th' table! Ye hide there and ye don't make a noise and ye don't come out until I say!" She stowed the crying, frightened girl under the table, dashed to the counter, snatched a cleaver from the chopping block, and whirled around.

The succubus crossed the threshold.

"Get *out!*" Brittyn snarled. Cords stood in her neck. Her face was flushed. Her eyes blazed. "Ye leave us be!" She cut the air with the knife.

Sylyth came on, unperturbed by the threat.

Brittyn did not wait. Though she had struck a truly violent blow only once before in her life, she sprang forward like a cornered badger and brought the cleaver down with all her force.

THOCK!

The blade bit deep into Sylyth's shoulder, staggering the succubus. Brittyn jerked the cleaver free. Blood fanned the air. Screaming in primal fury, Brittyn raised the blade to strike again.

Sylyth swung her uninjured arm. The blow appeared casual, but it was inhumanly strong. Brittyn flew backwards and crashed down on the counter, scattering pots and shattering bowls. Groaning, dazed, blood trickling down her cheek where a shard of pottery had sliced her open, the shepherdess struggled to rise. The succubus was between her and Aura now.

Shoving off the counter, Brittyn attacked again. This time the succubus was ready. The blood spurting from her shoulder had subsided to an ooze; no weapon forged of such common stock could truly harm a fiend. Even so, she had no intention of being subjected to another such hurt. She knocked the cleaver from Brittyn's grasp. Her other hand slashed down, fingers hooked to rip the flesh right off Brittyn's face.

The shepherdess twisted aside at the last instant. The claws tore through her hair and raked open her scalp. The pain was hot and blinding as a bolt of lightning. She had no recourse as the succubus grabbed her, lifted her overhead with hideous ease, and slammed her on the floor.

The breath blasted out of Brittyn. Through the haze of pain she heard her daughter wailing. Then the world slipped sideways toward a great blackness.

Sylyth stepped over Brittyn. The woman was not dead, but she was no longer an obstacle to what the succubus had come for.

Shoving a chair aside, Sylyth stood before the table. Beneath it, huddled back against the wall, was the cringing vessel for the spawn. The succubus extended her claw. "Come forth."

Aura screamed.

Sylyth drove her fist down upon the table. It split in the middle, one side collapsing over Aura like a tent. "Come forth!"

Aura screamed again.

Brittyn shattered a chair over Sylyth's back.

Grunting, the succubus pitched forward. Brittyn grabbed a broken chair leg and battered Sylyth's head and shoulders until the succubus crumpled and was still.

Gasping, Brittyn took a step back.

Fast as a snake uncoiling from a basket, Sylyth twisted to her knees. Brittyn swung the chair leg. Sylyth caught it. The slap of wood against her palm was loud as a ballista crack. For an instant they held poised like that, shepherdess above succubus. Then Sylyth's other hand shot up.

Her talons pierced Brittyn's stomach like a spear.

Brittyn's eyes flew wide. Her bloodied mouth opened in speechless agony. The chair leg slipped from numb fingers.

Sylyth rose, twisting her hand in Brittyn's body. The shepherdess screamed. Sylyth tore her claws free.

Brittyn fell heavily to her knees, swayed, and toppled. Blood from her gored belly soaked though her blouse, puddling on the floor.

Dying.... Brittyn fought the pain and the rushing dark. She would not let her child be harmed. Not while there was one single breath left in her body.

She looked desperately about. Saw a flash of steel.

Sylyth bent for Aura again. It was time to take the vessel and be gone from this place. She needed to heal and she would have to feed; already she could feel the spawn hungering within her.

Tossing the ruined table aside, Sylyth reached for Aura, who flung her chubby hands up in useless warding.

"Don't ye dare touch her!"

Sylyth had no capacity for amazement, but she felt something like it as she looked slowly over her shoulder and saw the woman there.

Brittyn was standing again. One hand clutched her wounded stomach, the other held the bloodied cleaver. The knuckles fisted around the wooden handle were white as bone, and her face had gone equally pale save two spots of febrile color on her cheeks.

The succubus turned to face the shepherdess. She saw how Brittyn's legs were trembling with the just effort of standing. Smiled coldly.

Brittyn sensed Sylyth had seen past her bluff of strength. She swallowed hot blood. Forced herself to stay upright. "Aura! Mama loves ye—remember that!"

"Give me the child and I will spare your life," Sylyth said again.

"Ye'll not have her! Never while I live!"

With all a mother's love, Brittyn flung herself at the succubus one last time.

15

Artelo Sterling rounded the last bend in the road below his hillside cottage.

The knight had made the three-day journey from Duralyn with little rest, but if his body was weary, his mind was reposed. The emptiness of snow-clad days and the solitude of snow-clad nights had given the knight the space he needed to accept the events that had unfolded before the steps of Castle Aventar.

There, in the bleakness of a wintry afternoon, Artelo had made the cruelest choice in his life—for the second time.

He had let Solsta go.

The story of the Crown of Teranor and her knight and the misadventure of their love was long and tangled, full of all the ill twists of Fortune that attend such tales. Artelo, who had thought of little else since that same Fortune had thrust him, after a three-year absence, back into Solsta's presence, did not want to think on it any longer.

Over and again Artelo had weighed his heart against his choice: the flame that still burned for Solsta against the duty and love he bore his family. Over and again he came to the same answer: the one he had come to three years ago after the Battle of Hidden Vale, and three weeks ago during the tortuous sea voyage to the isle of Elsmywr to rescue Argentia

Dasani from the clutches of a mad wizard, and finally three days ago upon the steps of Castle Aventar.

Part of his heart might always belong to Solsta, but it was a part that lived in the past. The rest of it, the rest of him, was bound to the life he had made in the present. *Here. Home....*

Artelo looked up at the cottage, quaint and simple but still perfect and all he needed. He had been too long away. He did not regret going after Argentia, but now that he had returned no summons or appeal would draw him from this place again.

So resolved, he hitched his borrowed steed to the post beside the water well. He would bring her to the barn later. Tomorrow Pandaros could ride her back to Duralyn. Right now, the only thing Artelo wanted was to hear his daughter's gleeful laughter as he caught her up and spun her about.

Instead he heard silence.

No birds. No sheep. No Brittyn whistling in the cottage. Nothing. *Something's wrong....*

Sudden fear made Artelo's mouth run dry. *Calm down!* a voice in his mind said. *There's nothing wrong....*

He did not quite believe that voice, however, and he hurried up the hill, slipping twice on the snow-covered slope, catching himself with his hand, not feeling the bite of cold against his fingers or the jarring wince in his shoulder, still sore from the nearly crippling blow dealt him in the conflict on Elsmywr, desperately hoping to catch a glimpse of Brittyn in the window that would show him he was a fool to worry.

He reached the terrace. An odd snow creature—three great, lumpish balls stacked atop each other with a single stone for an eye in the topmost—greeted him. Brittyn and Aura must have built it. The creature made Artelo smile for a moment. Then he looked past it.

The cottage door hung open on twisted hinges.

Oh no. Please no.... Artelo drew his blade and rushed into his home. "Brittyn! Aura!"

No one answered, but the scene screamed at him: shattered furniture, smashed pottery, and on the wooden floor Brittyn prided herself on keeping clean, so much blood.

Artelo felt sick. He stumbled in a circle, staggered into the bedchamber.

That room was also empty.

Artelo fell to his knees beside the bed, clutching the blanket in his hand. What had happened? Whose blood was that? Where were Brittyn and Aura and—

Pandaros! Had the wizard saved them? If they had been attacked by goblins from the Gelidian Spur, which was not so distant as Artelo would have wished, had Pandaros managed to get Brittyn and Aura away to safety?

Jerking to his feet, Artelo sprinted from the cottage. As he crossed the threshold, he saw a thing he had missed when he rushed in: a splash of red upon the snow.

The bloody footprints dragged a trail across the white ground. Someone had survived in the cottage and made for the barn.

The knight ran, oblivious to the jumble of other tracks that crossed the snow-covered yard toward the woods. He burst into the shadowy space of the barn, shouting for Brittyn and Pandaros.

Froze in horror.

Brittyn was there, her back to him as she struggled to lift a saddle onto their horse. She was uncloaked and barefoot. Blood ran from beneath her torn skirt and down her calf in a scarlet ribbon.

She did not turn at Artelo's call or as he ran to her. Only when he grabbed her shoulder did she react, screaming and wrenching about, tearing away from him, bumping against the horse, which whinnied and shied as far as its tether would allow.

The saddle fell, crunching down on Brittyn's foot hard enough to break bones. She did not flinch, did not even feel it. Her world was already boundless pain.

Artelo could only stare at her. On Brittyn's blood-streaked face was a look of abject terror. Her gray eyes were haunted and mad. Her blonde hair was clotted with gore. Below her breasts, the tatters of her white blouse were soaked crimson.

"Artelo!" she gasped. Hope brightened her gaze for an instant. She reached for him. Her legs buckled.

He caught her.

"Brittyn! Brittyn!"

16

Sylyth had left Brittyn for dead.

The final attack against the succubus had failed. Sylyth simply met Brittyn's mad rush with outstretched arms. They grappled, but the shepherdess was too wounded to hold against Sylyth's fiendish strength. She did not even have time to scream for Aura to run before Sylyth flung her into the wall.

She smashed down, the breath blasted from her in a bloody gasp. This time she could not rise. She tried, fighting the waves of blackness rolling over her, struggling to get to her feet again, to get to Aura somehow, but her body would no longer obey.

Her last vision as she sank beneath ebony waters was of the monstrous thing that had invaded her home finally seizing her daughter, lifting her....

Mercifully, she drowned before she heard Aura screaming.

Time passed.

How long Brittyn lingered in the pitch she would never know, but at last, infused with the most primal force of all, she clawed her way back to the light of consciousness.

Entered a world of pain.

Everything hurt. The pain in her stomach—like a white-hot poker had lanced her—was so excruciating that the wounds to her head, the broken ribs, the sprained knee, were deadened. The gash bled freely but it bled slowly. Left her with a sliver of a chance.

Aura....

This was Brittyn's only thought. It had brought her back. It gave her trembling strength enough to first crawl, then to rise. "Oh," she gasped, trying unsuccessfully to straighten. "Oh Aeton...hurts.... Please...."

That she was likely dying she knew abstractly. That her body was in agony she knew for fact. She would not let either truth matter.

Aura....

That thing had taken her daughter. *I'll find her....* Beyond this thought, nothing could take hold in Brittyn's mind, which had all but shut itself down in an effort to stem the killing pain. She knew only that her daughter was gone and that she had to find her.

Aura....

Clutching her wounded stomach, which was seized with agony worse than the worst cramp, the shepherdess started limping. One leg was dragging badly—a shard of wood was impaled in her thigh—but she made it to the counter. There amid the shattered plates and glassware Artelo had given her on their wedding day was a dishrag.

Brittyn grabbed it and stuffed it into the gash in her belly. Her scream was a protracted hiss. Her eyes watered, her nose dripped bloody mucous. For an instant she was certain she would fall again and clutched the counter desperately for balance.

Breathing heavily, she gathered herself and shuffled forward, one awkward step at a time. She cut the soles of her bare feet on the debris, but somehow crossed to the cottage door and out into the yard.

Cold assailed her: she had no cloak, no boots. If she realized this, she showed no sign, merely kept limping along, head bowed, breathing labored, leaving a bloody trail in her wake. She was existing solely on will and instinct: one sustained her, the other guided her to the barn.

She did not see Orsey until she almost bumped into him.

The horse shied at first, still skittish, but the evil that had so agitated the animal was gone, and it calmed quickly enough to Brittyn's scent and the soft clucking she was unaware she was making as she leaned heavily against the horse's strong neck, fumbling with the lead.

After what seemed an eternity, she managed to get the tether free from the post. "Go on," she whispered. Orsey obeyed, walking back into the barn with Brittyn stumbling alongside. He stopped near his stall, and Brittyn, who by now could barely stand, lay against him, battling to stay conscious, exhausted by her exertions.

Cold.... Her feet were already an ugly red, but the cold she truly felt— and feared—was a deeper, more insidious chill in her chest and stomach. It was a cold such as she had never known before. One that made her want to fall down and sleep.

Just a while. Just rest a while....

She almost did. Her eyes closed, her knees weakened eagerly, but at the last moment another thought of Aura burst up in her mind and she bit down on her tongue, sending fresh blood sliding down her throat.

This new pain was like a slap of icy water across her face. She pushed away from Orsey and stumbled across the barn, past the wagon, past Artelo's piled terrace stones, to the table where the saddle sat.

With every swallow she tasted more and more blood. With every step she hurt unto death. It seemed she would never be able to lift her arms and take the saddle, but she did. She could not hold it, however, and the moment it had scraped over the edge of the smooth wood that her father had carved and lathed winters ago, it fell heavily to the hay-covered floor.

Brittyn fell with it. The jarring impact was as if she had been hit by a giant's club. She felt the rag slipping free of the wound in her stomach. Stuffed it back in. Fresh tears mingled with the blood on her cheeks. She uttered a long groan, shoved back, and used the saddle as a step to lift herself to her feet once more. She swayed, hunched as a withered crone, but she stayed up. After a moment trying to catch a decent breath, she took the saddle's pommel. *Come on, ye damned thing....*

She could not ride bareback, so she had to have the saddle. She dragged it across the barn, pausing halfway to vomit a brackish fluid that was mostly blood. Gasping, gagging, her head swimming so badly she hardly knew if she was moving at all, she staggered up from her knees once more and went on.

When she was beside Orsey at last, she faced her fiercest challenge. *Please, Bright Lady, let me help my Aura,* she prayed, clenching her hands on the saddle. Strength that should have been impossible allowed her to jerk the seat off the ground. She staggered, trying to force the saddle high enough to straddle the carthorse's broad back, but she was too weak and it was slipping—

A hand clamped on her shoulder.

Brittyn screamed, wheeling and tearing away from the thing holding her. Orsey flinched in surprise. The saddle, which had been poised precariously between the horse and the shepherdess, slipped from Brittyn's grasp. It fell upon her bare foot with a sickening crunch, breaking bones.

Brittyn felt nothing. She was too busy trying to make sense of the thing before her: not the woman-guised creature that had stolen her child, but a form that was somehow familiar and a voice that was somehow familiar.

Dreaming, ye fool, and ye've no time for such now. Ye're on your own, and Aura needs ye.... She blinked and shook her head but the figure did not disappear.

"Artelo!" She reached for him. Her legs buckled.

He caught her.

17

"Brittyn! Brittyn!"

Fighting back the horror and shock, Artelo lowered Brittyn gently down and cradled her in his arms. Her eyes had slipped closed. She barely seemed to be breathing, and she was very, very pale.

So much blood.... "Brit! Oh God, oh my God—what happened? Brittyn...." Artelo peeled aside the tatters of Brittyn's blouse and saw the rag. It had been beige once; now it was a deep maroon, sopping with blood from the hole punched into Brittyn's stomach.

Artelo pressed his hand to the hot, sticky mass. *If I can just stop the bleeding....* But even as that thought flew up, the part of him that had seen and dispensed many mortal wounds knew it was a false hope.

No! She'll live. She has to live! "You'll be fine, Brit. Do you hear me, honey? You'll be fine...." Tears slithered over Artelo's lips as he pressed them desperately to Brittyn's, as if his kiss could break this spell of doom.

Brittyn stirred against him, her eyes opening. "Ye...came back...."

"I'm here. I'm not going anywhere." Artelo looked around frantically. His hold on sanity, so firm and sure only minutes earlier, was slipping. "Ah, God...."

Sterling! A voice barked in his mind: Gwydityr, Master at Arms in the Academy and a model of decisive action. *Puling won't save her....*

What would? He had to help Brittyn—but how?

"Pandaros!" Artelo shouted. The wizard could teleport her to Thackery. To old Devlin, the apothecary whose tried and true hands had once saved Artelo's life. He could save Brittyn as well. There was still time. There had to be time.

Brittyn felt Artelo's arms around her again. That overwhelming sense of safety and security she had always known in his embrace wrapped her like a hearth-warmed blanket. He had returned. He had kept his word. Everything would be all right again. They were together: she and Artelo and Aura....

Aura—

Shaking off the lassitude spreading through her like some slow, sweet heat, Brittyn rallied. Artelo was here now. He would save Aura. *Aye—he must....*

First he had to know.

Brittyn's hand clenched on Artelo's arm. She sat sharply forward, her eyes suddenly wild.

"No, Brit! Stay still!"

"No! Ye listen! Aura...."

"Aura? What about Aura? Where is she? What happened?"

"Took her...."

"What! Who? Who took her?"

"Lady...." Brittyn managed. Runnels of bright blood drooled over her chin.

"What lady?" In his agitation, Artelo almost shook her.

"Tried. I tried...." Brittyn choked and shuddered violently. Her head fell backwards, spilling her crimson-streaked hair against the ground.

"Brittyn! No! Stay with me!" Artelo held her fiercely to him, willing her to keep fighting. "Don't leave me, Brit...."

With a supreme effort, Brittyn forced her head up and clung tightly to Artelo's shoulder. "Promise...ye'll save Aura. Promise me!"

"I promise. On my life I swear!" His tears splashed her face like hot rain.

Brittyn smiled an eerily contented smile and raised her bloodied palm to Artelo's lips, as if she had heard the last thing she needed to hear from him.

"Brittyn?" His voice was more sob than whisper. He stroked her hair back from her brow. The light in her eyes was dying.

Brittyn hitched in a sharp gasp of air. Her eyes focused once again, fixing Artelo in their dove-gray depths. "Ye...were still the best thing... that ever happened t' me...."

"Brittyn—no! Please don't go...."

But she was already gone.

18

"We're closed," Del Kardee snapped when he heard the knocking at the door to the Speckled Tortoise.

It was after two in the morning. He had just turned out the last of the patrons. All his care now was to have the bar wiped, the floor swept and mopped, and to be climbing the steps to his room before the hour was out. He hated this part of the job he had inherited from his father more than any other, but if he did not do it and do it well, he would have his mother to answer to.

Why hadn't the gods seen fit to take her instead of his father, Del frequently wondered. The answer, he suspected, was that the gods had no desire to keep Mavia Kardee's company in Aelysium, and the demons in the Fel Pits were probably afraid she would take over the place. Regardless, Del was stuck with her for the foreseeable and grim future, and—

The door to the tavern swung open, letting in a blast of winter night.

Del looked up sharply. He had locked the door. He always did. The one time he had forgotten, his mother had strapped him raw. "Thieves live in Thackery too, you simp," Mavia Kardee had said. "And more than just those your worthless father lets rob us with drinking on credit. Leave that door unlatched again and you'll only know the look of it from the outside. You mind Mother now."

A vicious lash with a black leather belt punctuated each of those last words. For a woman who was all skin and bones, Mavia wielded that strap with the strength of one thrice her size. The secret—though she would never tell her son this—was all in the wrists.

Del glanced reflexively at his mother's stool, which stood empty now that she had retired to her own chambers. Her voice echoed in his head: *Thieves....*

Could it be? Del ducked down behind the bar, heart pounding as he grabbed for the cudgel that had been his father's pride. He stood up, pointing the gnarled wood at the door, where a weirdly hunched, cloaked figure was crossing the threshold. "Hey! I said we're closed! Get out or I'll give ya a taste of Skull Cruncher!"

The figure came forward another step, into the light of the bar's lamps. Cradled in its arms was a small form wrapped in a blanket. "Help me. Please...."

"Brittyn?" Del lowered Skull Cruncher in astonishment. He had hardly even seen Brittyn Mayfair in the last three winters, but prior to that, when she was spreading her legs for Gasten Crond, she had been no stranger to the Tortoise. He came out from behind the bar. "Gods above! Brittyn, what happened?"

Brittyn's face was bruised and swollen. One eye was completely shut beneath a purpled lid. Blood trickled from a nostril and from split, puffy lips.

"Brittyn? Who did this?" Del paused, choosing his next words carefully. "Was it Artelo?" He knew firsthand that Brittyn's husband was capable of violence, but he had not seemed the type to turn his fists upon his wife.

For a moment Brittyn said nothing. Her face grew troubled and closed. Just when Del was certain she would not answer, she looked up. "Yes," she said. "Yes, Artelo. I took the vessel and fled."

"The what?" Del asked.

His confusion was mirrored for an instant on Brittyn's mangled face. "The child," she said quickly. "Artelo hit me. Hurt me...."

"Bastard son of a goblin whore!" Del's anger was not entirely feigned, but a calculating part of his mind—a part, loathe as he was to admit it, that came from his mother—was already thinking how he might finally gain revenge for the beating Artelo had given him and his friends at Brittyn's cottage. He still bore the scar across his forearm to remind him of that encounter. "Stay right here," he said. "I'll get the Watch."

"No!" With the sleeping child balanced in one arm, Brittyn seized Del's wrist with fierce strength. "No! Just a place to rest awhile. That's all. Please...."

That was not what Del wanted to hear. He wanted Artelo dragged off in chains, disgraced before all Thackery. "But I don't—"

Upstairs, a door slammed. Del jumped. *Oh hell!* He heard the staccato clack of hard shoes descending the stairs. A long shadow thrown by the lamp on the landing preceded his mother's appearance.

"Del Kardee!"

He winced but turned at the harpy's call. "Yes, Mother?"

Mavia Kardee stepped into the tavern. She was a blade of a woman dressed in funereal black—this had nothing to do with the passing of her husband; she wore that color always and only—with a hatchet nose and a face withered beyond its years, like a mummy entombed in the great pyramids of Makhara. Her hair was stern iron, drawn back in a severe bun, her mouth a humorless line. Her dark eyes stared with all the compassion of a crow's. "Warned you before about letting people in after clo—"

Mavia started. Her hand flew to her throat as if sudden pain had seized her there. She staggered backwards. For an instant Del thought she would fall. He reached reflexively for her, but she recovered and swatted his hand away. "What's this?" she whispered.

"Brittyn Mayfair, Mother. She's been hurt. Her husband, that bastard Artelo—"

"Brittyn Sterling," Mavia corrected, almost absently. She was staring intently at Brittyn.

"Please, give me a room to rest in," Brittyn said. "My child...." The little girl stirred in her arms, but did not wake.

"I'm going for the Watch," Del said, mustering all the assertiveness he could.

"You'll do no such thing!" Mavia's voice recovered its usual shrill tone. "Go up and prepare a room. Leave the thinking to them with minds to do it."

"Yes, Mother," Del said automatically. He had been a victim of Mavia's tongue all his life. The only response he knew to it was obedience. With a last glance at Brittyn, he went hastily up the stairs.

The two women were alone.

The moment her wretch of a son was out of sight, Mavia Kardee fell to her knees, caught Brittyn's free hand and pressed it reverently to her cold, bony forehead. "You've come. At last, you've come. Bhael-ur be praised!"

19

Sylyth looked down at the old woman. A gleam of smile flickered across her bruised lips. All was proceeding even better than she could have anticipated.

After dispatching the shepherdess, Sylyth had collected the child. Aura had resisted, screaming piercingly and beating at Sylyth, but she had no recourse against the magic of the succubus, who conjured a sleep upon her.

With the vessel secured, Sylyth went hastily through the cottage, seeking out other things. She took a skirt and blouse from Brittyn's closet, the cloak from the peg beside the door, the woolen boots from the hearth: items she would need if she was to pass safely as a human long enough to fulfill her destiny.

That done, she took Aura and set forth into a gray day that was painfully bright, though not as hateful to her as the stars had been at night. She wanted to be gone from the cottage. She was not yet as strong as she would become and some instinct told her it would not be safe to linger there to be discovered.

She went by untracked paths through the rolling, wooded lands that descended from the hills. Her destination was a nearby village known to her from Nema's memories, which had passed to her when she claimed that unfortunate girl's body for her birth shape. She could have reached it within an hour of leaving the cottage. She chose instead to wait.

The spawn within her was alive with hunger. It could not be long before she nourished it, else it would begin to feed on her, not realizing in its idiot gluttony that to do so would cause its own death when Sylyth died. But it also would not do for her to risk too much exposure. The succubus was powerful, but she sensed there were forces in this world that could check her, hurt her, even slay her. Best they knew nothing of her presence here until she was prepared to deal with them.

So she waited in the woods for day to turn to night. Came under cover of the delicious darkness to the village, seeking to sate her ravenous spawn. She found not only prey, but something of unexpected, perhaps vital, use.

Who would have believed that here in this remote place, this cluster of simple buildings that could not have been home to more than a few hundred people, there would be a devotee of Bhael-ur? But the demon god's ways were mysterious, and Sylyth felt that His favor was very much upon her now.

"Rise, woman," she said. "Take this child." She had almost said "vessel" again, but stopped herself. She had slipped in using that word before. While it would not have mattered to this woman, who was already a willing thrall, such a mistake might arouse suspicion in others, as it had for a moment in the man upstairs. Suspicion could lead to questions, which could lead to just the sort of trouble Sylyth was intent on avoiding.

Sylyth's human disguise was good already, and would become better, more seamless, the longer she was incarnate in flesh, but it was still a masquerade. She was an alien thing in these realms and ways. It would serve her well to be always mindful of that.

If she was careful, there would be no mistakes.

She handed over the child, who was still sleeping her unnatural sleep. Mavia stared at Aura with her crow eyes. The child, seeming to feel that gaze, moaned and turned her face away.

"A sacrifice?" Mavia asked eagerly.

"A treasure," Sylyth said. "Harm her and I will destroy you. Keep her safe and I will reward you." She used her subtle magic to comb through

Mavia's mind for secret desires. "New youth," the succubus said. "Beauty again. A life you will not have to waste here."

"Yes," Mavia whispered. She had taken off her black shawl and wrapped it around Aura, but she hardly seemed aware of her actions. An ugly rapture spread across her pinched face. "Praise Bhael-ur, how I've dreamed of it, how I've prayed for this deliverance."

"It will be," the succubus said. She winced, clutching her belly as the spawn's hunger struck her like a contraction. "Time grows short. If you would serve the Master, prove so now."

"Anything."

"I must have your son."

Mavia smiled. "With my blessing."

20

"Del?"

He turned at this tremulous call of his name. "Brittyn!" She was leaning easily in the doorway of the guestroom, all round hips and ripe breasts swelling against skirt and blouse. "I'm sorry. I'll have this room ready in just—"

"Never mind that." Brittyn came forward. It was a small room, and her presence seemed to make it even closer. Del could smell her perfume, a sweet scent like summer peaches, intoxicating. Even bruised and battered she was the most beautiful thing Del had ever seen.

She caressed his cheek. He could scarcely believe this was happening. How many nights had he helped himself to sleep with almost this exact fantasy? "But...Brittyn. What—"

"I said never mind." Brittyn took his hands and placed them on her breasts. "What you want will be yours. What I need will be mine." She pushed him back onto the bed, pouncing upon him. If Del noticed the change in her voice, he had no will to react to it. A fleeting thought of his mother

(*If she comes in....*)

assailed him, but even that was not strong enough to deter the passion Brittyn had awakened. He tore her blouse open, spilling free those breasts he had so often ogled from behind the bar, longing to touch, to taste. Now, finally, he could.

She freed him from his pants. Sank upon him in one swift motion, her wet heat enveloping him in the most unutterably exquisite sensation he had ever known. He tried to roll her beneath him, but she pinned him, riding him down. His climax came almost instantly, leaving him gasping in amazement.

"More!" she urged, still rocking atop him.

"Wait, just wait a little—"

She slapped him across the face, drawing blood. Del's eyes snapped open. "Ah! What the—"

She hit him again. His head rang. In his swimming vision, her black eyes blazed monstrously. Her voice was a growl drawn up from the Pits. "More!"

Dawn was brightening the east when Sylyth descended.

Her hair was tousled and sweaty from hours of relentless copulation, but she was glowing with vitality. All the marks of her battle with the shepherdess were gone from her face, replaced by winsome, rosy flesh.

Mavia was on her customary stool, waiting with the child, who was awake and looked up as Sylyth crossed to them. "Wan Mama." She snuffled miserably and started to cry.

"Hush, brat," Mavia warned sharply, raising her leather strap. Aura, by now all too familiar with that particular device and the pain it could cause, flinched and stopped crying.

Sylyth nodded, pleased. Controlling the vessel was important, as was keeping it healthy. She could do both with her magic, but that might make it imperfect for the spawn, which throve on corrupting purity. The purer the vessel, the stronger the spawn would emerge from it. If the old woman could play nurse effectively, freeing Sylyth to concentrate her efforts on feeding, so much the better.

"We depart," she said. For the moment, the spawn was sated. They would do well to be underway before the hunger took Sylyth again.

"Yes, Mistress." Mavia rose. She had not been idle in the hours of the night. A pack leaned against the bar. She slung it over her shoulder and collected a long black cape and a sturdy walking stick from beside the door. "Where you lead, Mavia follows."

"It is a far journey," Sylyth warned. "If you falter...."

"I'm more capable than you know," Mavia said haughtily. Then, realizing to whom she was speaking, she lowered her shrike-like head and added, "Mistress."

"We shall see."

They went out of the Speckled Tortoise. Though Mavia saw lights burning in several houses, the streets of Thackery appeared empty. She felt a great weight rising off her. She had survived her husband and her son—though at least Del had been useful in the end. After sixty-three miserable years, she was finished with this wretched place at last.

Spitting disdainfully on the stoop, she seized Aura's unwilling hand and followed the succubus onto the road that went west.

21

Hrutch Pentery scrunched his bushy brows in surprise.

Travelers on foot were rare enough in these parts, where the low hills made for arduous walking and many leagues lay between most villages, but to make the matter stranger still, this trio looked like women. *Aeton's bolts—believe they are....*

"Mavia Kardee, fine t' see'ee forth from Thackery this morn," he said, hailing them from the driving bench of his wagon as he slowed to a halt. "Who's this with'ee?"

"My niece and her daughter," Mavia said, conjuring the lie quickly. She had not expected to encounter anyone she knew on the road. While this meddlesome wood-carver was not Thackery-born, he did frequent the Tortoise on his trips to the village and it only took a drink or two for his mouth to start running.

"Hrutch Pentery." He doffed his hat. "Here now—stop that." Hrutch snapped his whip at the pair of horses, which had begun to whicker and shy nervously. "'Pologies. Never seen 'em take on so. Wither bound, ladies?"

"The city in the west," Sylth said after a moment's thought.

"Byrtnoth?"

"Yes. Byrtnoth." She savored the pronunciation.

"They're from there," Mavia added. "Taking me to my sister."

"On foot?" Hrutch scrunched his brows again.

"What business is it of yours, Hrutch Pentery?" Mavia snapped.

"Pardon, Mavia. Meant no offense."

Mavia nodded slowly. "They've no coin for a horse. My sister is dying and wished to see me before she passes." Mavia did not know where that story had come from, but it sounded plausible and, she hoped, dire enough to engender some generosity. Despite her boast of capability, she was tired already. If Pentery would take them on a bit in his wagon, she would be grateful for the reprieve.

"Can you bring us there?" Sylyth asked, stepping closer to the wagon. Hrutch's eyes lingered on her bosom. Del had popped several of the fastenings on her blouse in his hasty pawing. Sylyth had managed to make due by tying off the blouse at her midriff, but the plunge of her cleavage and inner swells of her milky breasts were on generous display. When she felt the man had looked long enough, she ran a hand with deliberate slowness through her blonde tresses, pushing them back to reveal her dark eyes.

Every carnal promise seemed to glitter in those onyx depths.

"Well now," Hrutch said, wiping at the back of his neck, which was suddenly flush with heat. "Seems I'm headin that way myself. Climb aboard."

PART II

Knight Errant

The spires of Castle Aventar, gleaming like upraised swords in the high sun, rose above the walls of Duralyn.

Artelo raced his horse harder, thundering toward the Crown City's western gate. Just days ago, he had sworn he would never return to this place. That this part of his life was once and for all in the past. He had broken that vow willingly, with neither hesitation nor the slightest remorse. He had no choice.

If he was going to rescue Aura, there was no other road but this.

How long he had knelt weeping in the barn Artelo did not know. All strength, all will had been stolen from him. Disbelief—the horror had not settled enough yet to be grief—had shaken the foundations of his world. This could not be happening. He denied it. Refused to concede that the laughing, vital young woman that had been his wife could now be this leaden, breathless, lifeless form cradled in his arms.

Not Brittyn. No....

It was Orsey who finally roused Artelo from this stupor, prodding him in the arm with his wet nose. *Get up,* the gesture seemed to say. *Get up and do what must be done....*

"No," Artelo groaned. "Get off, damn you!" He struck at the horse, which backed quickly away. But it was too late for Artelo. He looked down at Brittyn's body, then up to the shadowed rafters of the barn. "Oh God!" he screamed, his voice breaking moments after his heart. "How could you let this happen?"

There was no God. That was the answer. There could not be—for what power could have stood by, unmoved as stone, while his wife was slaughtered and his daughter taken? And was this his reward, then, for having ever been true to his principles, to duty and loyalty and the impulse to do good, to do right?

Even as that thought rose in his mind, another, full of a quiet certainty that rebuked his doubt, whispered that Aura was not yet lost to him. He remembered his promise to Brittyn. He would keep it, or he would join her in whatever awaited them beyond this world.

Gently, tenderly, Artelo laid Brittyn down, closed her eyes, and folded her hands atop the gash in her stomach. As he crossed the hay-strewn floor and retrieved a saddle blanket to shroud her with, he thought of how she had bid him go off to rescue Argentia and to return safely to her. She had always worried for him like that, yet he had come safely home and she had been the one to die in his embrace minutes after his arrival.

Oh Brittyn.... Artelo lay the heavy blanket over her body. Kissed her lips, which were still soft. Pressed his forehead to hers, missing her already as the reality of her death began to sink its stony weight upon his chest. She was beyond his touch, he knew. Nothing would bring her back. It was fallen to him to put right what she had left behind.

Galvanized, Artelo came to his feet with an almost violent motion. He had to know what had happened here. Who had besieged his home and taken his daughter—and why?

He gazed around, his good hand clenching and opening reflexively, the knuckles cracking. *Pandaros....* What had happened to the wizard? Had he been part of the battle? Had he been killed, or taken like Aura?

Artelo's gaze lifted to the loft. By some tacit agreement neither he nor Brittyn had climbed to their tenant's aerie, preferring to respect his privacy. Artelo was beyond such niceties now. He mounted the ladder into the loft.

The knight had seen many monstrous things in his days. His sword had felled strange creatures in a haunted forest and a magical mist; slain hobgoblins, giant spiders, unquiet skeletons, and even a vampyr. He had faced a demon, seen it die, and had walked through the carnage of a field of fiends charred to ashes by dragonfire. On his last, fateful venture to the isle of Elsmywr he had done battle with things that were both man and beast: the nightmare children of a wizard's insane imaginings.

All of that did nothing to prepare him for what he found in the loft.

Artelo descended swiftly, actually leaping down the last few rungs to the ground. He bent forward, shuddering out an unsteady breath, trying to keep his gorge from rising. He closed his eyes. The bloody vision remained: a horror—but worse, another mystery.

Pounding the steel-capped stump that had once been his left hand against his thigh in frustration, Artelo dropped to his knees beside Brittyn. "Where is she? Where's Aura?" he asked helplessly. "What did you mean? Who took her? What lady?" He had no idea who Brittyn could have meant. He had passed no one on the road, so whoever had taken Aura had either gone north toward the Gap Outpost or had taken to the woods. *How will I find them?*

Inspiration struck him. He scrambled to his feet and rushed outside, scouring the white ground. He was no tracker, but in the snow....

There! A single trail of footprints led away from the cottage. Artelo followed them down the side of the hill, across the road, and to the woods.

Beyond the barrier of brambly thicket, all was dark. A jay made its angry cry. Artelo peered in and cursed. He could see the broken branches where his quarry had entered, but nothing beyond that. The wind had blown much of the snow off the trees. What lay on the ground was a jumbled mess. He thought about going in anyway, but he knew he would never be able to find the track in such conditions.

You know who can....

You're mad. She's halfway across the crowndom, part of him protested. *You'll never find her in time....*

That almost threw him, but the answer came in yet another flash: so simple that Artelo laughed. It was a low sound, not quite sane. "Yes, I will," he said. "I will."

First he had to tend to Brittyn.

23

It was the hardest thing Artelo had ever done.

Everything else had held the chance of reversal or redemption. Even giving up Solsta to her duty to the throne, though it had torn his heart out at the time, had held some possibility for change. Here there was none: only the immutable finality of the Harvester's reap.

Brittyn's internment took the remains of the day. During those hard-worked hours, Artelo kept madness at bay by constantly reiterating that there was nothing he could do for Aura right now. Above all, he reminded himself that whoever had taken his daughter had taken her for a reason. If they had wanted to kill her, they would have done so at the cottage.

He hoped.

Please keep her safe, he prayed. *Please....*

That prayer became Artelo's mantra as he loaded the stones he had been saving to build the terrace into his wheelbarrow and rolled them up to the copse that crowned the hill above the cottage. It took five trips to get the entire load moved. By the end he was sweating and trembling with the exertion. His arms, though strong and used to labor, ached almost too much to raise them.

It was more than fatigue, he knew. His heart was not in this hateful task. But he persevered. In a small, secret clearing where he and Brittyn

73

had made love many times beneath both sun and moon, and where they had often taken Aura picnicking in fair weather, he built his wife's cairn.

It was a rude work. He lay the stones in an oblong shape, creating a hollow space, like a tub full of blackness. When he judged he had built as much as he could and still left himself enough stones to make the roof he stopped.

Went down for Brittyn.

Artelo had always assumed he would be first to die, and that Brittyn and Aura and whatever other children Fortune had graced them with would carry on. That was the way that seemed right to him, but Fortune had other plans. Artelo could—and did—hate Her for it, but he could not change Her.

Always, Fortune rolled as She willed.

So he took Brittyn from the defiled barn to the cottage. There he stripped and washed her body clean of blood and grime, and dressed her in the gown she had wedded him in: white silk with a powder-blue lattice. That she had kept it safe in a cedar trunk to one day give to Aura he would not let himself think on, just as he would not let himself think on the many things they had planned together and now would never do.

Instead, as he set the wedding garland, its bluebells, cockles, and white roses now dried and yellowed and

(dead)

brittle, on Brittyn's brow once more, Artelo thought of all the good. All the love they had shared. The home and the family they had made together.

All through the preparations he held to those things. As he gathered Brittyn into his arms one last time to make the grudging journey up the hillside he held to them even harder, weeping freely as each step brought him closer to the final parting of their ways.

Eventually, that climb ended in the copse. With the same slow gentleness that he had once used to set her upon their nuptial bed Artelo now lay Brittyn in her last bed. He knelt beside the half-formed mound of stone and took a rock in his trembling hand. "I can't do this," he whispered. "I can't...."

But he had to. Brittyn was lost to him. Aura was not. Yet....

Ye promised.... Brittyn whispered across an unbridgeable gulf.

"I know," Artelo said. "I know."

He set the stone resolutely in place, and all the others after it, until there was but a single space remaining.

Into this Artelo thrust a torch. "Good-bye, Brittyn," he whispered to the smoke that rose from that hole and spiraled toward the first stars of dusk.

⚬⚬⚬

Artelo rode through the night and the next days with only the barest rest, driving his horse into a lather. A man possessed of a single purpose, he came exhausted to Duralyn.

And Solsta.

Solsta, whom he had spurned.

Solsta, whom he now had to beg for mercy and aid in his greatest need.

24

"These people are *starving*, Lord Trike," Solsta Ly'Ancoeur said.

Her voice rang through Castle Aventar's throne hall, and a hush fell over the Peerage in their booths along the walls. The Crown leaned forward on her throne. Her hands gripped the arms of the chair. "The storm has wiped away their stored goods, destroyed their homes. They will *die* if they are not given aid, and you are making mouths about the costs to your own enterprises to lend them aid."

"Pardon, Majesty," Lord Trike said quickly. He had the floor and stood at the base of the steps that marched up to the throne. "I meant no disrespect, but only to point out that for resources to be diverted from my lands and my people—"

"At *our* bidding," Solsta interrupted. The hush among the gathered nobles deepened; they knew from experience that Solsta's adoption of the royal pluralism was a sure sign of her ire. "We are aware that these are not your people, Lord Trike, but you are the nearest source of succor for the people of Urna. Lord Blayke has already done all he can to help his own. He calls for aid and the Throne will answer—through you."

"But Majesty—"

"No." Solsta shook her head. The Mark of her rule, a blaze of white in the forefront of her chestnut tresses, shone in the light of the great chamber. "We could command you to our will, but we do not choose that course. Rather we ask you one last time, Lord Trike: Will you deliver the aid, or shall we send it with our knights? This can be done, and help will come to Urna, though not as swiftly. People will suffer, people will die, and we will hold you accountable. So—what say you?"

For a moment it seemed Trike would continue to argue. He was trying to curry coin for his own lands in exchange for his aid to Lord Blayke's people in the neighboring valley, who had taken the brunt of a vicious winter storm. It was neither an unreasonable request nor one that would likely have been denied. Solsta was free enough with the royal coffers if she felt the cause was just—a little too free for the tastes of her treasurers—but for some reason Trike's words had struck a raw nerve and roused her.

It was hardly surprising to those assembled in the hall. The Crown had been in a black study for days. No one knew the cause exactly. It was rumored she had gone on some secretive journey with the Archamagus and her closest friends and returned in this distemper. Whatever the case, her normally equable demeanor had been cast aside and the Peerage was seeing the steel will and strength that were often beguilingly disguised by a lovely young woman who did not quite stand five feet from head to toe.

It reminded many of them of her father.

"My people are at your disposal, Majesty," Trike said, bowing.

Solsta nodded. Some of the electric tension in the air dissipated. "Well chosen, sir. Let it be heard that should such a time come when Fork or River's Bend has need, I will remember Lord Trike's wisdom this day and shall repay it in kind."

Trike smiled and bowed again.

"I will be visiting Urna personally, Lord Trike," Solsta added. "Do not disappoint me."

"I will not, Maj—"

This time the noble was interrupted by shout from outside the doors. "I will see her now! Solsta!"

The Sentinel knights in the hall snapped to the alert, their black-and-gold ranks closing to form a series of protective rows upon the steps leading to the throne. Above them, Solsta was already on her feet. "Open those doors!" she commanded, hurrying down the steps until she reached the first row of Sentinels. "Let me pass. There is no danger."

The ranks of Sentinels parted. The door wardens obediently opened the massive double-doors to the throne hall.

Artelo Sterling shoved his way through the knights who had been blocking his path. He staggered forward, struggling not to swoon.

Solsta brushed past an astonished Lord Trike, her ankle-length white skirt swirling as she broke into a run, gold boots clipping against the marble floor. She heard the surprised muttering and murmuring in the Peerage. Paid it no heed. All her care was for her knight.

She reached him just as his strength finally failed and he slipped to a knee before her. "Artelo? My God—what's happened?"

"Brittyn's...dead," Artelo gasped. "Aura...taken...."

25

Solsta paused outside the doors to her chambers, steeling herself.

When she had first heard Artelo's voice, her heart had leaped up, thinking that he had changed his mind and had returned to her after all. The moment she had seen Artelo's anguished face, however, she had known her hope was blasted.

Still, she had never expected the words that he had spoken.

They had been lovers once, when he was a Guardian knight and she the Princess, before duty had torn them apart. Since then, perverse Fortune had twice brought Solsta and Artelo back together. Each time they had been forced to face the truth that matters were far from settled between them; that despite the courses their lives had run, their deepest hearts were still for each other. Solsta had embraced this truth. Artelo had fled from it.

Now, barely a week removed from their last storm-charged and awkward parting, he awaited her in the sitting room of her chambers, where Solsta had ordered him taken after he collapsed in the throne hall.

She nodded at the two omnipresent Sentinels flanking her doors. She hated this formality and their presence so near to her private spaces, but the Archamagus was adamant that the guards be stationed there at all times, and Solsta, who had survived the assassinations of her parents and her husband, could not well deny their necessity.

Artelo looked up as she entered. For a moment, they simply stared at each other across the small chamber. The door closed behind Solsta with a quiet click.

"I hope you're happy," Artelo said. "You've destroyed everything I have."

Solsta had taken a single, tentative step toward him. Now she stopped in confusion. "What do you mean?" she asked, her dark eyes wide.

"What do I mean?" Artelo echoed. "What do I *mean?*"

A strange thing had happened to Artelo as he rode the last distance to Duralyn. For the early part of the journey from his home to the Crown City, he had been consumed by fear for Aura and sorrow over Brittyn. Those things had churned in him, boring a hole in his heart. Into this space had come a rush of acute guilt.

His family had been destroyed because he had not been there to protect them. *If you'd never gone to help Argentia, none of this would have happened,* a malicious voice whispered. He had no recourse, no defense against its battering insistence.

The guilt festered, in Artelo's heart. Became a monstrous rage that roared louder and louder within him as he passed through the rings and arches of Duralyn and on to the castle. It had burst forth when the Sentinels had denied him entrance to the throne hall, and it surged up again now.

"It's all your fault!" Artelo railed, rising to his feet. "If it hadn't been for your summons I would have been there to protect them!"

"I never sent for you!" Solsta shouted back. It had been the Archamagus who had requisitioned Artelo's aid against Mouradian of Elsmywr. Solsta had been the most surprised of all when the knight had arrived at the castle to pledge his sword to the task. "Never! Ralak sought you out on his own because he thought you could help!"

"I did help. Look what it's brought me! Look—" Artelo trailed off, sinking back down on the couch, burying his face in his hand, overcome with emotion.

All the anger and profound hurt melted out of Solsta. She crossed to the couch and touched the back of Artelo's bowed head. The feel of his hair was familiar though more than three years had passed since she had last run her fingers through it. "Oh, Artelo, I'm so sorry...."

Artelo shoved her hand aside. "Get away from me!" he snarled, his pale blue eyes glaring as he raised his head. "I don't want your apologies! I don't care what you think or what you feel, God damn it! All I care about is Aura. Now are you going to help me or not?"

Solsta sat beside him: near, but not so near as once she would have. Her voice was very small. "I promise I will help however I can, but please, Artelo, I don't understand any of this. What happened?" She reached for his arm. Thought better of it and lowered her hand to her lap. "You said Brittyn was killed and Aura was taken. By who? Goblins? Bandits? Artelo, what happened? Tell me, please."

Artelo looked at Solsta for a long moment, appraising her as he might a serpent. She felt such hate in his gaze that she wanted to cry, but held to her composure.

Looking away again, Artelo unfolded his tale, his voice often dropping to near inaudible levels as he relived the agonizing discoveries. He spared Solsta the details of Brittyn's death, wanting to hold them close and silent in his heart, but told of chasing the tracks to the woods and his plan to enlist Argentia's aid to carry on the hunt. "She's the best tracker I know. She'll find Aura."

Solsta took a deep breath. She was nearly overwhelmed with all she had just learned, but what gave her pause was her sinking certainty that the solution Artelo had fixed on was not nearly as straightforward as he believed. "Artelo, we don't even know if Argentia's still in Harrowgate."

Artelo shook his head. "It hasn't even been a week."

"You saw what she was like on the dock," Solsta reminded him. "With Argentia, a week is more than time enough for her to move on. She was already running."

Artelo started to retort, stopped, and cursed under his breath. Solsta was right, as she was usually right. "Ralak. Yes! Ralak can find her. He did before."

"Ralak's not here," Solsta said. "He's returned to Elsmywr to oversee the destruction of Mouradian's laboratories."

"Then contact him," Artelo snapped, the rage rising once more. He mastered it quickly, before it could undo the chance Solsta was offering. He looked her in the eyes again, and now his own were not full of cold hate, but hot tears at the thought of the danger Aura was in. "Please."

26

"Majesty?" Ralak the Red canted his head in surprise when the mist in his oculyr cleared to reveal both Solsta and Artelo Sterling. It was unlike the Crown to disturb him at his work, and the knight should not have been there at all.

"We need you here," Solsta said without preamble. "Artelo's wife was murdered and his daughter taken."

"Murdered!" Ralak exclaimed. "Tell me."

Leaning on his omnipresent rune-carved staff, the Archamagus listened as Artelo again told his tale. Like Solsta, he kept silent, only a narrowing of his dark eyes or the occasional twitch of his lips betraying his concern. "You have no idea who might have done this?" he asked instead of answering the knight's closing plea to deliver him to Argentia.

Artelo shook his head. "None. Not the killing or the kidnapping. I thought Pandaros might have taken Aura, saved her, but he's dead, and before..." He swallowed hard. Made himself continue. "Before she died, Brittyn said it was a lady."

"Pandaros?" This time Ralak's frown was complete, creasing his forehead with deep lines. *Why is that name familiar?* "Who is this Pandaros?"

"I told you, he was our farmhand," Artelo said, growing impatient. "I found him and a girl dead in the loft." He closed his eyes briefly against the image of the gutted carcass, the desiccated corpse, the rivers of blood.

"You did not tell me his name," Ralak corrected.

"Pandaros Krite. Why the hell does it matter what his—"

The magic of the oculyr blinked out.

"What hap—"

Artelo's words were again cut off, this time by a silver flash that lit up the sitting room as Ralak materialized out of the aether. The chambers and halls of Aventar were proofed against such magical intrusion, but the staff Ralak wielded, a token of power wrought by Dimrythain, the first Archamagus, had created those wards and granted each of successive Archamagus the power to bypass their shields of invisible fire.

Ralak nodded to the Crown and then turned to Artelo. "This may prove painful to you, but we must go to your home, Sir Sterling, and we must go quickly."

"What do you mean? I told you, there's nothing there. I need to—"

"Quickly," Ralak repeated. Before the knight could react, the Archamagus seized his arm with a surprisingly powerful grip. "Majesty, we shall return."

"Wait!" Solsta cried—but they had already vanished in another scintilla of light.

27

"What are you about!" Artelo demanded.

They were standing in his cottage, where two months earlier the Archamagus had appeared and set in motion the events that had wrought the destruction of Artelo's world. His anger helped him shake off the dizziness of walking the aether, which took a heavy physical toll, though the travel itself was a matter of moments. "I need to find Argentia, damn it!"

"Patience," Ralak said, glancing around the wreck of the kitchen. *Shadowaether....* He could sense the lingering taint of the dark magic. *As I feared....*

"You know something about this, don't you? Was Pandaros involved?" Artelo spat the question with such vehemence that Ralak thought however horrible Pandaros' death had been—and he suspected it had been horrible indeed—the foolish young man had been fortunate to die before Artelo could lay hold of him.

"I know nothing," the Archamagus replied calmly. "Though I expect that is soon to change."

Recognizing that it was useless to press the cypheric Archamagus further, Artelo followed Ralak out of the cottage. He was all right until he pulled open the barn door. Then he saw the saddle blanket that had covered Brittyn and his chest hurt as if an ogre had punched him. He fought against the tears.

When Ralak set a hand on his shoulder Artelo jumped in surprise. "Go and tend your cottage," the wizard said.

"My cottage? What the hell are you talking about? We have to find Aura!"

"The road to your daughter begins here, but to find it out is wizard's work," Ralak replied. His face was very grave now. The reek of shadowaether was much stronger. It was coming from above. From the loft. "Go and put your home right. Make it fit for your daughter again. Leave me to my task."

When Artelo was gone, Ralak summoned his magic, levitated to the loft, and surveyed the carnage. The rank, brimstone stench of shadowaether lingered in the air, so noxious he could almost taste it. Everywhere around him was the evidence of Pandaros' dark practices: pentagram, black tallows and sackcloths, potions and censers.

None of this was surprising to the Archamagus at all, but the depth of Pandaros' carelessness was. The blood-etched pentagram, which a good magus would have checked at least thrice before trusting his life to its wards, had at least four flaws that Ralak saw at a glance, any one of which would have been fatal to the diagram's warding power.

Ralak shook his head in disgust. It was worse than carelessness, it was arrogant stupidity. *Promitius was right to cast you out, boy,* he thought.

While that was true, it was also the source of the present catastrophe.

28

Ralak had first heard the name Pandaros Krite several months earlier, when Promitius of Valon had called him to his home to report the theft of his medallion of summoning. The loss of such a token of power was never to be taken lightly, but before Ralak could deal with that problem, the even graver menace of Mouradian and his army of simulcra had swept him up.

Now—and all too swiftly—the stolen medallion had returned to haunt him.

Ever since Artelo had named Pandaros, Ralak had been certain the apprentice had used the medallion to summon something beyond his control. The only question had been what.

From the butchery he found in the loft, he feared he knew.

His eyes went to the body on the bed. The woman had been spilt open like a rack of beef left upon the block when the chef turned to tend some other task. No weapon had caused the damage. It appeared she had been ruptured and pried apart from within.

Yet hers was not the corpse that told all the tale. There were many things of this world and others that Ralak knew could inflict such wounds. Spells he kept in his own arsenal could make a man's organs burst in their sacs, his blood boil in his veins.

There was only one thing, however, that the Archamagus had crossed in all his vast studies that could do what had been done to Pandaros Krite.

What remained of the apprentice was a husk. The flesh was withered to the bones within the torn remnants of his black robes. His mouth was a rictus of pain—or perhaps, even at the end, pleasure—exposing dried gums and teeth that appeared much too large for his shrunken face. His nose was a pit and his eyes were likewise gone, sunken into their sockets. His hair was a fine white silk, like cobwebs long rotted upon the head of an ancient, corrupted statue. His spindle-stick hands clenched only air. His splayed legs looked like a chasecrow's after summer heat and autumn frost had their way with the effigy.

"Succubus," Ralak muttered, moving nearer to the mummified corpse. Nearby, beneath one of the black tapers, he saw a pile of ash in which a few scraps of parchment that had not completely burned remained. He recognized them for the last of a scroll—very likely the scroll that had brought forth the demoness.

A scroll without which there was no way to banish her back to the Fel Pits.

The Archamagus started violently. *Where is the medallion?*

Checking his anger and his fear, Ralak searched the loft. He shoved aside hay and cluttered arcana.

Found nothing.

He closed his eyes. Conjured the aether, seeking the presence of any powerful magic token. Usually such a trick worked only if the device was empowered, but if it had been recently used, there might be enough of an afterglow to guide him.

Nothing.

Cursing, Ralak reached into a fold of his robes and drew forth a small oculyr. He passed his hand over the crystal ball. It clouded with aethereal smoke, and then cleared to reveal a portly figure in brown robes.

"Archamagus? To what do I owe this honor?" Promitius of Valon asked.

"I have found your wayward apprentice," Ralak said.

"Where is he?" Promitius exclaimed.

"Dead."

Promitius met this news with a moment's silence. "Then I have failed him completely." He shook his head.

"You do not know even the half of it," Ralak said ominously.

"What do you mean?" Even as he asked the question, Promitius' eyes widened with recognition. "My medallion?"

"Gone."

"Gone?"

"Perhaps I should say 'taken.' Taken by the thing your fool apprentice summoned."

"What thing was that?" Promitius had dreaded this moment since discovering Pandaros had vanished with his medallion. When his own efforts to locate the boy failed, he had no choice but to seek out Ralak's aid.

Ralak's eyes glittered deeply. "That is what you must tell me."

"How? Ralak, what would I know—"

"Do not think to trifle with me, Promitius of Valon!" the Archamagus said. "Without a summoning scroll, the medallion is useless. Where did that scroll come from? It was taken from your stores, was it not? Stolen along with the medallion."

"I—don't know, Ralak. I have many scrolls." Promitius' jaw twitched nervously.

"How many are to summon succubi?"

Promitius did not answer save to dart his eyes away from the Archamagus' glowering countenance. "How many?" Ralak repeated.

"Many. I could not help myself," Promitius whined, seeing the disgust on Ralak's face. "You don't know...their touch, the pleasure. No woman could—"

"Enough!" Ralak snapped, making Promitius flinch even though leagues separated them. "Do you know the name of the one Pandaros summoned?"

"I don't know. I didn't know he'd taken a scroll. I didn't think to check."

"She burned the scroll. I need not tell you what that means."

"Then the name will not matter," Promitius said. "All is lost. She has the token. She will breed."

"I am aware of the dangers," Ralak said crossly. "Cease your babbling, Promitius. Find the name. Make another scroll to control this fiend."

"That will take much time."

"Then I suggest you begin immediately."

"I will do as you ask," Promitius said. "But Ralak—please, old friend. Consider what will happen if this was known. I would be disgraced. Ruined."

"I will deal with you later," the Archamagus promised.

Without waiting for a response from Promitius, Ralak dismissed the image from the oculyr. He knew it was doubtful that a scroll of sufficient power to command the succubus back to the Fel Pits could be made swiftly enough to serve them, but the name of the fiend had other uses. It could only help to know it. *So let that fool search it out....*

Ralak looked around the loft again. Perhaps there was some other clue, something he had missed. Or perhaps he might discover the succubus on his own. Wherever she had gone, she could not yet be far.

He settled himself into a cross-legged position. Folded his hands into the sleeves of his red robes. Closed his eyes. Opened himself to the aether.

For many hours the Archamagus cast his spells, seeking for the succubus. But she was not using her own magic or her true form and so remained hidden from his questing eye.

A creaking of the ladder brought him back: Artelo, his work in the house completed.

Ralak rose, brushing off his robes.

"Well?" Artelo was physically and emotionally exhausted. He had barely slept in three days and was almost too tired to move, but he needed to know what Ralak had learned. "Who took Aura? Where is she?"

"We must return to Aventar," Ralak said. "There is more than just your daughter's life at stake now."

Artelo grabbed Ralak by the front of his robes. "Shut up! I don't give a damn about anything but Aura! Do you understand that? You'd better, because—"

A pulse of aether flung Artelo back. He skidded across the loft and fetched up against the defiled bed.

"Enough," Ralak warned. His eyes glittered dangerously for a moment, then softened. "I am deeply sorry for your loss, Artelo, and for the theft of your daughter. If you think me—or worse, the Crown—to blame for your own choices, then I am sorry for that too. But so be it. I am the Archamagus of Teranor. To me is given a weight of responsibility far greater than yours. A grave mischance has struck. The whole world may again stand in danger for it—and your daughter is the fulcrum on which all now pivots."

"What...do you mean?" Artelo gasped. In his overtaxed and weakened condition, the magical blow had struck him much harder than Ralak had intended. He was still trying to catch his breath.

The wizard went over and helped the knight to his feet. "Let us return to Aventar. This tale the Crown must hear as well, and I would not spend the time to tell it twice."

29

An instant's aetherwalk later, Artelo and Ralak entered the Crown's chambers.

"Sit," Solsta bid. "Take some tea, please." Herwedge, Solsta's highly efficient butler, had been dismissed for the night, so she poured fresh cups herself, appraising Artelo carefully as he took his from her and then sank into a chair. "You look so very tired."

In truth, Artelo looked like hell. Years earlier, the knight and his companions had journeyed far and fought brutal battles to rescue Solsta from the vampyr that ruled Braken Swamp. She remembered waking in the dungeon to see Artelo before her. He had looked bad then; he looked worse now. Black bags hung beneath his wild eyes, his cheeks were scruffed with stubble around his normally trim moustache and goatee. *How is he even going on?* Solsta wondered. She knew, of course. *His daughter....*

"I have the Unicorns ready to ride," she said. "We will hunt whoever has your daughter to the ground and bring her back."

"I wish it were that easy, Majesty," Ralak said, shaking his head. "But it is not. What has taken Artelo's daughter cannot be overcome by normal force of arms."

"What are you talking about?" Artelo demanded. "Will you just speak plain, damn it!"

"It is a succubus. A powerful and very dangerous demoness."

"A demoness? A *demoness* has Aura?"

"Yes," Ralak said. "I am afraid so."

"How could a demoness have taken Aura? How is that even possible?"

"It was possible thanks to your farmhand, Pandaros Krite. He summoned the succubus."

"That son of a bitch! I'll...." Artelo trailed off. Pandaros was already beyond any vengeance he could wreak. *You got off easy, you bastard....*

"I don't understand," Solsta said. "How could a farmhand summon a demon?"

"Pandaros was not really a farmhand. He was a thwarted apprentice magus who aspired beyond his talent and was expelled from his master's house," Ralak said. "Alone he was little threat, but he had stolen a medallion, a token of summoning. With its power, he brought the fiend forth, and it proved beyond his control. It has fled now, with the medallion and Sir Sterling's daughter."

"But why?" Solsta asked. "What does it want with Artelo's daughter?"

"To make a vessel for its spawn."

Silence hung in the sitting room in the wake of Ralak's words. Not even Artelo could speak. His cup trembled violently in his hand. He managed to set it on the nearby table and then looked up at the Archamagus. "It can be killed," he said. "Tell me it can be killed."

"With a weapon of sufficient craft."

"What weapon?" Then he remembered there was such a one, a blade that had been instrumental in the defeat of the demon Ter-at. "Scourge!" He looked to Solsta. "Please, I need that sword."

"Scourge is gone," Ralak said, sparing Solsta the pain of a reply.

"What do you mean?"

"It was given to the dragon as wyrgyld for its aid against Mouradian."

"So we'll get it back. Give it something else in exchange."

Ralak shook his head. "A dragon will never part with the least of its treasures. No, I am afraid that sword is beyond us."

"Then— There must be another way." Artelo rose and started pacing. "I can't just let Aura die. She's all I have left."

Though it nearly broke Solsta's heart to hear those words, she found the right ones of her own. "You'll find her," she said, rising and moving instinctively closer to him. "Artelo, I *know* you will. You came for me when I was lost. You *will* save your daughter."

"Indeed," Ralak said. "There are always other ways, but first this thing must be found."

"I thought we went back to my barn so you could find it," Artelo said.

"I went seeking answers. That was not among them."

"Then it was a wasted trip."

"Hardly. I learned much of great import, which you have yet to hear."

"The only thing I want to hear is how to find my daughter!"

Ralak frowned. "So I see," he said. Then he nodded, as if resolving some internal debate. "Very well. I suggest you make ready."

"For what?"

"The aetherwalk to Harrowgate."

It took a moment for Artelo to understand what the Archamagus was saying. Then he nodded, his eyes lighting with purpose. "It's about damned time."

30

The true purpose of the aethergate in the Monastery of the Gray Tree was to allow the Crown's escape if Aventar should ever fall to siege. It was useful this day in sparing Ralak from further exhausting his powers by making yet another long journey in the aether.

In a flash of time, Artelo passed by the sparkling way from the monastery to Coastlight Cathedral in Harrowgate. He was met by Colla, the city's High Cleric.

"Is she still here?" Artelo asked her when he had recovered from the aetherwalk sufficiently to speak without feeling like he was going to vomit. The magical travel did not usually affect him so badly. *Tired,* he acknowledged. He did not want to think about how long it had been since he had eaten something not dried and pulled from a saddlebag, or since he had slept.

"Would the Archamagus have sent you else?" Colla replied, but not unkindly. She was a short woman with brown hair damp from a bath framing a pretty face. She looked altogether too cute and youthful for the gravity of her position until she settled her eyes upon you. In their brown depths were purpose and wisdom and compassion that beguiled her years. She was dressed not in her clerical raiment, but in a simple blue robe that looked very old and well worn, and a pair of faded pink slippers. Artelo remembered that when he first met her, Colla had been a simple cleric in a small village called Sharelywys, and a shepherdess, as well. The recollection made him ache for Brittyn.

Colla must have sensed his pain, or seen it flicker across his face. She touched his forehead gently, like a mother determining a child's fever. Her fingers began to glow.

Artelo flinched from her touch, which she had meant to draw some of the weakness from him. "Peace," she said. "You need rest. I know you will not heed that advice, but at least let me help you."

Artelo shook his head. "Just tell me where she is."

Sighing at the knight's willfulness, Colla lowered her hand. The nimbus of the healing power bestowed on her by Aeton's grace dimmed away. "On the beach, as has been her habit each night since her return."

"You're spying on her?" Artelo was surprised.

Colla smiled again, this time a cynical gesture that hardened her pretty features. "Did you think the clerics of Aeton merely healers and confessors? We have many duties. As for Lady Dasani, let us say that there are those who felt it would be prudent to keep a watch upon her for her own safety. She has suffered much and is not of a right mind. If you must approach her, do so with care."

"*She's* suffered? Damn it, I don't care what she's— You've no idea—" Artelo waved his hand dismissively. "Never mind. Just show me where I can find her."

Colla looked at Artelo for a long moment. He met her gaze defiantly until she turned away and tugged a silken cord hanging beside the door. Somewhere in the cathedral a single bell tolled. A moment later the door to the aethergate chamber opened. Another cleric entered and bowed to Colla. He was a man of some fifty winters, with thinning, sandy hair and a bushy moustache.

"Maren will show you the way," Colla said to Artelo. "When you are finished, whatever the hour, return and I will see you sent back to Duralyn."

"Thank you," Artelo said, managing not to sound too churlish.

"Aeton's Light follow you," Colla said, lifting a hand in benediction.

Artelo was already headed for the door.

31

The beach was dark and empty. Silvery fog wormed up from the sea. The chill, wet air was full of a sense of the end of things, of land swallowed by the immeasurable water that crashed incessantly against the shore.

By pale moonlight, Artelo trudged along the scrabbly beach. Had it really been just a week since he had disembarked at Harrowgate's docks, the battles of Elsmywr behind him, anxious only to return to his family? He felt as if he had aged a thousand years in that time. His family was a union shattered: his wife gone forever, and his daughter.... He could hardly bear to think on the fate Ralak had told him awaited Aura.

The knight quickened his pace. As he moved farther from the lights of the city and the pier, the moon slipped behind a cloud. The darkness grew more pronounced, until he could barely see. He stumbled, cursing. *Where the hell is she?* Maren had brought him only to the edge of the beach. "She is there," the cleric said, pointing through the gloom.

Artelo had seen a solitary figure down by the water, but now he feared his eyes had played some trick on him. *It wasn't that far. I should have reached her by now....*

He stomped on, squinting. The moon eased from behind the clouds again, and he saw he had not been deceived.

She was there: a tall silhouette in the shallows of the surf.

Artelo shouted to her. No answer. Perhaps the wind had stolen his words.

He shouted again. Still no answer. He went closer. Reached for her shoulder. "Argentia."

"Don't touch me."

She did not turn to face him, so Artelo stepped into the water beside her. The low waves splashed over his boots. Under the clean scents of sand and salt, a rank odor reached him. In the moonlight, he could see her clothes were filthy. Her head was swaddled in a black scarf. The night hid the rest of her burns and scars, but he remembered they had been extensive and awful.

Colla's warning rose in his mind: *If you must approach her, do so with care....* He wondered suddenly if this was such a good idea.

"Please, just hear me out," Artelo said. "Something terrible has happened."

"Leave me alone." She steadfastly refused to look at him.

"Please—"

"Go."

"I'm not going anywhere! Brittyn's dead, my daughter's been taken by a demon and I need your help!" Artelo shouted.

She did turn to him then. Her cobalt eyes shone above the dark scarves masking her face. "I can't help you."

"What the hell do you mean? I can't track this thing, but I know you can. That's what you do."

She shook her head. "Not anymore."

For a moment Artelo was silent, stunned by what he was hearing. "Please, I—"

"No."

The rage boiled up in Artelo. "No? *No?* You can't say no! You *owe* me. I saved your life!" This was something of an exaggeration—despite their best efforts, the company that sailed to rescue Argentia had not reached her in time to do anything except bring her back from the island—but it had an effect.

"You *saved* me?" she shouted back. "Look at me! Better you'd left me to die!"

"Don't make me wish I had!"

Her eyes flashed. "Get out of here." The warning in her voice was unmistakable.

"If you don't help me my daughter is going to die!" Blood was pounding in his temples, but Artelo forced himself to be calm long enough to voice one final plea. "If not for me, then do it for her. She's an innocent little girl. She did nothing to deserve this fate!"

"What did I do to deserve mine?" She turned away.

"No! You *will* help me." Artelo grabbed for her.

She spun with all her uncanny speed and lashed her bare foot into his chest.

Artelo went sprawling backwards into the shallows. He thrashed in the shockingly cold water, sputtering and gasping but more astonished than hurt. He sat up. A wavelet slapped across his back, soaking him further. "God damn you, Argentia!" he roared as she ran up the beach. "I thought you were my friend!"

If she heard, she gave no sign.

Kept running.

32

Later that same night, a pair of Sentinels escorted Artelo from the Monastery of the Gray Tree back to Castle Aventar.

He was bedraggled and beaten, his clothes sodden and full of sand and salt, but none of that mattered. Argentia's rejection had given him a new focus for his rage, from which he drew new strength. He would have begun the hunt for the succubus that very moment—if only he knew where to begin.

I can't believe she betrayed me.... When Artelo had dragged himself out of the water Argentia had already disappeared in the dark. Furious, Artelo took a few steps after her before deciding it was worthless. She had made her choice. Even if he chased her down and fought her, there was still no way he could force her to help him.

He was on his own.

Bitter, he left the beach and returned with Maren to Coastlight Cathedral. Neither the cleric nor Colla asked what had happened on the beach. There was no need. Without so much as a word of thanks, the knight walked the aether to Duralyn, crossing the thousand leagues between the two cities in the blink of an eye.

The rage followed him. When he entered Solsta's chambers and found Argentia's butler Ikabod and her dog Shadow had joined the Crown in her vigil, it erupted.

"I am deeply sorry for your loss, young sir," Ikabod said, bowing to the knight. His disappointment when Artelo entered alone was great, but he hid it behind an etiquette bred from a lifetime of service.

"Too bad your mistress didn't feel the same," Artelo snarled. "We should have let the dragon finish its work!"

"I beg your pardon, sir!" Ikabod drew himself up to his full height: a tall, thin old man in an immaculate black livery. "I will not hear you speak so of Lady Dasani, whatever your cause."

"I'll speak how I please, old man."

Shadow raised his lupine head off his big paws and growled low in his throat.

"Stop this, all of you!" Solsta said. "Artelo, what happened? Where is Argentia?"

"In Harrowgate. Let her rot there."

"But what happened?" Solsta pressed. "Is she all right?"

"I don't give a damn if she's all right. All I care about is finding Aura—and she doesn't." He glared angrily around the room, surly as a dwarf in need of a drink. "Where the hell is Ralak?"

"Here."

With a flash that startled Solsta—though she should have by now been well used to the Archamagus' sudden appearances—Ralak materialized in the chamber. He nodded to the Crown and ascertained from Argentia's absence the result of Artelo's trip to Harrowgate.

"Where's Aura?" Artelo demanded.

"I do not know," Ralak said.

"You don't know? What have you been doing all this time? All your magic, you can't even find one missing little girl?"

"Be calm!" Ralak commanded.

Mirkholmes, Solsta's pet meerkat, jumped off the couch where he had been resting and looked about in alarm. The little animal had pilfered spells from the Archamagus many times. When the wizard raised his voice Mirk always feared he had been found out and was but moments from being turned into a worm. That did not seem to be the case tonight, but the sensible meerkat still took shelter behind Shadow's black-and-silver bulk.

"I grow weary of this churlishness, Sir Sterling," Ralak said. "Will you hear me or no?"

"Artelo, please, just listen to what Ralak has to say," Solsta said, stepping between the two men. "There are other things you must know. Things that will help you save your daughter."

"Fine," Artelo said grudgingly. "Talk."

33

The Archamagus had spent the time of Artelo's absence pouring over centuries of obscure writings about succubi, looking for any advantage against their foe. He explained to Artelo the nature of a succubus, how it lived only to breed and how its spawn, being part man, was not subject to the barrier magic of the Shadow Gate. "A demon loose upon this realm cannot summon others of its kind, but the spawn of a succubus can. To do so it requires a token of power, which its mother already has. If the spawn comes into possession of that medallion, Teranor will once again face war from the hordes of the Fel Pits."

"I told you, I don't give an orc's ass about any of that. What does this have to do with finding Aura?" Artelo asked.

"Much," Ralak said. "The succubus is powerful, but checked by its nature. It must feed on men until its spawn is formed and then it must go to a place of darkness to give birth. Until that time, your daughter is safe. The creature will neither harm her nor allow any harm to come to her."

"You seem to know a hell of a lot about this thing, so why can't you find it?"

"Its magic prevents me. With each feeding, it drains the life-essence from its victims. Its power grows and its guise becomes more fully human. I cannot track it through the aether, as I might were it in its true shape, but I will find it nonetheless."

"How?"

"As I told you, it is bound for an evil place. A shimmyr, where the passage between the Fel Pits and our plane comes easiest. A place like the cave atop Mount Hoarde."

Artelo remembered that cave very well. It was there that he and Argentia had fought the final battle against the demon Ter-at and its troll ally. "If you know all that—"

Ralak shook his head. "I do not know which shimmyr it is making for, nor would I wish to guess. There are many more than you might believe. I must wait for the signs."

"Signs?" Artelo echoed. He did not like what he was hearing at all. "What signs?"

"Other victims like Pandaros. They will show the course the creature has chosen. Once I know that, I can anticipate its destination. Until then, we must all be patient."

"Like hell! *That's* your plan, great Archamagus?" Artelo spat. "You expect me to just wait around and hope you're right about this thing and what it might or might not do to Aura? Are you completely mad?"

"I know it is difficult advice, but you must trust me. The answer will come in time enough to rescue your daughter."

"Artelo, Ralak is only trying to help you," Solsta said. "We all are—"

"No! No more help! You've all been enough *help* already. If I hadn't gone after Argentia to begin with, none of this would ever have happened. Now you tell me to *wait* while Aura gets farther away every hour? I can't. I won't."

Artelo wheeled around and wrenched the door open. He shouldered the astonished Sentinels aside and raced down the hallway. Shadow barked loudly.

"Majesty, should we sound an alarm?" one of the Sentinels asked. His hand was already on his silver trumpet.

"No. I forbid it." Solsta stepped forward. "Let him go. Let him be. Send word immediately that he is to pass unchallenged, even from the city, if he wishes."

"At night, Majesty?" the Sentinel asked. With sundown, the gates of Duralyn were closed and did not reopen until dawn.

"I have spoken," Solsta said, her voice full of a quiet weariness as she looked out the doorway where her love had vanished. She remembered the times he had charged to her aid, first rescuing her from the vampyr, then coming to Mount Hoarde and taking the sword Scourge against the demon—never hesitating, simply doing what he knew he needed to do.

Now he was flying off against impossible odds to find his daughter. Though Ralak said it was all but fruitless, Solsta somehow believed that if there was even the slimmest margin of success, Artelo would find it.

More troubling than Artelo's rash departure was Argentia's flat rejection of the knight in his obvious need. *The Argentia I know would never have done that....*

Solsta feared that woman might be lost forever. That what had returned from Elsmywr was burned not only in body, but in spirit.

Sighing, Solsta turned away from the door. There was no way they could help Argentia. It seemed for the moment they could do nothing to help Artelo, either.

PART III

The Road West

34

Artelo was gone from Duralyn and out into the night before he calmed enough to realize he had no idea where he was actually headed or what he meant to do when he got there.

He had raced through the rings of the Crown City, meaning to do *something* for Aura. To do anything but accept Ralak's ludicrous counsel and sit and wait for an answer while his daughter was out there in the clutches of some fiend: frightened, cold, hungry, lonely for her parents and her home and all the familiar, comforting things that made up her whole young world.

Spurred by these wrenching thoughts, Artelo had actually drawn his sword, prepared to fight his way past the Gate Warders if he had to, but they had opened the great doors to the city and let him pass without even slowing him.

He slowed now, however, dropping his overtaxed horse to a walk. He looked up at the star-dusted heavens. *Am I going mad?* The night remained still and silent, so he turned his questioning inward.

He did not have to look far for the answer. His wife had been murdered, his daughter taken, his friends had deserted him. If any man in Acrevast was right to question his sanity, it was surely the son of Alidar Sterling.

Still, he was troubled by his behavior, particularly by his lack of self-discipline. He was a knight, after all, yet since his return from Elsmywr he had behaved with anything but the dignity and restraint befitting his station.

No, that's not true.... Faced with the choice of Solsta or Brittyn, he had held to his marital vows and left the Crown behind. Would that stand as his last testament to his chivalric code? He prayed not, but since then he had seen his life sucked into a vortex of pain and death that had been beyond his coping. Rage had been his only shelter. Now he wondered if it might not be a prison as well.

It was not so much his anger at Argentia that cut at his conscience—she had betrayed their fellowship and deserved his wrath—but at Solsta and Ralak, who at least had tried to help. They had continued to do so even after his stormy exit, he realized. Only an order from the Crown could have made the Gate Warders stand down and let him pass.

Solsta.... Artelo did not rightly know why he was so angry with her and Ralak, or why he felt so adamantly that regardless of his own responsibility they should not be exculpated from Brittyn's death and this whole nightmarish affair, but he was, and he would continue to be until his daughter was safe in his arms again.

Only then could he contemplate forgiveness—of them for their part, and of himself for his.

If Aura dies....

Murderous thoughts flashed like white-hot meteors across Artelo's mind. He faced them down. Aura was not dead, and he refused to think of her so. *I'll get you back, pumpkin,* he swore. *I'll bring you home. I promise....*

Artelo rode on, heading west at as arduous a pace as his mount could stand. He crossed the bridge fording the Valdenthal, the mighty river still sluggish, waiting for the thaws in the Gelidians to set its waters roaring through springtime.

He was brutally tired now and half starved. He had exhausted his rations and all but emptied his waterskin. He bitterly regretted shunning Colla's offered aid. In their own strange way, the priests of Teranor were as powerful as the magi—more powerful, some would say—and the

High Cleric's healing grace, never dispensed lightly, would have served Artelo well.

No help for it now...

He continued on. Made his camps brief, preferring to doze in the saddle and at least keep moving. He was still unsure what he was moving toward, however, and the time he was awake he spent wrestling with doubt and fear and anger, trying to fuse them into some constructive purpose: some starting point from which he could begin to chase down the fiend that had stolen his daughter.

Three days later, he reached the turn for the Gap Road that would lead him home. No clear idea or brilliant inspiration had illumed him. With almost bottomless disgust Artelo realized that Ralak had been right. There was no real course but to wait. Worse, he would have to face the Archamagus again, like a child come creeping back to his parents after a tantrum.

It galled him, but he would do it if it meant finding Aura.

In the meantime, Thackery was only a couple of hours down the road. He would find the cleric Hozlizem there and have him hallow Brittyn's stones, assuring her spirit peaceful repose. That way at least some good would come of his temperamental departure from Duralyn.

Artelo walked his abused horse into the village. Thackery was arranged much as any hamlet in Teranor: trade shops, a tavern, a hostelry, and a small church all lined a main thoroughfare that was transected by residential streets of quaint, thatched cottages. Cart paths extended from the village through the surrounding farmland, and all was lorded over by Crond Manor in the shadows of the foothills to the west.

It was a quiet place. Today it was too quiet.

Artelo hitched his horse to the post in front of the Speckled Tortoise and patted its trembling flank in thanks for its mighty efforts. As the horse bent its head to drink from a trough of stagnant, almost brackish water, Artelo realized what was wrong. Not only were the streets of Thackery mostly empty—he had seen perhaps a half-dozen people, and they had all looked at him suspiciously, though he knew each by name—but the windows of the Speckled Tortoise were all dark and the tavern door was shut.

Artelo did not frequent the Tortoise, but he had been past the tavern more times than he could count picking up supplies or dropping off wool or milk or cheese from their farm. He had never seen the Tortoise closed before. *Never even heard of it....*

It was none of his business, he knew, but he found himself approaching the door, impelled by something more than curiosity. The vague unease that had crept up on him as he walked through the village now wrapped about him like a cloak of shivers. He half expected to hear a scream as he reached for the knob.

Locked.

He hesitated for a moment, feeling the weight of the ominous silence, then raised his stump to knock.

"Don't bother."

Artelo wheeled, his hand dropping to his sword, his heart leaping in surprise.

Behind him stood Devlin, the apothecary and village healer for cases not extreme enough to require Hozlizem's unction.

"What happened?" Artelo asked. The wizened apothecary was one of the few people in Thackery that the knight genuinely liked.

Devlin shook his gray-haired head. "Best we don't talk of such things on the street." He gave a judicious nod. Artelo saw that the few people who were about were watching them with more than passing interest.

Devlin took the knight's arm. "In my shop—hurry now."

35

It was cool and dark in the apothecary. The air was gritty with the residue of alchemical powders. There was clutter everywhere; more than Artelo ever remembered seeing in the normally meticulous space. "What happened?" Artelo asked again.

Devlin hung the wooden CLOSED sign in the window and drew the curtain behind it. "Sit down," he invited over his shoulder.

"No, thank you. Can't you tell me what this is about?"

The old man turned and fixed Artelo with a careful eye. "Del Kardee is dead. Murdered."

"What? How? When?"

Devlin, who seemed to have been studying Artelo's reaction to this news, nodded as if he had satisfied himself on some point. "Curious you should ask. Folk believe you killed him."

"That's insane! I didn't kill anyone. Why would—" But even as he asked it, he knew the answer, or thought he did. *Because of what almost happened to Brittyn. Del was part of that. They think I waited three years to take revenge....*

"Because your wife and daughter were seen leaving the Tortoise early on the morning Del was found," Devlin said.

"What?" Artelo could only whisper. Shock and confusion whelmed him. The little strength remaining to him flooded out of his body. He sagged into a faded leather chair. "That's impossible," he said faintly.

If Devlin heard, he did not reply. He went into one of the back rooms and returned a few moments later with a cup of cold tea. The drink had a pungent odor. Serrated green leaves floated on the amber brew. "Drink it all," the apothecary said. "The leaves come from Nhapia. Great healers, the Nhapians. Renowned for their herbal medicines. Right now you look to me like a man who could use some medicine."

Artelo sipped the tea. It was crisp and minty and refreshing. He took a larger swallow. "Good, no?" Devlin smiled. "Not elven esp, grant you, but it will help you, I think."

Artelo, who'd had the potent elven drink on several occasions, actually managed to smile back. "It's very good. Thank you."

Devlin let Artelo drink in silence for a few minutes. He went to the door and moved the curtain slightly to peer out into the empty streets. It seemed they still had time. He turned back to Artelo, meaning to ask him a question, but the knight spoke first. "When?" he said.

"Pardon?"

"When was this? Del's death?" Artelo was leaning forward in the chair, the pieces of a dark puzzle beginning to fall into place in his mind.

"Some five days ago. The Tortoise didn't open at noon. People wondered for a few hours. Finally some of them got to knocking. No one answered, so Fenerd Kemp brought a bar from his forge and pried open the back door. He and some other men went in. They found Del in an upstairs room. Murdered—or worse."

He described the body, which he had been privy to see before it was taken for burial. As he spoke of withered cornhusks, the cup began to tremble violently in Artelo's hand. "What's the matter?" Devlin asked.

"Who saw my wife?"

"Dommen."

"Dommen?" Dommen was a half-wit boy who performed odd jobs around Thackery and its neighboring farms. He had helped Brittyn at the cottage during her pregnancy. Artelo knew him to be honest enough, but still a fool. "How? Is he sure?"

114

Devlin spread his thin old hands. "He seemed sure. At least, as sure as he ever is. It was early morn and he was delivering milk to Dol Bartlet's. He saw three people by the light of the Tortoise's door lantern: Mavia Kardee, your wife, and your daughter. He was across the street and he hid when he recognized Mavia. She was always cruel to him, you know."

"How did you learn all this?"

"Two days ago, some men came to my shop to ask me if what they'd heard about Del's body was true. By chance, Dommen was here to collect my order for the herbalist. He overheard Butchwald Farady mention Mavia's disappearance. People were wondering, of course, what had happened to her. Most figured if either of those two was to murder the other, it would have been Del's knife in her heart. In any event, Dommen told what he'd seen. I don't know how many believed him, but I think enough did that—"

"Never mind that," Artelo interrupted. "Did he say which way they went?"

Devlin nodded. "He said he watched until they were out of sight. He was afraid to come out until Mavia was gone. They left town headed west."

Artelo leaped up, galvanized. He had given the succubus a five-day head start with his wasted trip to Harrowgate, but perhaps there was still time to make up for it. "Devlin, listen to me. Brittyn can't have been here five mornings ago. I don't have time to explain now, but I didn't kill anyone, I swear to you. You'll just have to trust me."

"Wait!" Devlin said. "There is more you must know!"

"No time. Not now." Artelo crossed to the door.

It opened before he could reach it.

A dark-skinned man stepped into the apothecary. The polished belts and buckles of his Watch uniform gleamed in the soft light. "Artelo Sterling," he said. "I arrest you in the name of the Crown."

36

Jaru Ben'Aboden, Captain of Thackery's Watch, was a tall man from the Sudenlands. His dark eyes were calm. His helm sat tight on his caf-colored head. His arms were by his sides, his hands in easy reach of his sword and dagger.

Behind him was a younger man, also in uniform: his deputy. The deputy's sword was drawn and his eyes darted nervously around the room. Ben'Aboden merely looked at Artelo. "Will you come quietly?" he asked.

The Watch Captain spoke with almost no Sudenland accent, a sign that he had been raised in or at least spent many years in Teranor. He projected the sure, placid confidence of a seasoned professional. Artelo figured he would have much more trouble getting past Ben'Aboden than his deputy, despite the fact that it was the deputy who was supposedly ready for resistance.

Perhaps it would not come to fighting. Artelo had never attacked a servant of the Crown before. There was something about the idea that did not sit well with him; it would be like striking at a brother. Still, as when he had ridden with his sword drawn against the gates of Duralyn, he would do what he had to do here as well.

Aura's life depended on his freedom.

"What charges are brought against me?" he asked.

"Murder," Ben'Aboden replied.

"Whose murder?"

"Let's start with the two bodies found yesterday in your loft. I don't know why you'd be fool enough to return here, but I thank you. Makes my job much easier."

"I was trying to tell you," Devlin said to Artelo, who was stunned. "News of what Dommen saw traveled fast. Captain Ben'Aboden went to your cottage."

Artelo could piece together the rest for himself: Ben'Aboden would have seen the open door to the cottage, the signs of struggle. A search of the property would have brought him inevitably to the loft.

"Whatever you may think, I did not kill them," Artelo said. Nothing was going right. He had finally gotten a line on Aura and now this.

Ben'Aboden shrugged. "That's for the Magistrates to decide. My job's only to keep you until they come to collect you for your trial. Now I ask you one last time, out of respect for your station: will you come quietly?"

Artelo closed his eyes for a moment. "I will," he said.

Ben'Aboden nodded. "Well chosen. Kensel, take his weapon and bind his hands."

Artelo smiled and raised his stump. "It won't be necessary," he said. "I told you I'll come quietly."

"Take his weapon," Ben'Aboden repeated.

The deputy, Kensel Marin, stepped forward. Artelo's sword was scabbarded at his left hip. Kensel could not reach it with his own blade extended, so he put the weapon up between him and Artelo. Reached with his left hand toward the hilt of Artelo's sword.

Artelo's right hand speared crosswise and down, catching Kensel's wrist. He yanked the deputy forward and headbutted him in the nose. Kensel cried out as pain burst through his face like a shooting star. He was spun around. An iron-hard band clamped across his chest. Dazed, he barely felt the blow from Artelo's steel-capped stump that struck his sword hand and sent his weapon clattering to the floor.

"Stop!" Ben'Aboden unsheathed his sword.

"Don't move!" Artelo said. His right arm kept Kensel pinned against him. *Snick!* A knife blade sprang from his enchanted wristcap. He pressed the edge to Kensel's throat. "I didn't do anything you think I did, and I've no wish to harm either of you, believe me, but I am leaving here and I will not be stopped. Now drop your sword," the knight said.

Ben'Aboden read the terror printed clearly on Kensel's bloodied face. He weighed the odds that he could strike Artelo before the knight cut his deputy's throat. They were not good. "You will hang for this, Sir Sterling," he said as he cast his sword aside.

"Perhaps, but not today. Get down on your knees."

Ben'Aboden complied. He knew what was coming next. Artelo would hit him, hoping to knock him out. It was what he would have done had their situations been reversed, and there was a risk to it. Artelo had to get near enough to land a blow, which meant Ben'Aboden would also be able to reach the knight. He still had his knife. If Kensel could somehow twist free or distract Artelo...

The Watch Captain tensed to spring.

Snick! The wristknife retracted into its sheath. Artelo drove his stump in a hard uppercut, crunching Kensel's jaws together. The deputy's legs were jelly as Artelo shoved him forward. His dead weight crashed onto the surprised Ben'Aboden, who was helpless when Artelo stepped in and clubbed him over the head. A second blow put the Captain down to stay, pinned beneath the already unconscious Kensel.

"What have you done?" Devlin whispered.

"What I must." Artelo felt sorry for the Watchmen, who had only been trying to do their duty, but they never would have believed him if he told them the truth, and even if they did come to believe, he would have been too long delayed.

"But why? You did not kill those people they found in your loft—I could read that truth in your eyes—and I know you did not kill Del Kardee. Hozlizem sensed great evil at work in that chamber. Unless you are a magus of extraordinary power or a poisoner without peer, I know of no way you could have done what was done to Del."

"I didn't," Artelo said. "I told you that."

"Then why are you doing this?"

"To save my daughter."

"Aurora? But what—"

"There's no time for me to explain," Artelo said. "Will you help me?"

Devlin looked long and hard at Artelo. Nodded slowly. "I will do what I can, within reason."

"Then listen. Brittyn's dead—murdered, along with the two Ben'Aboden found in my barn."

Devlin paled. "Dear God, but how?" The apothecary had known Brittyn literally all her life, having assisted the midwife at her birth. "Why did the Captain make no mention of this?"

"He didn't know," Artelo said. "I built a cairn for her atop the hill before Ben'Aboden ever arrived. I need you to take Hozlizem there. Have him hallow the ground. Let her spirit rest in peace."

"If what you say is true, who did Dommen see outside the Tortoise?"

Artelo took a deep breath. He knew Dommen certainly had not seen Brittyn. He must have seen Aura and the succubus. Shape-shifting had been a trick the demon Ter-at had used many times to evade pursuit and to walk unseen by the wizards whose magic could hunt it out in its true form. *And Ralak said this one was in a human guise...*

"He saw Aura and the thing that killed Brittyn and I guess Mavia Kardee, though I don't know what that's about," he said. "I can't explain now. I have to go after Aura."

"You'll not get far on that horse of yours," Devlin said. A conspiratorial light was in his eyes. "Take the Captain's. It's in a paddock behind the mercantile. It will be one less horse they have to chase you with when they recover."

"Steal a horse?" Somehow that thought was appalling to the knight.

"If you want to make more than a league a day. I've tended my share of horses. Yours is in no condition to go on. Wait here a moment." Devlin headed for the back rooms of the apothecary again. A few minutes later he returned with a worn pack stuffed with food. "Not much, but it will get you started down the road."

"Thank you." Artelo knew he had imposed a great deal of trouble on the old apothecary, but the circumstances had left him no choice. "I am in your debt."

"Nonsense. It is my vocation to give aid to those in need, and you clearly are in need."

"Will they cause a problem for you?" Artelo asked, gesturing at the fallen Watchmen.

"The Captain? Doubtful. I suppose he could arrest me for abetting you, although I can always tell him you forced my compliance at swordpoint." Devlin chuckled. "No, I think I will be well enough. The village is full of fear now, but that will pass soon if nothing else goes amiss. Let people think what they will. I am old enough to know truth when I hear it, and too old to pay mind to the chattering of fools. Now go quickly, before they wake."

"When they do, tell them to contact Ralak the Red at Castle Aventar. He can vouch for my innocence."

"I will do that." Devlin handed Artelo the pack and opened the back door. "Keep to the backstreets. Most of the town is probably out front waiting to see you brought forth in irons."

"Have Dommen tend my sheep," Artelo said, digging some coppers out of his purse and giving them to the apothecary. He added a gold mark. "And take that for yourself, for the supplies. And don't forget Hozlizem. Please, that's the most important thing. And thank you again, for everything."

Devlin said. "Fortune follow you, Sir Sterling."

"Pray She follows my daughter."

37

Artelo rode his stolen Watch horse (the saddle had been conveniently resting on a nearby fence post) out of the village. He was a fugitive now. He did not like the way that term rang in his mind. He hoped Devlin would tell Ben'Aboden to contact Ralak and that the Captain would do so.

If he did not, Artelo might find himself not only riding after Aura, but riding ahead of a pursuit of Unicorn cavalry knights.

He could not control that, so he refused to waste time thinking about it. Again he reminded himself that he was only doing as he must to rescue Aura.

God, what a fool I was! he berated himself. He had raced off to Duralyn and never even thought of checking Thackery. He could have had Aura back by now. *This could all have been over....*

But he had failed. He had been too blinded by grief and fear to think clearly and he had gone storming off on exactly the wrong course, letting the fiend that had taken his daughter slip away behind him. If Aura died now, he had no one to blame but himself.

I won't let her die, he swore. *Please, Aeton—one chance to make this right....*

Driving his heels into the sides of his horse, Artelo spurred down the North Pass, chasing the succubus toward the setting sun.

38

Sylyth moaned.

She locked her ankles hard on the small of the man's back, holding his heavy weight down against her, urging him on. His thrusts grew more frenetic. Soon he would burst his hot seed in her.

The succubus gave an expert swivel of her hips, clenching her hidden muscles tightly. The man sweating and gasping above her groaned and arched suddenly upward. "Oh gods!"

Yes! Sylyth gloated. *Feed, my spawn! Feed....*

Outside, a steady rain beat against the window. This was Sylyth's fourth man tonight but she was nowhere near tired. She would never tire. Only the sun would put a temporary hold on her insatiable appetite. She could take three, perhaps even four more before day came and the stream of customers dried up until the next night, when the doors of the Pink Tulip would open once more and cycle would begin anew.

Finding the brothel was yet another sign that Bhael-ur's dark favor rested on the succubus. The Tulip served Sylyth's purposes perfectly and eliminated many of the dangers of the road....

Hrutch Pentery's wagon had brought the succubus and her companions eleven days west of Thackery.

Hrutch Pentery had not been with them after the second day.

Sylyth, still glutted from her feeding in the village, had only teased and tasted the wood-carver that first night. She took him on the next, out in a field off the North Pass, beneath a black velvet sky full of those hideous stars. Hrutch was good: strong and vigorous. It took her almost all night to be done with him, but in the end his bulky frame was wasted down to a chasecrow carcass that she was able to carry with one hand and toss into a convenient copse of alders and spruce.

His strength was her strength now, feeding her spawn, augmenting the magic of her disguise. She was very nearly a perfect imitation of Brittyn. Her nails had shrunk from talons to shapely but sharp lengths. The few wounds that had remained from her battles were healed. Only her eyes could betray her, and in time even those would only be noticed by a person of excruciating discernment.

But the horses were still a problem.

They were hateful creatures, the succubus thought, innately capable of sensing what she was. She would have enjoyed ripping them open, watching their innards splash and steam upon the dirt of the road, but she knew they needed the animals to better complete their journey.

Since the horses would not tolerate Sylyth's proximity, she left the driving to Mavia, who perched upon the board like a stormcrow and whipped the team with the same vigor that she had once whipped her son. The succubus sat in the wagon amid the boxes of Hrutch's wooden carvings. She found the various animal shapes and symbols inane totems. The ones carved from ash and holly and oak made her flesh itch horribly when she touched them. If nothing else, however, they served to keep the child occupied.

Aura was another annoyance. The child cried often, calling for her mother or father or for food. Sylyth was astonished at how much so small a creature could eat, and thanked Bhael-ur that the wood-carver's wagon had been well laden for his journey west. She was glad to feed the child; it stopped her whining and kept her healthy. The stronger the vessel, the better chance it would survive the entry of her spawn.

For her part, Aura was as confused as a child of three could be, and very scared. The old woman hit her and yelled at her, terrorizing her so badly that now she actually stopped crying at just a glance from the vulture-eyed hag, but it was the other who truly frightened her.

The woman who looked like her mother was not her mother. An older, more rational mind might have been driven into madness trying to reconcile this impossibility, but Aura had a child's simplicity and thus no difficulty at all accepting what her heart told her was true.

Still, it frightened her. Being touched by the Bad Lady was like when she had been playing in the mud and a worm had wriggled across her ankle: her flesh felt as if it was going to crawl right off her bones in revulsion.

She had no real way to articulate her feelings, and so, surrounded by hate and evil, she regressed in her behavior. She began to wet herself—something she had not done in more than six months and which provoked more strikes and screaming from the mean old woman—and all but stopped speaking except to call for her mother or father or when she was hungry.

Mostly she slept.

Rocked and lulled by the motion of the wagon, Aura found refuge in dreams, where a woman veiled in celestial light whispered comfort to her....

They journeyed on, following the North Pass toward the Hills of Dusk. On the third night out from Thackery they came to a farmstead, and Sylyth discovered that dogs were far worse than horses.

39

They had stopped under the pretense of shelter from a spring storm. Soaked and huddled on the doorstep, they waited as the heavy footfalls and the barking of dogs approached from within. Sylyth could smell the men. She licked her lips greedily.

When the door opened it revealed the farmer, his two sons, and the dogs: a pair of stocky, fierce-looking black-and-tan beasts held on short tethers by the two boys. The instant they saw the succubus, the dogs burst forward, pulling free of the leashes. A chaos of shouts, screams, and snarls battled the shriek of the wind and the pelting rain. Sylyth recoiled, but not fast enough.

The first of the dogs barreled into her, jaws snapping on her upraised arm. Sylyth howled, staggering back, losing her footing on the soaked ground and going down hard. Thrashing in the puddles, the hot, hairy beast scrabbling atop her, she smashed her fist into the dog's head with such force that she broke its grip on her arm for an instant and was able to shove the dazed animal away from her.

The second dog hit Sylyth before she could recover, burying her in a rush of fur and fangs. The succubus was pinned on her back and the dog would have torn her throat out, but the farmer dove atop it and wrestled it off long enough for Sylyth to scramble up. "Wait!" he cried, but Sylyth, clutching her wounded arm, was already fleeing to the wagon.

"Please, tell her to wait." The farmer looked up at Mavia. "Don't know what got into 'em. They're the calmest dogs anyone could wish. Swear it by Aeton's light."

Indeed, now that the succubus had been routed, the dogs were markedly different. The one that had bitten Sylyth came slinking back toward the door and the one caught by the scruff of its neck in the farmer's firm grasp was whimpering. Neither seemed remotely threatening.

"Bring her on back, let my wife tend her arm," the farmer pleaded.

"A curse on you and your kin for this foul hospitality," Mavia said. Leaning forward, she spit in the farmer's rain-soaked face, then turned on her heel and stalked after her Mistress.

The wagon rolled into the storm-ridden dusk.

By morning, Sylyth was ravenous. She could feel the spawn within her, its hunger a thing awake and keening. There was nothing she could do to sate it. Draining Mavia's life and essence would only sustain her own form; it would do nothing for the spawn.

She needed a man, and soon.

But they were in an empty stretch of land. That day and the next passed with no sign of human habitation. Sylyth grew desperate. She could feel herself weakening as the greedy spawn drew its nourishment from her womb.

Finally, six days west of Thackery, they reached the village of Hamlyn. Nestled in the hills on the north side of the road, it was smaller than Thackery—home to perhaps seventy people—but still boasted a tavern, the Hog's Breath, with boarding rooms.

After securing one of these, Mavia went forth to to seek the village apothecary. Aura had caught a cold thanks to her trip through the rain, which Mavia had spitefully neglected to shield her from (she hated the puling, stinking little brat and could not stop hating her, despite the warning from Sylyth that the child was to be unharmed). Mavia made the illness sound much worse than it was, earning the apothecary's quick response.

Geoff Taryson was narrow-faced man of fifty, balding, and almost as thin as Mavia herself. He had been ministering to the ill of Hamlyn and the travelers passing through the village on their way to and from Byrtnoth for thirty years, so he was well used to calls for aid at all hours of the night and from all manner of people. He went hurriedly and in good faith, suspecting nothing.

Only when he entered the chamber did it become apparent that much was amiss.

There was indeed a child sleeping in the room's single chair, but on the bed was a woman who appeared much more in need of aid. She was stark naked and shaking as if wracked by some fever. Her hands were twisted claws, one arm was swathed in blood-stained bandages, and there was something terribly wrong with her eyes: they seemed to have no irises.

"What is this about?" Geoff asked as he heard the door close behind him. "You said a child was—"

Mavia struck him across the top of his head with her walking stick. Stunned by the surprising force of the blow, Geoff dropped his satchel and stumbled toward the bed. Inhumanly strong hands seized him and pinned him down. The woman with the strange eyes loomed over him.

"I starve," Sylyth hissed. Her hand closed between Geoff's legs, sending a bolt of pleasure such as he had not known for a decade or more through him. He tried to struggle, but already he was drowning in the erotic promise of those black eyes: a promise he did not even want to resist. The succubus mounted him with quick expertise, and the rest of Geoff Taryson's life shot away in a tumescent arrow of fatal delight.

After the apothecary, Sylyth was strong enough to hunt on her own. By the time the trio slipped back to the wagon and rolled away under cover of the last hours of the night, Hamlyn had also lost its baker, its butcher, its smith, and its mayor's son. The succubus came to each like a dark, wanton dream, choosing a shape culled from their fantasies. She took them quickly, tapping each for all his worth and moving on to the next and the next, until she was at last sated and her human guise was flawless once more.

They continued their journey into its second week. Between Hamlyn and Byrtnoth they found three more farmsteads.

All of them had eligible men.

None of them had dogs.

40

Byrtnoth reminded the succubus of the brimstone citadels that towered amid the flaming lakes and burning deserts of the Fel Pits.

The city was built on five tiers up the side of a hill. The nobility dwelt in the uppermost tiers, the wretched and impoverished in the lowest. Between were the various mercantile districts, streets full of shops and taverns and inns.

Everywhere, there were people.

Sylyth had never seen so many. There were endless streams of men; such numbers that she almost swooned with lust. Yet she knew she must be cautious. If she was to remain safely in this place and feed until her spawn was fully formed, she could not kill with abandon as she had in the village and at the isolated farms. She had already left a trail behind her, as if a plague had visited the North Pass. It would not do to let that trail follow her to the city, where she sensed there were wizards and clerics and guards with stern steel, all of whom could do her and her plan great harm if they discovered her.

Sylyth was not worried. The first days with the spawn were the most dangerous. That was the time it grew fastest and its need for an almost constant supply of food made her insanely ravenous. She could not help but glut herself on every man she encountered, taking all their seed, all their essence.

Those days were behind her. No longer starving, she was much more in control of herself. She could take what she needed now, leaving the men weak but alive.

The only question was where to bring her victims.

Sylyth knew nothing of Byrtnoth or any other human city, but Mavia did. She had been born in Byrtnoth and lived her first ten years there, before what her father had referred to only as "the Trouble" sent them east to Thackery.

They left the wagon at the first tier's public stable. Mavia did not know the place she was looking for by name, but she would know it when she saw it, and she was sure there would be one. If the stories she had overheard her father telling were true—and he had spoken with great authority—there were likely dozens.

They walked the streets. Mavia had Sylyth put on a hooded cloak. Under the influence of the succubus' dark magic, Brittyn's simple beauty had become a smoldering force that drew men like metal to a lodestone, and some of those skulking in alley mouths were of the sort that would as quickly kill you as look at you.

The first tier of Byrtnoth did carry on some legitimate trade, but the majority of these businesses were just fronts for illicit activities carried out in backroom gaming parlors and seed dens. It was across the street from one such place, a tavern called Rat's, that Mavia found the Pink Tulip.

She was surprised that the place would make so little an effort to disguise itself. Perhaps such things were no longer so frowned upon as they had been in her father's day. The cunning part of her mind also wondered if they should not push onward and search for another place instead of settling on the first one they had come across, but she was weary, her leg ached like a bastard, and the wretched child was crying again.

They entered and were greeted by Matron Weyzl and her two thugs: giant men wearing tunics of leather over bulging muscles. Weyzl was a short, plump woman with a braid of dishwater gray hair dangling to her knees. She was skeptical when Mavia approached her about work until

Sylyth lowered her hood and unfastened her cloak. Then Weyzl's eyes lit with a piggish light, like winter sun striking off coins in an alley.

Mavia brokered the arrangements with the same ironhanded sense she had used to run the books of the Tortoise for so many seemingly endless years. Sylyth was granted the Tulip's plushest suite, which caused no small row among the established but clearly inferior whores in Weyzl's stable. Mavia and Aura were placed in an attached room with a viewhole in the wall that looked through a mirror in Sylyth's chamber. Weyzl thought she had achieved a marked victory in weighing the split of coin heavily in her favor, but that was only because Mavia could not have cared less how much coin they took in. She had plenty of her own with her and a feeling that wherever they were heading, coin would not be a necessity.

In the five nights since her arrival, Sylyth had left enough men sated, drained, and almost delirious as they stumbled out of the Tulip that Weyzl believed Fortune had shown upon her at last and with ultimate grace. When every one of those men returned at least once over the ensuing nights, the Matron started giving serious consideration to releasing all her other girls. With Sylyth alone she could turn a tidy profit for much less expense. In all her years in the business she had never seen men so besotted as they were with Sylyth. It was almost like witchcraft.

Mavia sat behind the mirror and watched Sylyth with her latest victim. Since coming to the Tulip, Mavia had watched every one of the succubus' encounters. They were all of a pattern. The man would enter. Sylyth would remain behind the curtains of the bed, using her magic to touch the man's mind, finding his secret fantasy. Then she would approximate that shape, part the curtains, and the coupling would begin.

This time the succubus was wearing the guise of a tanned, black-haired Nhapian. Mavia felt no desire as she watched the bodies writhing together through the gossamer veils—that furnace, never hot in her to begin with, was long cold—but she did feel a sense of growing darkness and power in her Mistress. She reveled in it, understanding that she was privy to a great display of Bhael-ur's design. Her long faithfulness to the demonic god had been rewarded, and would continue to be rewarded.

Young again, yes.... It was a chance to rectify all the errors she had made in her first seventy-three years. Perhaps in Byrtnoth, perhaps in some other city. Or perhaps her Mistress would have some particular place in mind for her, some particular service she wished Mavia to carry out.

The details did not matter. Mavia knew that all would pass however Bhael-ur ordained it. She would obey her dark god's will.

She took a length of beads from a pocket. They were a prized possession: wood from a willow that had been struck dead by lightning. The beads had been carved into tiny, horned skulls. Their black surfaces had been worn almost gray by the oils of Mavia's fingers and forehead. Closing her eyes, she clenched the beads in a gnarled fist and began to pray.

Time passed.

The door between Mavia's chamber and Sylyth's opened. The succubus was there, framed in pink light from the room behind her. She wore a shift of silk mesh that barely reached her thighs and left little that it did cover to the imagination. The medallion of summoning hung about her neck. She was in her Brittyn form again. Her blonde tresses were mussed, her face and throat flushed with the afterglow of hard sex, but the hungry look was still in her dark eyes.

"Bring me the next," she said.

Artelo followed the corpses west.

Near sunset of his second day out of Thackery, he met a small, three-wagon caravan headed toward Duralyn. They had pulled to the side of the road. Across a field, vultures circled overhead.

The wagoners were setting camp. One of the men hailed Artelo. The knight was going to keep riding, but there was something frantic in the man's gesture, so he slowed his horse and stopped.

"Good evening," he said. He was wearing his armor, which usually commanded the attention of Teranor's commoners, most of whom had never seen a knight. These were no exception. The women and children—there were eight that he could see—lingered back by the wagons, pointing and whispering. The man who had hailed Artelo stepped forward. He was in his middle years, a farmer by the look of him, likely with the last of the winter's potatoes and roots loaded on those wagons.

"Good ev'nin likewise, sir," the farmer said, doffing his patched hat and bowing his weathered head to Artelo.

"Is something amiss?" Artelo already regretted stopping. Probably the farmer was going to offer for him to share their camp, gaining a measure of protection through the night in exchange for a meal.

"Mayhap, sir. Found a body, sir. Saw them buzzards circlin somethin fierce over them trees. My boys went to check what were down there.

Thought mayhap twere a deer or such we might profit off." Artelo nodded, not really interested. The roads of Teranor were dangerous places. People died on them all the time, killed by sickness or storms or bandits.

"Weren't no deer, though. Was a man, sir, and he died awful. Like naught I've ever seen. Beggin your pardon, sir, but the womenfolk are nervous it's not safe to camp if whatever did this might be out there?" He gestured vaguely in the direction of the field.

Artelo nodded again. Part of his mind was urging him to move on already, that he was wasting time, but another part was nagging him that he had a duty here. A lone man killed in the wilds was probably a hunter or trapper who had run afoul of a bear or wolf or mountain lion, which likely meant no danger to a large group with a good fire going. But probably was not certainly. If the man had been killed by bandits or by goblinoids—a remote possibility this near to Duralyn, but still a possibility—they might still be about, in which case the caravan might need protection through the night after all.

There you go again, the other part of his mind said. *This is exactly the kind of thinking that set you off after Argentia and got Brittyn killed and Aura kidnapped. Haven't you learned anything?*

Artelo actually shrugged his shoulders in answer to that interrogation. What he had learned by the sheer fact that he had stopped here at all was that this was who he was. He could not turn his back on those who might be in need. Brittyn had known it. She may have resented it at times, but it was also the thing she had most admired about him. If he buried that part of him with her, how was he honoring her memory?

How are you honoring it if Aura dies? Remember your promise?

If she dies in the next five minutes there wouldn't be a goddamned thing I could do about it!

That seemed to quiet the nagging voice. Artelo exhaled a long breath. The farmer was looking at him strangely and twisting his hat in his strong, brown hands. The rest of the caravan had gotten very quiet.

"You two found the body?" Artelo pointed to the farmer's sons.

"We didn't do nothin, sir," the older of the boys said, wringing his hat in a manner similar to his father.

"I didn't say that you did. Show me where you found it." Swinging down from his saddle, Artelo strode after the farmer's sons. The grass was low and stiff beneath his boots. They made for a copse of alders and spruce. "In there, sir," the boy said.

For a brief moment Artelo wondered if this was some elaborate set-up to draw him off the road and ambush him. But the boys were unarmed. They looked farm-strong, but unless they had two or three more men with weapons lurking in the trees, they had no chance against him in a fight. Still, Artelo had been trained to be cautious. "Wait out here," he said.

"Yes, sir."

Artelo went into the trees. No attempt had been made to hide the body. The moment Artelo saw it, all thoughts of ambushes flew from his mind.

"Aeton's bolts!" Artelo bent beside the body. The corpse had the same withered appearance as Pandaros. It had once been a man; parts of a beard still tufted the mummified jaw. Now it looked like a chasecrow. It had no eyes; the birds had gotten those, as well as the nose and lips. Scraps of dried flesh had been pulled loose from the face and chest, left to hang like cured meat.

Artelo straightened and returned to the wagoners. "Sir, what is it?" the elder boy asked. "Some danger here?"

"Danger, yes," Artelo said. When he had seen the body, his first thought was that the succubus and Aura might be somewhere in the area. He quickly realized that was unlikely. Ralak had said the fiend needed to feed its spawn. It would not risk hiding on a roadside to prey upon whatever happened to pass by. It would make for a city, or at least a village. "But not here. Not any more. Set your camp. Start your fire," Artelo said.

"Beggin your pardon, sir," the other boy said. He was fair and freckled like his brother, and looked to be a year or so younger. "We was thinking before you rode up, sir, that it don't seem right to just leave the body like so."

"You want to bury it," Artelo said.

"Yes, sir."

"You have spades in the wagons?"

"Yes, sir. Good 'uns, too."

Artelo nodded. "Go tell your father all's well, and bring a spade for me. Three can dig faster than two."

"Yes, sir. Right away, sir."

The ground was hard, but the trio was up to the task. By the time the last of the light was leaving the land, the work was done. The farmer invited Artelo to camp with them. The knight accepted.

He shared a meal of beans and sausage in a rich, red gravy: the first good meal he had taken in too many days. They talked of crops and the land. The farmers were surprised to find a knight so versed in the agrarian ways. "My family owned land," Artelo said by way of an explanation. That made him think of Brittyn and their cottage—a life lost to him now—and the shadow hooded him. He excused himself from the fire, tended his horse, and retired.

At dawn, he was on the road west again.

42

Artelo saw no other signs of his quarry until he reached Hamlyn. When he rode into that village it was as if he was entering Thackery all over again. He knew almost instantly that the succubus had stopped there ahead of him.

Stopped, and killed.

There were few people on the streets, but Artelo got what confirmation he needed at the Hog's Breath. Again his armor carried weight. Once people started talking, the tales and rumors flowed as if the village had been baiting its breath for the past five days, waiting to loose these pent fears. One of the murders—there had been five, including the mayor's eldest son, Artelo learned—had taken place in an upstairs room in the tavern. The others had been in various homes. All had been in the same night.

Feeding, Artelo thought. *Gorging itself....* What if the thing's spawn grew fully and was ready to emerge? According to Ralak, that was when Aura would come into danger.

I have to find her first....

On his way out of the village, Hamlyn's lone Watchman stopped him and asked, "You hunting whatever monster did this?" He was a veteran soldier, wearing a heavy conscience as plainly as his battle scars when he introduced himself to Artelo. There had not been five murders in this sleepy village in the last five years; now there had been five in one night.

Artelo nodded. For a nervous moment he had been sure his fugitive status had outpaced him and this man would try to arrest him as well.

"Good," the Watchman said. "When you find it, make sure you strike it down with Hamlyn's name on your tongue."

"I will." Artelo wondered how many other names he would be adding to that list before he finally crossed paths with the fiend.

By the time Artelo reached Byrtnoth, the list had grown by seven.

These dead were divided over three farmsteads. At one he found a widow and her two young children. At the next, a widow who had lost both her husband and her father. At the last, a girl of his own age who had awakened five mornings past to find her father and her three brothers dead and shriveled in their beds. Artelo met her as she was fixing a wagon to a horse. "Leavin," she said. "Nothin for me here but pain." She had blonde hair and gray eyes and reminded Artelo so much of Brittyn that he had to ride on before he started weeping.

43

It was late in the afternoon of a day that had seen storm clouds gather since midmorning when Artelo reached Byrtnoth. No rain had fallen yet, but it was coming. The cold air was charged. A restless wind stirred. Thunder grumbled impatiently as the pall of evening dropped over the land.

Artelo rode to the gates of the tiered city bearing his own storm with him. He was weary in heart and body, but his anger still gave him strength to carry on. He had started his journey focused solely on Aura, but what he had witnessed along the way had heightened his hatred for the succubus. Not only was there Brittyn to avenge, but more than a dozen other innocents. It stirred the righteousness in him. If he could save Aura and end this fiend's existence in the process, he would gladly do so.

First he had to find them.

Byrtnoth was nowhere near as large a city as Duralyn or Argo or even Harrowgate, but it was still an impressive place. Storm shadows had fallen over the upper tiers, draping the mansions of the nobility in mourning cloths. Five levels of the city stood between the knight and those great homes. He doubted the succubus was in one of them, but he could not be sure. Even so, there was a lot of city to search before that became a concern. *I need a lead,* he thought. *Please, Bright Lady, just one lead. Help me find Aura....*

Inside the gates, he paused long enough to once again put his armor to good use and ask some questions of the Watchmen stationed there. He had little hope—people flowed in and out of Byrtnoth like leaves in a stream, heading east to Duralyn or south to Timber Cross and the Mir River cities—but to his surprise one of the guards actually remembered seeing Aura and her captors.

"Strange group," Laeonus Castlebright said. He was tall and handsome, with a youthful light in his hazel eyes. He might have seen twenty-five winters. Artelo marked how clean and polished his uniform was, and how serious his demeanor. He was reminded of himself a lifetime ago.

"Two women and a child on a wagon. Don't see that much. Not safe, especially not for a woman beautiful as that one," Laeonus continued.

"I was their escort," Artelo improvised. "Took ill in Hamlyn."

The guard's eyes narrowed. He backed up a pace. "Catching?"

"No, no, I'm fine. Ate some bad meat. Anyway, they didn't want to be delayed, so they went on with a man from the village to guard them."

"No man. Not unless he came in before or after them. Those three came alone."

Artelo made a face. "Villagers," he muttered. "Probably ran off after the first night with the coin I gave him. Did you happen to give them the name of an inn? I'd like to catch up with them again."

"I didn't, but they stabled their wagon and horses. Maybe one of the boys there can help you, although five days on I doubt that lot'll remember."

"Worth a try," Artelo said. *At least I know for sure they're here—somewhere....*

He clasped Laeonus' forearm, thanked him, and walked his horse to the stable. The wind had stolen the last, fleeting warmth from the day. *Might not snow, but winter's teeth will be in this rain,* the knight thought as a crash of thunder split the heavens. Moments later, the first drops of that sleety rain began to fall.

Cursing under his breath, Artelo ducked into the stable. Amid the good smells of hay and horses, the five stable boys showed Artelo the wagon the two women had left. "Everything's in it still, sir," the lead boy said. He was perhaps fourteen and feared Artelo meant to accuse them of robbing the wares. "We didn't touch nothin."

Artelo peeled back the canvas and looked inside. There were only boxes full of wooden carvings. Still, he could almost feel Aura's presence lingering there. *So close now....* "Two women and a child," he said. "You saw them?"

"One old, one young, and a baby. They were hurryin. Old woman paid the fees."

"Which way did they go?"

The boy shook his head. "I didn't see, sir."

"I did," another piped up. Artelo turned to him. "I...followed 'em out, sir. I's done my shift and that lady was...."

"Go on," Artelo said. Outside, thunder rattled and the rain fell harder.

"Beautiful, sir," the boy stammered. "I wanted to see her again." The others laughed. Artelo silenced them with a glance.

"Where did they go?"

"Into a...a harlot house, sir." The boy flushed and looked down at his manure-stained shoes.

Of course.... Artelo felt like a fool for not having thought of it himself. The succubus needed men. Where better to get them than a brothel?

He ruffled the stable-hand's wild blonde hair. Digging into his purse, he pulled out some coins. Passed them among the boys, even those who had not spoken. Then he held a gold crown between his thumb and forefinger. "One last question: the name of this harlot house?"

The blonde boy grinned from ear to ear. "Sir, the Pink Tulip."

44

Artelo ran through the storm.

The rain beat like a timpani upon his chain corset and armored breastplate. His boots splashed in deep puddles that sprayed up to soak his pants. He was already so wet it hardly mattered. He kept on going. The stable-hands had told him the way to the Pink Tulip, but the pouring rain and dismal gloom confused everything. Had he made a wrong turn?

There was no one he could ask. The few people still about on the streets in the miserable weather were hardly stopping to give directions. Artelo ran on. Up ahead, through the nimbus of a street lamp, he saw a sign for Rat's. *That's it!* The boys had said the brothel was opposite the tavern.

Across the dark street there were dark buildings. One of them was the one he sought. Artelo forded the flooded cobblestones, wiping his drenched hair out of his eyes. Lightning jagged. He searched in the glare. Found the door marked with a carved flower. *The Pink Tulip…*

Were they here? Had they moved on already? Even if they had, there would be information to help keep him close on their trail. But he did not think they were gone. This felt like the right place. He remembered something Argentia had told him once, about being able to sense when a hunt was close to its end. He had not understood or really believed her then. He did now.

Artelo grasped the door handle. There would be enforcers of some sort waiting within. It was even possible that the succubus had turned the whole brothel to her defense. *Doesn't matter. I'm getting Aura back. If I have to cut down every whore and patron in this place to do it, I will....*

He opened the door.

45

Speed, surprise, and viciousness were Artelo's allies.

He burst out of the rain and into a smoky lounge full of pink lamps glowing over silk-draped couches adorned by scantily clad women. There were men as well, seated and standing, chatting idly with each other or with the women, drinks in their hands, pipes in their mouths. The gray haze in the air was scented with spicy seed.

At the rear of the room, near a curve of ascending stairs, stood Matron Weyzl and her two thugs. The Matron was smoking a thin, straight pipe with a very small bowl and wagging her finger in mock reproach at a small, richly dressed man who was reaching into his jacket for his purse.

Artelo barreled across the fleecy golden carpet before anyone in the hazy lounge could begin to react.

Matron Weyzl could not believe her eyes. Her pipe fell unheeded from her mouth. She had a long-standing relationship with the Watch in Byrtnoth. They left her establishment alone and she provided whatever services they required free of cost. So why was there a knight of the Crown charging at her—and with a sword drawn?

"Stop him!" she shouted at her guards.

The two hulks surged off the walls. They were ponderous men who relied on brute force and intimidation to win their battles.

Artelo was trained to deal with brute force, and he would not have been intimidated by the likes of these two were he still a novice at the Academy.

Plus he was angry.

It was a bad combination for Matron Weyzl's guards.

A mace swung in from the left. Artelo parried the blow out wide. A simple reverse slash would have split the thug's broad belly wide open, but even in his rage Artelo retained enough of his code that he would not kill needlessly. Instead of the fatal riposte, he countered with a left hook that crunched his steel wristcap into the guard's jaw. Bloody spittle and several teeth flew from the thug's mouth as he pitched forward like a felled tree.

The other thug tried brain Artelo from behind, but the knight was already ducking away. As the mace whistled harmlessly past his head, he spun around and kicked the man squarely in the groin.

The guard made a weird whining noise and fell to his knees. A chopping blow from Artelo's wristcap dropped him atop his fellow guard in a mountain of unconscious flesh.

The lounge erupted into screaming chaos. Whores and patrons crashed into each other, all rushing for the door. Matron Weyzl, staring at her fallen guards, had time for a single thought—*They're a complete waste of my coin*—before Artelo set the tip of his blade against her plump chin.

"The woman with the child—where is she?" Artelo said. Weyzl's piggish eyes darted from side to side, trying to find her lie, and Artelo knew he had the right place. "Where?" he demanded, dimpling her flesh with his sword.

"Up the s-stairs. Far end of the h-h-hall!" Weyzl sputtered. It would be bitter to lose the new girl—she realized that she did not even know her name—but she could not spend her profits if she was dead.

"If you're lying, I'll cut your tongue out," Artelo promised.

"I'm not!" Matron Weyzl shrieked, tears spilling down her doughy cheeks.

Artelo was already past her, running up the stairs. He raced down a red-carpeted hall, never breaking stride, and threw his shoulder into the door.

Like everything else in the Pink Tulip, the door was ornate in appearance but cheap in substance. Artelo knocked it mostly off its hinges, smashing through in a spray of wooden shrapnel.

The man mounting Sylyth on the bed twisted toward him, anger quickly turning to surprise and fear at the sight of Artelo's rain-glistening armor, wild eyes, and shining sword. He rolled away from Sylyth and threw his hands up. "Easy, friend."

"Get out." Artelo commanded. The man scrambled off the bed and ran naked out the door.

The succubus, hissing like a wildcat, retreated to the far side of the room.

Artelo should have been stunned by what he saw: the image of Brittyn was almost perfect. But one look at the eyes of the figure cringing in the corner spelled all the difference in the world. Those soulless black pits held nothing in them of the woman who had been a wife, a mother, a lover, a friend. They held nothing human at all.

Artelo leveled his blade at the succubus. "Give me back my daughter!"

Sylyth was terrified. She was naked and unarmed, and while she had her great strength, she feared the man's sword. It was only steel, and could never kill her, but if it pierced her belly it might kill her spawn, which was too weak yet to survive such a trauma.

For a moment her terror was so great that Artelo's words failed to register. Then they did, and Sylyth understood who her enemy was and how she would defeat him.

She summoned her magic and extended her hands, beckoning. "Artelo...."

At the sound of his name sliding like honey off those sweetly curved lips, Artelo paused. Despite himself, his resolve slipped. A wave of raw lust whelmed him. He wanted only to drop his sword, catch

(Brittyn)

the succubus in his arms, carry her the short distance to the bed, and bury all the pain that had tortured him this past fortnight in the liquid warmth of her body.

"Yessssss," Sylyth whispered. "Come to me...." She rubbed her

(*Brittyn's*)

stiff-nippled breasts and licked her lips. "Take me...."

Artelo stepped forward, his sword slipping in his grasp. A blast of thunder split the night. Somewhere nearby, a child

(*Aura?*)

cried out in fear.

The sound broke Sylyth's spell. Artelo steadied his blade. Fresh anger surged through him as he realized what he had been about to do. Growling furiously, he raised his sword to strike down the succubus.

Mavia Kardee stabbed him in the back.

46

The knife, guided perhaps by some malevolent force as much as by aim, entered a seam in Artelo's armor and sank deep into his flesh. He dropped his sword. Staggered forward.

Sylyth darted past him.

No! Artelo swiped at the succubus. His fingers clutched through her hair. Closed on empty air.

His assailant twisted the blade in his back, ripping it free. Pain volcanoed through Artelo. He turned clumsily. Fell to his knees.

A black-clad specter loomed. Steel flashed: the knife coming again.

Artelo caught the woman's skeletal wrist, jarring the knife from her grasp.

He surged up and drove his stump full force just below the crone's sternum, doubling her over as—*Snick!*—six inches of cold steel from his wristcap plunged into her chest.

"Gaaah!" Breath and life blasted from the old woman, but still she clawed at Artelo. He shoved her away. She collapsed in a heap. "Mistress!" she gasped, blood foaming from her lips. "Help me!"

Sylyth, already in the adjoining chamber, did not even spare Mavia Kardee a glance.

Artelo stumbled after the succubus, but fell before he could get to the door. *Hurt....* He could feel the blood of his life flowing down his back. It was hard to breathe. He struggled to his feet.

Have to... Have to save....

He collapsed again. Heard distant voices. A child screaming.

Aura....

Everything went black.

47

Sylyth ran through the storm.

She had paused in Mavia's chamber only to grab Aura, slapping the child viciously across the face to stop her screaming and slinging her over her shoulder like a sack of potatoes. Then she raced down the hall and the steps, glancing back with every other stride, certain the knight would be behind her.

She made it out the door and into the press of whores and patrons gathered outside the Pink Tulip. Forced her way through the crowd. Icy rain pelted her. She realized she was naked. Spying a whore who had wrapped herself in a blanket, Sylyth veered over and shoved the girl down, stripping the covering. The whore screamed. One of the patrons grabbed for Sylyth. She let some of the demon flash up in her black eyes. The man blanched, stumbling back, and then Sylyth was through the crowd and into the storm-dark night.

She ran for blocks on end until she found an alley shadowy and twisted and secluded enough to suit her purposes. She plunged into its recesses, fighting through spilled trash and scattered refuse, chasing rats from their hiding places beneath rotted crates.

At last she stopped, gasping, drenched, and shaking. The lizard part of her mind that had triggered her instinct to escape receded. She began to think again.

Aura stirred, recovering from the stunning blow and the jouncing flight. Sylyth hunched down and drew the blanket over her, shifting it to keep Aura as protected from the storm as she could. Unbidden, a human memory imprinted during her birth from Nema's body rose in Sylyth's mind. She lay Aura's head on her breast, so the beating of this body's heart might comfort her, as Nema's mother had done for her.

While Aura, who was still dazed, quieted, Sylyth pondered her situation. Her time among the humans was almost ended. The spawn was nearly fully formed now, though no outward sign of it was evident.

She would not need many men, but she would still need one.

"Hear about the Pink Tulip?" Harcor Braze asked as he stepped into the gatehouse for the midnight shift change.

"Hell of a thing," Laeonus Castlebright replied, removing his helm and running a hand through his matted blonde hair. "I heard two dead—the guards or something."

Harcor shook his head. "I heard just one dead. Some old lady, not the guards. The knight that attacked the place, he's still alive. At least, he was."

"I think I spoke to him earlier," Laeonus said. "He was asking about that old woman...." He trailed off. Had he been responsible for the old woman's death by putting the knight on her track?

"Guess he found her," Harcor said, laughing. "Here's another thing, though. What in the hell was a Guardian doing this far from Duralyn?"

"Don't know."

"Ask me, that's the weirdest part." Harcor looked at Laeonus curiously. "You all right? You don't look so good all the sudden."

Laeonus forced a grin, shaking off his troubling thoughts. "Just tired."

"Then get home. Quiet rest."

"Quiet watch."

The two Watchmen clasped forearms. Laeonus left the gatehouse. The Watch barrack was several blocks away. The storm had passed, but the air was full of thick mist. Laeonus walked slowly through the fog.

Lost in questions of conscience about murderous knights and old women, he almost did not hear the child crying or the voice calling to him:

"Help me. Please help me. My child needs help. Please...."

A cloaked form materialized through the mists. Laeonus dropped his hand to his sword. He was halfway between the barrack and the gatehouse. The street was poorly lit and Byrtnoth could be a dangerous place. It was not unheard of for a lone Watchman to be set upon in the night, though rarely in this part of the city.

"Who goes there?" he called, his young heart quickening as he fumbled his moonstone from its pouch and raised it. He had never faced any real danger at the gates. If he faced some tonight, he prayed he would do so bravely. "Stop in the name of the Watch."

The cloaked shape stopped just beyond the stone's light. "Help me. Please...."

He heard the voice more clearly this time. Caution was forgotten in a burst of chivalry. "What is it, Lady?" He hurried to her. She was wrapped in a sodden blanket, part of which was bundled over a child cradled in one arm. "Aeton's bolts! It's you! You're

(beautiful— God, so beautiful....)

the one the knight was looking for!"

"Knight!" she spat. "Pig! My husband. He beat me. I ran away. He came after me. Killed my mother. I ran again. I think he's chasing me."

"That bastard!" Laeonus felt a flush of heat as his temper rose. Damned if he would suffer a lady to be ill-used. He might only be a Watchman, but he understood honor as well as any Guardian, Sentinel, or Unicorn.

Sylyth forced herself not to smile. Men were inordinately easy to manipulate; nowhere near as challenging as demons. "Please, you must help us," she begged, drawing closer. Her black eyes shone like onyx in the misting dim. The damp air filled with a scent of rampant orchids, making Laeonus' head whirl with lusty fantasies. Sylyth came closer, reaching for him.

Stole him with a kiss.

48

Artelo woke.

He came back jaggedly, struggling up through the layers of unconsciousness that lay over his mind like warm blankets on a deep winter's night. Fragments of memory returned, sluggish and dim but gaining in momentum and clarity until—

"Aura!"

Heart pounding, his daughter's name echoing in his mind, Artelo sat up. Pain speared through his back at the sudden movement. Gasping, he collapsed.

"Lie still," said an unfamiliar voice. "You will undo all that has been done to save your life."

Much more slowly this time, Artelo propped himself up on an elbow. He was in a bed in a room he did not recognize. A mirror hung over a small bureau. A table and a chair were set before a small window. In the chair was a tall, thin man in brown clerical robes.

"Where am I?" Artelo asked. He felt weak and dizzy. His back was in agony.

"Rat's," the cleric said. "Hardly Castle Aventar, I grant you, but enjoy it while you may. I fear your next accommodations will not be so comfortable."

Before Artelo could ponder what that cryptic response meant, the black tide dragged him under again.

When Artelo next roused, it was to daylight streaming through the small window. The pain in his back was still there, but it was dull compared to what he remembered.

The cleric was also still there, seated in the same chair. Perhaps he had never left. The two men regarded each other in silence for a moment. Artelo shoved the blankets down. He was in his breeks, but his clothes were piled on the table. His weapons and armor, however, were absent.

The cleric shook his head. "You are much too weak to rise."

Artelo's head was swimming. He clutched his hand to his forehead, fighting to stay conscious. "There was a child. A little girl in the brothel. What happened to her?"

"I do not know."

"How did I get here?"

"You were found in the Pink Tulip. They feared to take you any farther than this before you were treated. The wound was near the heart."

Artelo swung his feet to the floor. "I have to find her," he groaned.

"You cannot go."

"This is my daughter.... I tell you, I'm going."

The cleric shook his head. "You cannot go," he repeated. "You are in no condition to walk ten paces, and you are also under house arrest for murder. The only reason you are not in the dungeons is the severity of your wound. There are armed guards outside this door."

"Be damned," Artelo spat. He staggered up, but as soon as he tried to take a step a bolt of pain speared through him and he dropped heavily onto the bed, gasping. His heart and spirit were willing; his body had betrayed him.

He choked out a despairing sob. Fortune had granted him a chance to save his daughter and he had squandered it. He did not know how much time had passed. The succubus could be anywhere by now. *Have to find her again.... But how?*

The door opened. A man in the uniform of a Watch Captain entered, followed by a wizard in gray robes and two Watchmen. The captain was holding a sack in one hand. A vein pulsed high on his forehead.

Artelo wiped his teary eyes and tried to focus. *Arrested...* He could not be arrested. He had to find Aura. *Have to get out...* But this time, unlike in Thackery, there was no way he could fight free. He could not even stand up.

It was hopeless, but he had to try something. He would tell his tale, throw himself on their mercy. "Please, listen—"

"Shut up," the captain interrupted, glaring at Artelo. "I don't want to hear your voice. Were it up to me you'd rot in my dungeon until the end of your days, you murdering scum."

"But it is not up to you, Captain," the gray wizard said. "The Crown herself has commanded his release."

Artelo's surprise was complete. How did Solsta even know where he was, much less what trouble he was in?

"Two assaulted, one killed, and he walks free in my city," the captain continued, shaking his head angrily.

"Be still," the gray wizard said. "The Crown has spoken. There is nothing more to be said. This man is free—and rightly free, in my estimation. If you wish to learn why I judge him so, by all means remain. If not, take your men and go your way."

"If I were you, I'd leave Byrtnoth and never come back," the captain said, shooting a last venomous stare at Artelo. He dropped the sack, which struck the floor with a metallic clatter, and stormed out. The other two Watchmen followed him.

The wizard listened to their footfalls recede and shook his head in bemusement. He was old as wizards are old, his age impossible to truly determine. White hair framed a face lined by many winters, but his gray eyes held a bright and youthful sparkle. There was a sense of calm power to his bearing. When he looked to Artelo again, he smiled. "You must forgive the Captain; he is sometimes too zealous in his pursuit of what he perceives as justice," he said. "I am Gartekian the Gray, head of Byrtnoth's Watch magi."

"What happened? Can you tell me? My daughter was—" Artelo started coughing, his wound exacerbated by so much sudden stress.

"Peace," Gartekian said. "This much I can tell you: your daughter is gone from the city. Wither I cannot say, but I know one who perhaps can." He gestured and an oculyr materialized in his hand. "Look," he said.

The depths of the glass ball swirled to life, aethereal smoke clearing to reveal a red-robed figure at a cluttered desk.

"Ralak!" Artelo exclaimed.

"Welcome back to the world of the living, Sir Sterling," the Archamagus said. "I understand you were nearly lost to us."

"That thing escaped and it still has Aura!"

"I am aware."

Artelo's anger surged at the mild response. "God damn it! Do you know where it is?"

"No. But I know where it is bound."

50

Ralak did not, in fact, know where the succubus was bound—at least, not for certain.

He had learned of Artelo's flight from Thackery from Captain Ben'Aboden. The information that Artelo had headed west allowed Ralak to direct his search for the shimmyr.

One look at the course the fiend had chosen made it obvious to the Archamagus that Byrtnoth would become a feeding ground. Ralak called on Gartekian to alert him to any sign of the demoness. It was not beyond possibility that they could take the succubus before she ever managed to bring her spawn into the world.

Gartekian, however, reported no evidence of the fiend. "She was more subtle than we believed possible," the gray wizard admitted to Artelo. "Using the brothel to take men in quantity, she avoided the need to drain each victim to death. There were no corpses to discover, nothing to point to her presence."

Artelo's attack on the brothel had provoked an investigation. When Gartekian was told of the strange beads discovered on the old woman, he began to fit the pieces of the puzzle together. Questioning Matron Weyzl left little doubt that her "prize girl" was none other than the succubus.

Gartekian scoured the city, but to no avail. He informed Ralak of what had transpired. The Archamagus relayed the news to Solsta, who issued a command for Artelo's immediate release.

His hunt for Aura could begin again.

The Archamagus had narrowed Sylyth's destination to one of two places: Volg's Tree in Grimnoir Wood or the Fel Tarn of Cragyntor. Artelo listened to Ralak reason between the locations and agreed with the wizard's assessment of which the succubus would choose. He claimed that path for himself, leaving Ralak to cover the other in the eventuality that they had guessed wrongly.

"If it comes to that and you fail, I will avenge my daughter," Artelo promised. It was difficult for him to even accept that the scenario might play out in that way, but the possibility was there and he could not pretend otherwise.

"You will not have to," Ralak said. "If I fail, it will be with my death."

A course to pursue and the freedom to pursue it did not mean Artelo was able to so quickly resume his chase. His wound had been grievous and it took four more maddening days of rest and healing before he was recovered enough to rise again. It was only the hard-acknowledged truth that he was no good to Aura if he collapsed during the chase or could not fight to save her that kept Artelo from losing his mind completely.

As soon as he could move about again he made ready for his departure. Gartekian returned while he was packing.

"I have news," the wizard said. "First, do not forget this." He handed Artelo an oculyr.

"What news?" Artelo asked, taking the crystal ball and shoving it into his pack.

"The demoness may not be traveling alone. One of our Watchmen is missing. By all accounts, he disappeared sometime after your battle with the demoness. We do not know, of course, that those two things are intertwined, but I find it doubtful this fiend would risk travel unescorted."

"Doesn't matter," Artelo said. He glanced at his chain corselet, which lay upon the bed. Saw the slice in the steel links where the old woman's dagger had pierced a seam. It was sufficient answer to the question of Mavia Kardee's role in her own disappearance. Had she been leagued with Pandaros and the succubus from the beginning? Artelo wondered. Likely he would never know, just as he would never know why Pandaros had summoned such a monster in the first place. "I killed her last guardian. I'll kill this one too, if I must. Nothing will keep me from my daughter."

Gartekian nodded his white head as if he had expected no other answer. "You know your course," he said. "Remember: summon Ralak before you engage the fiend. You must not try to battle her alone. You will need the Archamagus to prevail."

"Somehow I doubt it'll be that easy," Artelo muttered.

51

Furnished with fresh supplies and all the hope he could muster, Artelo set out from Byrtnoth. He rode west of the tiered city, tracing the course of the Sylvastrym through the Hills of Dusk. Twilight came strangely early in the Hills. When it did, Artelo set camp and built a bright fire. The Hills were full of night-stalking creatures that hated men—but not nearly as much as they hated light.

Still, the knight slept poorly when he slept at all. Several times he awakened to the sounds of skulking things, and once to see red eyes watching him from the shadows.

He went on unmolested, however, trekking through brown hills where the sun rarely shone and the wind blew steady and cold. It was a lonely road. He was fearful for Aura's safety, but he knew he was doing all he could to get her back. The wound that would not heal was Brittyn. He missed her and the good and simple life they had made together. Times had not always been perfect, but he had loved her and she had loved him, and he hurt every time he thought of waking in their cottage and facing the day without her smiles and laughter. He was sure he would not be able to do it.

Ye will, Brittyn's voice whispered on the dark wind in the night. *Ye'll have Aura back, and part of me'll live on in her....*

There was some comfort in that thought—so long as he did not lose Aura as well.

A fortnight out from Byrtnoth, Artelo came to Frostwood.

The Sylvastrym ran its wide, clear course amid the white firs, gray needles, and rare silverleafs. Its incessant burble and the soft tromping of his horse's hooves over the needle-carpeted earth were often the only sounds Artelo heard. On his journey to rescue Solsta from the vampyr, the knight had braved the clutching dark of Grimnoir Wood: a haunted place if ever there was one. While similarly quiet, Frostwood bore none of the eerie malignancy of Grimnoir's twisting shadows and brambled paths. The elf forest's stillness had a solemn majesty. It was a place of wondrous natural beauty and daunting age. Of much enchantment and many ghosts.

Artelo rode beneath its spired canopies and felt small.

On the third night, he came to Rime.

By the tales Artelo knew from those who had been to the elf city, Rime should have been a ruin, its beauty razed, its inhabitants slaughtered by the demon and the troll during the quest for the Wheels of Avis-fe. The knight had been prepared to find the remnants of that destruction. What he discovered were alabaster palaces, sparkling fountains, silverleaf gardens, and crystal-lanterned footbridges mounting to arboreal dwellings.

Rime had been restored to all its splendor.

And it was not deserted.

As Artelo rode into the elf city, he saw a light ahead, glowing red against the dusk. Curious but cautious, he dismounted and moved quietly forward. A winding path led him to a courtyard enclosed by a ring of slim silverleaves. Artelo stopped and peered between the trees.

In the center of the courtyard was a small campfire. A solitary figure, cloaked and hooded, was seated before the flames. Its head was bowed, its back to Artelo. If it was aware of his scrutiny, it did not move to acknowledge his presence.

An elf? The gray-green cloak looked like the cloaks favored by the elves Artelo had met at the Battle of Hidden Vale. A slender sword—very much an elvish weapon—was scabbarded across the figure's back.

The wind freshened. Artelo smelled the inimitable scent of esp brewing over the fire. *Definitely an elf. What's he doing here?*

The simple answer was that this was an elf wood. If Rime had been rebuilt it stood to reason that the elves had done so in order to live there again. *But why only one?*

Elves were fey creatures, and might be using their magic to conceal themselves, but Artelo did not think so. For all its beauty, Rime felt cold to him, like a mausoleum. He was confident that the city was empty of any living thing save for himself and this stranger.

"Hail," Artelo called, emerging from the trees.

The hooded head lifted.

"You're late," said Argentia Dasani.

Interlude

The burned woman stood before the sea.

She had retreated through the dark down the beach until she was certain the knight was not following her and his angry cries had faded in the windy distance. She had fled him and her duty to their friendship just as she had fled her other friends on the docks a week earlier, unable to face them.

Unable to face herself.

She had tried. As the *Reef Reaver* voyaged back from the isle of Elsmywr, she had stripped away the bandages swathed about her limbs and torso and face and stood naked before the mirror in her cabin.

A crusty, black monstrosity peered back at her from the glass.

Her red hair, once long and lustrous and bright as a cardinal's plumage, was a ragged shock of singed edges. Her face resembled a cindered apple. The charred flesh mottling her body was cracked, reptilian. The silver-and-sapphire ring that had adorned her navel had melted away. Her dragonfly tattoo was gone as well, but in some perversity of Fortune the brand that the wizard Mouradian had placed upon her hip—an M inscribed in a circle—remained untouched in a patch of pale skin: a further reminder of her defeat and disgrace.

Some months earlier, she had been captured by Mouradian's assassin and imprisoned on Elsmywr. Her every attempt to escape the island had been thwarted. She had ended with her spirit wrested from her body and locked in a magical diamond while her form was used to make an army of simulcra ten-thousand strong.

It was because of her friends that she had been restored to her body and the wizard and his monstrosities destroyed, but her freedom had come at a cost. She faced it in the cabin's mirror.

Smashed the glass apart in a screaming fury.

All she had suffered in her thirty-two winters could not compare to this. Burned beyond self-recognition, tortured by fragmented memories of her likenesses slain by the thousands upon a field of battle, she sought solace in solitude. Hid away for the entire voyage. Ran from the friends who had gathered to greet her at the dock.

For a week she lived on the streets of Harrowgate. She avoided all the places she knew and favored in the city, especially the Mast and Nest, where the wizard's assassin had murdered her lover and taken her prisoner. She slept her days away beneath sacks of garbage in rancid alleys. Made her meals of scraps scrounged from the trash. Spent her nights on the beach, staring out at the implacable sea, listening to the voice of her broken mind whisper that she should end the pain and suffering, drowning her body in the water just as her spirit had drowned in despair.

And then, tonight, Artelo had come.

She could not escape the echoes of what he had said: his call for aid, his demand upon their friendship. She doubted there was anyone truly qualified to track and kill the thing that had taken his daughter, but if there was such a person, it was her.

After all, she did not know anyone else who had hunted a demon to its death.

Yet helping Artelo meant breaking the paralysis that held her. Meant facing what she had become, accepting it, and moving forward through the rest of her life as a goblinesque monstrosity.

She could not do that.

She did not want to face what had happened. Would have given anything to change it. But nothing would change it. Ralak had told her as much. The damage from dragonfire could never be healed. It was a miracle she had survived at all, he said.

A miracle? More like a curse!

Artelo's voice came railing back at her: *My daughter is going to die! God damn you, Argentia! I thought you were my friend!*

"No," she whispered. "I can't help him. That woman's gone. Dead...."

Lost and broken and alone, she trudged farther up the beach, her bare, burned feet sinking in the wet sand as she listened to the roar of the endless surf, afraid to hear the storm wind that had begun to blow in her heart.

PART IV

The Road Back

52

Dawn found her passed out in a back alley.

She had wandered the night for a long time. Had no clear recollection of how she had come to this place—or what the noises intruding on her sleep were.

"Why'st all covered?" Something tugged at the black scarves on her face. There was a gasp. "Aeton—look at it!"

"Think's a goblin," another voice said. "Looks like a goblin."

"Bet it's dead. Smells dead."

"Search it. Maybe's got coin."

"Better check it's dead."

Something poked her in the ribs and she came fully awake. Her eyes opened. She realized the black scarves about her face hung askew, revealing the horror of her visage. "Get the hell away from me!"

The two forms that had been hunching over her fell back in surprise. They were dirty men in rags and tatters, almost like goblins themselves. One held a threadbare burlap purse, ready to add any coin they might find on her to their own collection. The other held a short stick that he swung back in startled reflex.

At the sudden movement her instincts took over. She snapped up, scattering the trash she must have piled over her to keep warm. Slashed her hand into the vagrant's wrist. The stick went flying up. She snatched it out of the air. "Get away!" she screamed again, sweeping the stick viciously before her.

The men wheeled and raced off.

She let them go. Dropped the stick. Adjusted her scarves. *Goblin....*

Her lip trembled. She had been young and beautiful once, with a whole life of adventures open ahead of her. Now she was this hideous, inhuman thing.

She sank down to her knees on the filthy dirt floor of the alley, buried her head in her hands, and wept at the unfairness of it all. When the tears ran out, she groped at the dragon's tooth token about her neck, hoping for some comfort. There was none. Instead, all the troubling memories of the previous night came rushing back: Artelo telling her his daughter was in danger, begging her to help him.

I can't....

She would run.

The *Reef Reaver* was in the harbor. It was her ship and the crew was loyal to her. They would follow without question whatever course she set. *But where would I go?* A place with no windows, mirrors, or streams where she might catch her own reflection? A place with no people to flinch and shun her when she crossed their paths? Even if she found such a place, she would still not be rid of her horrible, haunting memories; her despair and self-loathing.

Mouradian and his simulcra were dead, but it seemed the Island Wizard's victory over her lingered beyond the grave.

53

A fortnight later, she reached the end.

She did not know how much time had passed; days and nights had bled together. She slept as much as she could. The nightmares that harried her—ranks of corpses in her image, rising as if from the dead to pursue her, their flesh kindling as they gave ceaseless, fiery chase—were somehow easier to handle than the guilt that tormented her waking mind.

She turned to drink. The vagrants from the alley had lost their purse in their hasty flight. Since they had been trying to rob her, she felt justified in profiting from their defeat. There was not much coin, but it was enough to purchase liquor. Not the elegant, clear drink she favored, just a strong, cheap swill called rotgut.

Bottle in hand, she spent her days in dens of trash and filth, her nights roaming the streets. She frequently forgot to eat. Eventually forgot she was hungry. She would pick on a few discarded beef bones or an apple core if she found such things, but it was the liquor that sustained her. She was able to replenish her supply at a market stand where she had seen other vagrants and panhandlers make purchases. The rotgut was as nasty as its name but its heat dulled the wind of her conscience and made her misery more bearable.

Eventually exposure, squalor, and starvation wore her down. A phlegmy cough settled in her lungs. Sores sprouted amid the blisters that pocked her formerly lush lips. A fever was growing in her body.

She did not care.

Sickness had no more meaning to her than anything else. She continued on in her stupor, day after day, sinking deeper and deeper into drink and despair.

Then she saw the attack.

59

She had spent the last of her coin on another bottle of rotgut. As she slouched through the night, a filthy specter, clammy with fever, hot with liquor, pondering the vaguely troubling question of where the next bottle would come from, a voice cried out from the mouth of an alley: "Help! You there—help!"

She stopped and turned without really meaning to. Saw a well-dressed couple and a short man in dark clothing, a black fedora pulled low to shadow his face, menacing them with a long knife.

"Get help!" the noble cried again. "Get the Watch!"

The thief hesitated, ready to flee.

She did nothing.

The nobleman lunged forward. The woman tried to restrain him. The thief spun back. His knife flashed. The noble went down, gurgling from a slit throat. The thief dipped, snaring the noble's purse. Screaming, the woman grabbed him. He shoved her against the wall. The knife stabbed out again. The woman fell atop the nobleman. The thief stepped back, tipped his hat to the silent, ragged shape in the street, and dashed into the depths of the alley.

"Help," the woman gasped. Blood bubbled from her mouth with her last breaths. Her hand groped in the air: an accusatory claw. "Why didn't you...help? You could have..."

"No, I...." She shook her head, stumbling away even as the woman collapsed into death. A commotion grew behind her: people drawn to the screaming. They were not that far from Harrowgate's main square. There would be Watchmen about. If she was seen near the crime she would be suspected. Hunted.

She found another alley. Followed it deeper into the city, turning randomly at several interconnecting passages, fleeing the scene of the attack as guiltily as if her hand had struck the mortal blows.

In effect, it had.

She could have stopped the thief. A cry for aid, a movement forward to intervene, and the thief would have fled. She had sensed that.

A simple effort on her part and the nobleman and his wife would have been alive.

A sob escaped her. "I never thought—"

She would not let herself finish the excuse. There was no excuse. Not all of the wrongs of the world could be righted, nor had she ever felt it was her place to crusade to right them, but when she encountered them she had not readily suffered them to stand.

Tonight she had willfully done nothing and a man and woman had been murdered. She never would have allowed such a thing before—but then, she never would have turned from a friend in his need before, either.

What have I done? What have I become? She did not know the answer. Did not even know herself anymore. Was the woman she had always been truly gone? Was all that remained this vile husk, as burned and ruined within as without?

She had been hurt before, both physically and emotionally, but it had never changed her. She had always been able to rally. Now she could no longer find the strength. Every time she tried, she caught sight of her hideousness in a glass shopfront or a puddle and she was broken anew.

What's wrong with me?

The noble's voice: *Help!*

The woman: *Why didn't you help? You could have...*

Artelo: *I need your help!*

She was dizzy. Her heart was racing. Sweat burst out in beads on her veiled brow. She wobbled. Raised a hand to steady herself against the wall. The bottle was in her fist. She looked at it with a species of dawning revulsion. Flung it away—but never heard it shatter.

Wha—

She came to with her face pressed against the rough, cold dirt of the alley. *Blacked out....* It had happened so suddenly that she did not even realize she had fallen until she was down.

She started to rise. Doubled over instead, tearing the scarves from her face, knowing what was coming, hating it, but helpless to stop it as the bile squirted hot and sour down her throat and fourteen days' worth of rotgut hurtled up in a steaming rush.

She vomited until it seemed she could not even breathe. When, at last, it was over, she moaned and slumped into her reeking mess, one leg pinned awkwardly beneath her, the other twitching spastically. Bright spots of heat swirled behind her eyes. Her pulse thundered in her ears.

She flopped onto her side, wiping lamely at her soiled mouth, trying to spit the noisome taste away between gasps for breath. Tears trickled unbidden from her eyes.

It was then, burned and blackened amid the trash and her own stinking vomit, at the lowest point in her entire life, that she at last found the courage to face what she had become.

"I'll try," Argentia whispered. She did not know what she could do to help Artelo, or even if there was still time to help. *But I'll try,* she vowed, cobalt light rising in her eyes as she pushed herself up to her hands and knees. *Yes. I'll try...*

And for the first time since she had recovered it from Mouradian's assassin, the dragon's tooth token dangling about her neck glimmered.

55

"High Cleric?"

Colla woke to the sound of Maren's voice outside her door. "Yes?" she managed, groggy with sleep. "What is it?"

"Pardon for disturbing you, High Cleric, but there is something knocking below."

"If someone is knocking, let them in," Colla said, unable to contain her irritation at being awakened in the middle of the night for such a reason. "You don't need me to— Maren, did you say some *thing* is knocking below?"

"Yes, High Cleric."

Colla rose, draping her blanket about her. The wooden floor of her austere chamber was cold beneath her bare feet as she went to the door and opened it. She blinked owlishly in the light of Maren's taper. "What do you mean?"

"Latteus was on vigil. He answered the door, but he would not admit the...knocker. He said it looked to be a goblin."

"A goblin?" Colla had been raised in a village in the Lake Country and was a sensible young woman, hardly given to frightening at all— especially not at foolishness. "There are no goblins in Harrowgate. Even if there were, do you think one would come knocking on the door to Aeton's house?"

"No, High Cleric. But that is what Latteus said. A goblin with a woman's voice."

Argentia hammered at the door again.

Had she not been so desperately in need of aid that Colla could easiest provide, and had she not been so weakened by her sickness, she would have abandoned the cathedral a score of knocks earlier and sought some wizard to set her on her way.

As things stood, she was too exhausted to do anything but keep bludgeoning the door. It had opened once. It would open again. *When it does, I'm getting inside....* She had been too slow and, despite what she knew of her appearance, too surprised by the cleric's reaction to force her way in last time. *That won't happen again....*

But when the door did open a second time, Argentia did not need to do anything. Colla herself stood inside, flanked by two clerics. "Come in, please," Colla said.

Argentia stumbled forward. She steadied her legs beneath her, pulling away from the clerics who had reached to help her. Her head pounded, her eyes throbbed. "I'm...all right."

Frowning, Colla touched Argentia's forehead. She could feel the sickness lurking beneath the scabrous ruination of her flesh and the stench of her filthy clothes: a febrile heat, full of dark menace. "Take her above," she ordered the clerics. "Bring water from the font, and wolfsbane, rosemary, lemon, olive leaves."

"No," Argentia managed. She was dizzy but refused to fall. "No. Have to get to Dura—" She broke off in a fit of ugly coughing. "No time," she said when she could speak again. Her voice sounded thick and far away to her.

Colla shook her head. "To walk the aether now would kill you for certain. You need healing."

"I need to get to Duralyn."

"You will," Colla said. "After you are well."

"Now."

"Stubborn," Colla muttered, closing her eyes for a moment. "Forgive me."

Before the barely conscious huntress could react, Colla again raised a hand to Argentia's blackened forehead. There was a flash of white light.

Argentia toppled in a heap beneath the cathedral's soaring arches and frescoed vaults.

56

She woke to softness.

For the first few minutes she simply lay there with her eyes closed, not moving at all, just reveling in the feel of a pillow beneath her head; a mattress beneath her body instead of the hard, cold, pounded dirt of an alley; sheets and blankets layered over her instead of sacks of trash.

She inhaled deeply, freely, without any of the heaviness or pain that had made her labor for breath as her sickness worsened. The fever had broken and the soreness had fled her bones. She felt rested. She felt good. Yawning, she arched her back and stretched.

At the scraping of her arms against the sheets, everything almost fell apart again.

Argentia opened her eyes, dismay rising in her like a shadowy wave. For a few blissful moments she had forgotten what had happened to her. She pressed her blackened hands to her blackened face, fighting not to lose the ground she had gained in the last night.

And what happened last night? She was not sure. She remembered making it to Coastlight. Arguing with Colla. Then—nothing until right now. Was she even still in the cathedral? *I'd damned well better be....*

Spurred by her reawakened need for haste, she shoved free of the warm embrace of the bed. It was much less luxurious than her slow-waking mind had imagined: just an old mattress, a single cotton sheet, a thin wool blanket, and a lumpy pillow. Nothing was cheap or ill-used, but neither were they items of great expense. They were functional, utilitarian. She was fairly certain she was still in the cathedral.

Clothes....

Hers were nowhere to be seen, but there were two beige robes folded on a small table, and a pair of leather sandals on the floor. As she walked over, she noted that the narrow room had a wooden chest in the corner and a dresser with three drawers standing against the wall. There was no mirror. There was not even a window. She was profoundly glad of that; she was still afraid to be alone with the image of what she had become.

No more, she thought fiercely. *You have to beat this. You have to help Artelo....*

She studied the two robes. At first she thought one was an undergarment, the other a frock, but she saw they were identical save for one feature. She hesitated for a moment, plumbing the depths of her bravery.

Chose the robe with the hood.

It was a clerical garment of good broadcloth. The sleeves were long enough that she could make her hands vanish into them. The hood swallowed her head, letting her peer out from the safety of its shadows. The sandals laced up her calves, brown straps crisscrossing mottled flesh. She hated them. They were a bit loose in the heel no matter how tightly she pulled the lashes, and they were uncomfortable: flat, clunky, and low when she was used to her well sprung, perfectly battered boots.

Those boots, like so much else in her life, were gone now. She could not go barefoot on her hunt, however, so she would make do. *That's something I'll be doing a lot of,* she thought.

Before that bitter seed could take its eager root, she headed for the door.

A cleric was waiting in the dim corridor. He bowed to her. "Aeton's grace upon you," he said. "If you will wait here, I will inform the High Cleric that you are awake."

"I'll come with you. I don't have time to wait."

"I'm sorry, but the High Cleric may be indisposed," the cleric said.

"She'll see me."

If Colla was disappointed that Argentia had chosen the hooded robe, she did not show it.

"What happened to me?" Argentia asked.

"You needed healing," Colla said. "It has been accomplished."

"Thank you," Argentia said. Meant it. She knew that whatever aid the clerics had given her, she was far from healed, but they had done what they could. The rest would depend on her will.

She feared that it would be a battle waged in small steps over long years.

"You are remarkable," Colla said. "Sick as you were, to have recovered in three days. Most would have been bedridden for a week, if they survived at all."

"Three days? I was out for *three days?* God damn it!" Argentia swore, forgetting where she was in her anger over this unexpected delay. "You have to get me out of here!"

57

"If her Majesty could please remain still?"

Solsta was frustrated, and the polite admonishment from Ittorio Tyntoryn did not help. It took all her self-possession not to lash out at the painter, but her mood was not Ittorio's fault. She would be remiss to punish him for it, or for trying to complete her portrait to hang in the Hall of Crowns.

There was no single thing that was bothering Solsta. It seemed that of late everything had been conspiring against her. As she sat upon the posing stool in her silver coronation gown, it was the constant greedy squabbling of the Peerage that vexed her. With rare exception, the nobles of Teranor had scant nobility in their behavior. Her own father-in-law, one of Teranor's most powerful and influential Lords, had tried to have her murdered. She had no doubt that there were others in the Peerage who held secret daggers for her as well.

Unfortunately, the nobles were a necessary evil. The Peerage was an extension of the throne, providing regional governance integral to the stability of the realm. Solsta could not alienate them, but she wished she could make them see beyond their noses—or their purses. *Coin grubbing wretches, and I'll probably end up marrying one....*

That was a miserable thought, but one that seemed to be a reality of her future. The line of Ly'Ancoeur had to continue. She would have to find another husband.

She snuck a glance at Ittorio. With his fawn hair and doe eyes, the painter was softly handsome and could be quite charming. During their initial sittings a flirtatious banter had grown between them to the point that Solsta had toyed with the idea of taking him as a lover.

Then Artelo had returned, and Solsta's belief that she had finally put her feelings for the knight behind her was blasted. It had taken her days after his departure just to resume posing for the portrait. When she did so it was with an absence of play and a forced smile on her lips to conceal thoughts that turned again and again to Artelo.

The news from Byrtnoth reporting his injury had nearly stopped Solsta's heart. She had almost ordered Ralak to teleport her to the tiered city so she could be with him, but in the end decided against it. She was not sure if Artelo hated her. How much of his ranting had been grief and fear and how much what he truly felt? The hell of it was that even if he did hold her responsible for his wife's death and his daughter's kidnapping, she still wanted so badly to help him, to make things right for him again—but what could she do?

She had managed to be of some use by keeping him out of the dungeons, but she could not bring back his wife (and a small, jealous part of her was not sure that she would if she could), nor was it within the scope of her power to hunt down this demoness that had taken his daughter.

Ralak was doing all he was able to on that count. He had set Artelo on what he deemed the right course and stood ready to join the fight himself, but Solsta fretted that was not aid enough.

"Majesty, the royal pout is quite becoming, but are you certain that is how you wish to be immortalized?"

Ittorio's voice brought Solsta out of her brooding. "I'm sorry," she said, putting on the fake smile again.

A few minutes later, she suddenly rose. "Enough for today, Master Tyntoryn."

"Majesty, if I've offended...." The painter was genuinely confused.

Solsta felt badly for him. "Not at all." She managed to give him a true smile this time. "No fault of yours. I've something to discuss with the Archamagus. Mirk, we're leaving."

In the corner, the meerkat looked up from his work. He had a small piece of canvas on the floor, a palette of his own, and his paws were covered with red and blue paint. He was working on a sunset. Solsta, who never failed to be amazed by Mirk's abilities, thought the painting was actually quite good. "Come on," she said. "And wash your paws."

It was on the tip of Mirk's tongue to ask how he could both come with her and wash his paws at the same time, but something in Solsta's tone told the little animal this was not the moment to do anything but obey. He dunked his paws in a nearby bowl, rubbed them vigorously until they were clean, then scampered out to catch up with Solsta, darting around the two Sentinels who had fallen into step behind her when she left the room. "Mirk washed paws," he announced.

Solsta nodded, but did not reply. Mirk ran on ahead, always happy for a chance to snoop in the Archamagus' tower.

Solsta could have simply summoned Ralak, but she was not one to stand on such privileges. She had two legs and could walk on them as well as the next woman.

She knocked on the door to Ralak's tower. She did not have to do this, either, but such simple courtesies were both her breeding and her way of ensuring that no arrogance of power would attend her reign.

An eye opened in the door. "Majesty," came Ralak's voice. "I was under the impression you were taking your portrait."

"I was. May I come up?"

"Of course. Your timing is impeccable. I was shortly on my way to see you."

The eye closed and the door opened. Solsta and Mirk ascended a winding stone staircase. Ralak was waiting for them on the landing outside his chamber.

"Are you certain we've done all we can for Artelo?" Solsta said as she climbed the last steps. "I'm not sure we have. I know Magus Gartekian gave him the oculyr to contact you, but what if something happens?

There must be some way we can get a force of knights to this tarn. Could we send the Winds?"

The Winds were two-dozen Unicorn cavalrymen who rode steeds with magically shod hooves. They were the Crown's messengers, but Solsta saw no reason they could not perform other tasks as well.

"I do not think we will need the Winds," Ralak said.

"Something else, then," Solsta snapped. Sometimes Ralak's literalistic interpretations were positively infuriating. "Anything so Artelo won't have to face that fiend alone."

"He won't be alone, Majesty," said the hooded figure that emerged from Ralak's chambers.

58

"Argentia?" Solsta exclaimed.

The huntress nodded. Colla had graciously overlooked Argentia's angry speech and sped her on her way through the aether to the monastery in Duralyn. Ralak, alerted by the High Cleric, met her there and escorted her to his chambers. They had not been long about their conversation before the Crown arrived.

"Bright Lady be praised!" Solsta hugged Argentia hard. "I was so worried," she said, remembering the brief glimpse of the swathed, tormented woman she had seen on the docks of Harrowgate, before Argentia had fled. "Won't you take down that hood?"

Argentia made no move to reveal herself. Instead she turned to Ralak. "Just finish telling me how I can find this demoness."

<hr/>

At Solsta's request, they descended from the tower to a nearby sitting room. A map was brought showing the lands of western Teranor. "It is not enough to simply find the fiend," Ralak said after explaining what he knew of the succubus and his estimation of its course. "You will need some means to combat it. The magic of my staff will perhaps be enough, and Promitius is working on a scroll of commanding, but what we truly need is Scourge."

"What happened to Scourge?" Argentia asked. Ralak told her of the holy sword's ransoming to Dracovadarbon in exchange for the dragon's aid in the rescue mission to Elsmywr. The huntress lowered her hooded head; none could tell what darkness lurked in her thoughts, what fires in her memories.

"Mirk has sword." The meerkat hopped onto the table and brandished the miniature copy of the demon-slaying Scourge he proudly carried as his own weapon.

"Indeed," Ralak said. Solsta shooed Mirk down from the table. She was thrilled that Argentia had returned—it seemed the answer to a prayer—but the task of rescuing Artelo's daughter still looked grim.

"So it's bound for this tarn," Argentia said at length, bending over the map and tapping a charred finger on the spot marking Cragyntor. The rest of her hand remained hidden by the low cuff of her robe. "How sure are you?"

"It is impossible to say for certain, but I believe it will seek the Fel Tarn," Ralak said. "Volg's Tree has an evil history as well, but Grimnoir Wood is home to goblins and worse things that might prove a danger even to the succubus, especially in the hours of birthing, when she will be very weak. Also, the spawn will have no defense of its own. It must grow in the vessel until it gains its full strength. Then it will discard the vessel and begin its terror. Sylyth will want it as isolated as possible until that time."

"What do you mean *discard?*" Solsta asked. She knew that Artelo's child was the intended vessel, but Ralak had never mentioned what would happen to Aura after that possession took place.

"Trust me, Majesty, you do not wish to know," the Archamagus said. "Suffice it that Artelo's daughter will not survive the departure of the demon from her body."

Solsta shuddered.

"Where is Artelo?" Argentia asked.

"Byrtnoth," Solsta said. "Recovering from his wounds."

"And he knows where this thing is bound?"

"He knows as much as you know," Ralak said. "As soon as he can ride, he will make his course for the tarn. I can take you to him," he added.

Argentia scrutinized the map again. "Byrtnoth," she murmured, calculating distance and time. "No." She pointed to another spot on the map. Lifted her hooded head. "This is where I need to go."

59

The iron way.

Argentia had ridden in the rail carts three times before: twice departing from and once to reach the holt deep beneath the Gelidian Spur, where King Durn and the dwarves of Stromness dwelt.

This was the first time she had ridden as a prisoner.

Ralak had taken Argentia through the aether from Aventar to the East Gate of Stromness, which appeared as a stone bluff no different than any of the surrounding mountain facades. Though they were not at a great elevation, the wind was strong behind them, whipping at their robes, bending the lean spruces that dotted the cliffside.

"One thing more," Ralak said as they stood on the narrow path between two piles of boulders. They had already discussed the plan to summon Ralak with the oculyr once the succubus was discovered. Now the Archamagus reached into the aether and drew forth a small, silvery disc.

"Where did you get that?" Argentia snarled, recognizing the portable aethergate Mouradian's assassin had used to spirit her to Elsmywr.

"Peace," Ralak said. "It is of my own crafting, based upon Mouradian's design." He turned the disc over so she could see his magemark on the reflective surface. "An ingenious device, truly."

"Why give me one?" Argentia asked suspiciously.

"For Artelo's daughter. She will have suffered enough, I think, without the hazard of a long return through the wilds. This disc will bring you to Artelo's cottage."

"Why not just bring us yourself?"

"I will," Ralak said. "Presuming I survive the trial." He handed the disc to Argentia. "Consider this a last resort. Should all go amiss, at least we will have a chance to save the child."

Argentia hesitated. The disc brought bad memories, but she could not deny Ralak's reasoning. She put aside her feelings and shoved the slim disc into her pack.

"Remember," Ralak said. "The medallion is the key."

"I know."

The Archamagus caught hold of Argentia's arm. A fierce light was in his dark eyes. "If the succubus escapes with that token, even without Artelo's daughter, this will all begin anew once it is strong enough to breed again."

Argentia pulled free of Ralak's grasp. "It won't escape." She was annoyed at the way the Archamagus was reviewing these details, as if she was too dull to understand the task before her or the consequences of failure.

Ralak nodded. Then he tapped his staff against the stone. "Show thy truth!"

There was a glimmering across the wall. The illusion of stone was dispelled, revealing a set of mighty iron doors flanked by a pair of giant iron statues depicting dwarves in full plate armor. Dwarven magic had crafted and concealed them. The power of the Archamagus was enough to render them visible, but not even Ralak could force these gates to open against the will of the dwarves within.

With a groaning and grinding of metal joints and hinges, the statue on the left jerked forward and crouched ponderously. It held a massive axe in its huge gauntlet, the blade leaning over its shoulder. The iron whorls of its beard scraped the ground. "Who goes?" it asked in a voice like the ring of a hammer on an anvil in an empty cavern.

Argentia had seen the golems of Stromness before, but they never failed to impress her. A dwarven companion had once told her that the golems represented the pinnacle of dwarf craft: the perfect meshing of metal and magic. She was inclined to believe him.

"Ralak the Red, Archamagus of Teranor, and Lady Dasani of Argo, servants of her Majesty, Solsta Ly'Ancoeur, Crown of Teranor, humbly seek entrance to your mighty holt," Ralak said. He remembered a time when this would have been a laughable overture, but since the Battle of Hidden Vale had allied men, dwarves, and elves against the demons of the Pits, tentative trade relations had resumed between the long-isolated races. While merchants were not yet welcome to make the journey to the dwarves, ambassadors went between the undermountain kingdom and Duralyn, and the invocation of Solsta's name was sufficient to at least gain entry to the holt.

The golem rose with more creaks and groans, grasped the great iron ring in the center of one of the doors, and pulled the tremendous portal open. "Enter," it intoned.

"Go with all Fortune and all haste," Ralak said as Argentia crossed the threshold. "I shall await word from you."

The huntress might have nodded; there was so much gloom inside the entrance to the holt that Ralak could not be sure. As swiftly as it had opened the way, the golem was closing it again—though before it did Ralak saw lanterns moving toward Argentia: a dwarven welcoming party, likely armed to the teeth.

The door slammed closed. The golems resumed their boulder disguises. The iron portals glimmered back into stone.

Ralak lingered.

He was deeply troubled about Argentia. He had been with those who found her on the beach of Elsmywr, burned almost beyond recognition by dragonfire. He had sat with her on the journey back to Harrowgate and showed her—albeit against his will—the fields of dead simulcra: mirror images of Argentia that Mouradian had conjured to build the ranks of his invasion force. He had told her the hardest truth: that no power known to clerics or magi could undo the damage she had suffered.

And he had been there at the docks of Harrowgate, when Argentia had run.

Now she had returned to help Artelo. She seemed to have begun a journey toward some sort of acceptance of her fate, but Ralak did not like the way she was hiding herself in the depths of her hood. It bespoke self-doubt, fear, weakness: all normal things for one recovering as Argentia was, except they did not have the luxury of time for such healing to take its course. They were rushing into a battle against a foe unlike any they had ever faced. They would need Argentia at her brilliant best if they were to triumph.

Ralak was afraid that woman had been lost to them on Elsmywr...

60

"Flynt Flamelock I be," the leader of the dwarven Warders said, placing himself squarely before Argentia. He wore a beard as red and long and tangled as Argentia's hair once had been. When she saw it, a sudden tightness in her chest choked her up. "Weren't expectin no messengers from yer Crown."

"It is a most urgent matter," Argentia said, forcing her voice to work. "If you could take me to King Durn, I can explain everything."

"King Durn ain't here," Flynt said. "Gone t' our cousins in Delv t' promote trade wit yer cities. Jurgen Mace's Steward o' th' holt until th' King's return. Ye'll have t' speak wit him."

"Not much fer likin yer attire there," another of the Warders said. "Sure yer not no wizard?" Though they used magic in their crafting and forging, dwarves had a notorious distrust of wizards. Only clerics ranked lower in their esteem.

"I'm not a wizard."

A third dwarf stepped forward. This one was familiar to Argentia: Noli or Doli—she always confused the twin brothers. "If ye be Lady Dasani, then show yer face and Doli Stonedust'll vouch fer ye."

"I know you," she said. "But I will not show my face."

"Whyn't?"

"I have my reasons," Argentia said, her voice growing tight again. She had expected a gruff welcome—dwarves were hardly partial to strangers—but not this questioning. There was no way she could settle it according to the proof Doli asked for: she was unrecognizable. Knowing the temperament of dwarves, they would likely mistake her for some goblinoid spy and strike her dead where she stood.

The dwarves withdrew a bit and had a hushed argument. Finally, Flynt returned. "Ye'll be taken t' Elder Mace as yer askin, but unnerstand if yer not provin t' Doli here and now that ye be who ye claim ye be, we've no choice but t' take ye as a pris'ner."

Argentia said nothing.

"Right." Flynt motioned to the other Warders. "Search 'er down and bind 'er hands."

So Argentia was shackled and herded into the rail cart for the five-day journey west under the mountains to the central delve of the holt. Doli and Noli manned the handcart. They seemed distant and mistrustful. Argentia could not blame them. As she rode on, the lamp on the front of the iron cart piercing the endless black of the ore tunnel, the wheels scratching over the rails, she wondered if she had not made a mistake in coming to this place at all. What if the dwarves refused to deal with her because of her suspicious appearance? What if they decided to keep her prisoner? It was possible. She was in their realm, subject to their ways and laws.

Much hinged on her success in Stromness, and that success was less certain in Durn's absence. The dwarf king was a friend, but the same could not be said of all his people. What the views of this Jurgen Mace were on aiding outsiders would count for a great deal, and Argentia already had a bad feeling about that. Flynt had called him Elder Mace, which meant he was one of the old dwarven retainers, likely set in the old dwarven ways. Odds were he would be staunchly opposed to helping her.

Nothing I can do about that now…. She would just have to wait the journey out and learn what her fate would be.

She sighed in the depths of her hood, glad she had at least forbidden Ralak from telling Artelo she was coming. Better he be surprised than expect her and have her fail to arrive.

That thought weighed heavily on her. Though rushing over the rails at speeds exceeding the fastest horses was normally an exhilarating experience for Argentia, this time she found the trip robbed of any pleasure. The only comfort was the dark around her, which made it easier to almost forget her damaged appearance.

61

"Ye'll show yer face t' me or ye'll show it t' th' cistern walls fer th' rest o' yer days," Jurgen Mace threatened. On the raised rows of seats behind the throne where the Steward of Stromness sat, the Elders of the clan stomped their boots in approval. "Ain't n'er heard o' such disrespect."

"What're we expectin from a human," a dwarf in the gallery of the massive throne hall shouted, drawing scattered cheers and applause—a keen reminder to Argentia that there was not universal support within the holt for King Durn's treating with Solsta.

"Quiet," Mace growled. The hall fell silent. The Steward was old, even for a dwarf, with a white beard that reached past his knees and a scowl that looked as if it had been etched centuries ago and never shifted since. Argentia hated him on sight, even before he began haranguing her, but she needed his help, and it was obvious that in order to get it she would have to face the humiliation—and the risk—of exposure.

Of course, she did not believe seeing her face would make Jurgen Mace any more inclined to her favor, but he had left her no choice.

"Fine. Unbind my hands. Or come take down the hood yourself," she challenged.

Surprisingly, Mace hopped off the throne and stomped over to her. The two guards flanking Argentia bent her forward. The Steward grabbed her hood and shoved it down. "Drim be damned!" he exclaimed, leaping backwards. There was a chorus of grunted surprise—the equivalent of screaming from the stoic dwarven crowd.

"Goblin-kin!" Mace rang his sword free.

"No! Wait! You're making a mistake!" Argentia shouted as the guards dragged her to the ground.

Mace stepped over her, his sword dropping to touch her throat. "If ye ain't goblin-kin, what manner o' creature be ye? Speak or yer dead."

"Let 'er be!"

The voice came from beyond the trio of dwarves surrounding her. Argentia heard it and her heart leaped with sudden hope.

"Out o' me way ye damn fools!" There were sounds of a scuffle as the guards tried to block the newcomer's approach.

"Stand down, by Drim's anvil! What're ye about?" Mace demanded.

"Savin ye from a terrible mistake. Let 'er be. 'Tis th' Lady."

"Ain't no lady," a dwarf in the crowd jeered.

"'Tis th' Lady Dasani!" Argentia's supporter roared.

"Vouch yer beard fer it?" Mace asked after a beat of silence in which Argentia, still pinned by the guards, was not at all sure the Steward would not kill her anyway.

"Aye," said Griegvard Gynt. "Vouch me beard fer it."

62

"Burned by dragonfire, ye say?" Jurgen Mace asked.

He was seated on his borrowed throne again. Griegvard Gynt stood obstinately before him. Argentia had been released from her bonds, but was still flanked by the two guards. She had drawn her hood up once more and was listening to Griegvard make the explanation she likely never would have had a chance to make herself.

"Aye," the sturdy blonde dwarf said. "'Tis she, not fer doubtin."

"Dragonfire...." Mace mused. "N'er heard o' naught survivin dragonfire." The other Elders muttered their accord.

"I'm not fer knowin nor carin what ye heard," Griegvard said. "What I'm fer tellin ye's that she survived, and she's deservin better welcome'n this."

"I'll be judge o' th' welcomes in this holt," Mace growled.

Griegvard gave a respectful tug on his braided blonde beard and turned away from the throne. As he moved off to one side, he shot a glance at Argentia and rolled his gray eyes.

Glad of the hood that hid her smirk, Argentia nodded her thanks to Griegvard. She had met the dwarf when he guided her party across Nord to Togril Vloth's Ice Palace. He had joined her other friends to rescue her from Mouradian, and his timely appearance had almost certainly saved her life again today.

"Come forward," Mace ordered Argentia.

Argentia did. "My gratitude for your mercy, Steward Mace," she said. She was going to have to be at her most diplomatic if she was going to get what she came for. The murmur of approval from the crowd told her she had just won back something of the deficit she had made for herself.

"Bah! Be thankin Griegvard Gynt," Mace said. "Were up t' me ye'd be cold already. Ye should tell yer Crown 'tis dangerous sendin messengers that're lookin like goblins t' a holt full o' dwarves."

The Elders stomped their boots in agreement. Mace raised a hand for silence.

"I would tell her," Argentia said. "But I bring no message from the Crown. My business here is my own."

"Aye? What business be that?" Mace asked.

"I crave a boon of the King of Stromness. Since you stand so ably in his stead, I would make my need known to you."

Mace hesitated. His dark eyes narrowed suspiciously beneath his frosty brows, until they appeared no more than shadows flanking his beak of a nose. "What boon'd ye have?"

"I need a block of mithryl."

63

"Quiet!" Mace ordered as the throne hall of Stromness erupted into chaos at Argentia's words. He had to wave his hands up and down three times before the desired effect was achieved. He looked at Argentia. "Must be me hearin's goin," he said, sticking a finger deep into an ear and twisting it around. "Thought ye asked me fer a block o' mithryl."

"That is the boon I crave," Argentia replied, carefully maintaining her High Speech parlance, grateful again that her hood hid her face, this time so none of the dwarves would see the anger there. *Bastard—if you're going to say no, just say it....*

But Mace did not say no. He stroked his beard, appearing arrogant but sweating beneath his coat as he contemplated his suddenly precarious position.

To crave a boon of the lord of any land was a serious thing: a formal request for a favor or aid, fettered with all sorts of diplomatic implications. Those implications were what gave Mace pause now.

The Steward remembered this Lady Dasani: she was the troublemaker whose visit had drawn Stromness into battle with the demons several winters ago. He knew she was close to the throne of Teranor. Word of his response would reach the human Crown, and (a much more fearful thought) it would reach King Durn. Mace would be forced to explain why he had jeopardized the nicely developing trade between the two realms because he felt a block of mithryl was too precious to waste on a human woman, or whatever she was.

So he sat in silence, seeking a way he could escape this trap without parting with any of the holt's mithryl or ruining its relations with the humans. Not that he would have minded the latter himself, but Durn would. The king already knew many of the Elders did not support his decision to reopen trading. If he thought Mace had deliberately sought to sabotage his decree, the Steward's downfall would be swifter than a hammer-strike.

The quandary seemed hopeless, but finally a sparkle came to Mace's dark eyes. "Ye ask a great deal. Mithryl's dear and short in supply. What King Durn'd say I'm not rightly knowin. If I'm agreein when he'd be refusin, I'm a damn fool, and th' same th' other way 'round. So I'm fer thinkin we'll leave th' decision t' ye."

"How so?"

"'Tis me right as Steward t' set ye a task fer grantin yer boon," Mace said. "Did ye know this?"

Argentia nodded. Beneath her hood, her frown deepened. Once she had learned of Durn's absence, she had feared something like this would be the outcome of her request. The first time she had come here, the dwarves had put one of her companions to a trial by combat. They seemed to delight in such ritualistic tests; it was a part of their culture and custom, much as it was among the barbarians of Nord.

You are a bastard, she thought, knowing full well that Durn would never have subjected her to any such test. She had already proven herself honorable and true in the dwarf king's eyes.

Unfortunately, it was not Durn she was dealing with now.

"Name your task," she said. She was not at all sure she was up to facing whatever challenge the Steward had in mind, but if it would win her the mithryl she had to try.

Mace's yellow smile cracked open the snowy briars of his beard. "'Tis called Drim's Forge."

69

The challenge of Drim's Forge was simple: Argentia had to plunge her hand into a fire and hold it there until the sands of a glass ran out.

This was a traditional dwarven test of stamina, and not even a particularly difficult one for them. The skin of the deep-delving people was tough as stone, and their hands were frequently so calloused and toughened by their labors in the mines and workshops that they could endure all manner of burns without complaint.

For a human, however, it would be a grievous test indeed, which was why raucous cheering rang out in the throne hall upon Mace's announcement.

"Ye vouched fer her, so I'm fer thinkin we'll use yer forge," Mace said to Griegvard. He smiled at the blonde dwarf: the triumphant grin of one who knew he had escaped any fault. If Argentia failed the test, Mace could not be blamed for denying her the mithryl.

"If she passes...." Mace paused to let the laughter at that impossibility die down. "If she passes, 'twill be a block o' mithryl from yer own stores she takes."

"Wouldn't have it no other way," Griegvard said. Argentia could see the tension in the thick muscles of his neck and wondered if the Steward knew how near he was to provoking Griegvard into battering him to a pulp. She smiled at the thought.

Griegvard merely tugged on his beard and turned to Argentia. "Come on, lass," he said quietly. Had he known she was coming, he would have given her the mithryl without so much as a question, but there was no way out of the trial now. While he was somewhat consoled by the fact that Durn would be furious when he learned of this, that did not do him or Argentia much good right now.

Then again, maybe he was looking at this the wrong way. He knew Argentia much better than any of the other dwarves did. He would not wager against her somehow passing this test.

Which gave him an idea....

An hour later, Argentia stood in Griegvard's workshop. The furnace was an iron mouth carved into the stone of the wall. Its fires were stoked and crackling hungrily. The small chamber was chokingly hot; the fact that dwarves were piled into every bit of free space, standing on workbenches and chairs and overflowing into the corridor outside, did not help matters.

Mace bellowed for Griegvard. The blonde dwarf, who had been hustling about among his holt-kin, forced his way in, shoving a tattered notebook and a stick of charcoal back into his apron as he approached. "Aye, Steward Mace?"

"'Tis yer forge. Ye'll keep charge o' th' time." The Steward held up a glass of sand. "One minute," Mace said to Argentia as he handed the glass to Griegvard. "Not that ye'll be lastin that long."

Argentia said nothing. She was suddenly having trouble breathing. Memories of her own flesh charring away with a stench like over-roasted pig assailed her. The heat of the forge became the heat of the burning tower. Of dragonfire.

"Yer ready, then?" Mace asked, smiling his awful yellow smile again.

Argentia shuddered, fighting a wave of dizziness. She had rolled the voluminous sleeve of her robe back almost to her shoulder, exposing the ruin of her arm, which looked like a lightning-struck tree limb and made the dwarves point and mutter among themselves. Her hand was trembling so violently she was sure she would never be able to raise it, much less thrust it into the fire. How could she? Was she mad? She had been burned once—how could she willingly let it happen again? *I have to. I have to do this....*

"Ye know ye can't win," Mace said. "Cry off yer boon. Go yer way in peace," he offered.

"Go to hell," Argentia snarled.

"Ye had yer chance," Mace said, shrugging. He pointed at Griegvard. "Let's get this joke o'er wit."

"Aye, then. On me mark," Griegvard said loudly. "Go!"

Argentia did not move. Could not move. Could not do this.

"Too bad," Mace sneered. "Ye f—"

"No!" Argentia squeezed her eyes closed.

Rammed her fist into the fire.

65

The dwarves let out a great cheer as Argentia's arm went into the forge. The noise was part acknowledgement of her bravery, part anticipation that in the next instant she would be screaming in agony and plunging her arm into the bucket of ice water set on a stool beside her, the test failed almost before it began.

Instead, Argentia's arm remained in the fire.

At first she did not realize she felt no pain. All her will and adrenaline had been poured into the act of shoving her fist into the flame. Her teeth were jammed together against a scream that never came. Every muscle in her torso was locked against the instinct to yank her arm back out of the forge even as her skin crisped and blistered and burned away.

Yet there was no pain.

In the shadow of her hood, Argentia opened her eyes. Flames were licking over her arm, and she felt nothing.

Not truly nothing, she realized. There was a sensation of heat, but it was as if she had immersed her arm in a warm bath, not a roaring forge. She flexed her fingers. They tingled, that was all.

The dragonfire.... That was the only explanation. Her flesh, scorched by the hottest force on Acrevast, was impervious to damage from lesser flames.

Argentia looked at her audience. To a dwarf, they were staring in stunned shock. Jurgen Mace looked ready to pull his beard out by the fistful.

Bad choice of trials, friend, Argentia thought. She shoved her arm deeper into the fire, drawing gasps from the crowd, and turned to Griegvard, who was trying—and failing—to keep a tremendous grin off his face as he thought of all the gold he had just fleeced from his holt-kin. Together they watched the sands slip through the glass until the last grains had fallen and the trial of Drim's Forge was ended.

Argentia withdrew her arm and rolled down her sleeve again. "Fairly won?" she asked Mace.

"I.... Magic! Ye used magic t' cheat me!"

Argentia shook her head. "No magic."

"A retrial. I demand—"

"No bloody retrial!" boomed a voice from the doorway. Mace wheeled, leaping in fright as King Durn stomped in, his obsidian eyes fixed angrily on the Steward.

"I.... Me King, I was just...." Mace blubbered.

"Shut up, ye buzzard. Just coverin yer ass, that's what ye were doin. Now get out o' me sight before I stick yer damn head in that oven!" Durn bellowed. "Go on! Clear out o' here, th' lot o' ye!"

Yelping, Jurgen Mace fled Griegvard's forge with the rest of the crowd stumbling over themselves to follow.

"Pathetic," Durn muttered. "Can't bloody wait til me boy's beard's long enough fer 'im t' stand Steward." Shaking his head, he turned to Argentia.

"King Durn." She bowed in greeting.

"Lass, ye got th' guts o' a dwarfess," Durn said. To Argentia's great relief he made no comment about her appearance. "So what's this I'm hearin about ye needin some mithryl?"

"Yes, please. If you can spare it."

"Bah! Course we can spare it. How much?"

"Enough to forge a sword."

66

Argentia moved along the pathless ways of Frostwood.

She was ten days out of Stromness. The mithryl block hung in a sack beside her pack; even now she was amazed at how light the metal was. Her journey had brought her west and south out of the mountains. Though the days were turning toward spring across Teranor, winter held fast in the elevations of the Gelidian Spur. She was grateful for the fur wrap the dwarves had given her. The steep trails were windblown and tricky: slow going, but at least clear of ice-falls.

Once she was down into the foothills, the passage eased. She made up for the fact that she had no horse by sleeping only a few hours each day and walking by star- and moonlight, which gleamed even brighter against the black night in these wild lands far distant from any city.

For most of her journey she was not alone. By night she heard the wolves and the mountain cats on their hunts. By day she caught glimpses of bears in the hills, and saw many deer, rabbits, squirrels, and foxes in the vale. Hawks and eagles circled on invisible currents. Jays cried in copses.

When she reached Frostwood, all that changed.

She noticed it the moment she passed out of the early morning light and into the coniferous shadows. She had been in many forests in many parts of Acrevast. Most of them were full of noise, much as the vale and hills had been. Frostwood was different. There was a gravity to the elf forest. A weight to the slanting beams of white-gold light sifting down through the towering trees. A primeval aura that bent all things beneath it to reverent silence.

As she went deeper into the forest, surrounded by scents of pine, following paths that were not truly paths along the needle-carpeted ground toward the ruins of the elf city of Rime, Argentia felt a sense of peace so profound that she almost believed all might yet be well. At the least, she knew she had been right to return.

Night in Frostwood was mystical.

The stars and moon turned the trees to silver ghosts. At her camp, Argentia did not even make a fire, preferring to huddle in her fur wrap and let the beauty of the wood play out undisturbed around her. She even lowered her hood.

On past midnight, she was rewarded with a rare sight. An ivory owl stooped silently out of the diamond and obsidian sky to fall upon some unsuspecting rodent. It happened so swiftly that only the abortive death-cry of the prey as it was speared and borne aloft in one beautifully efficient strike convinced Argentia that she had not conjured the whole scene out of her imagination.

Yet that stood as nothing compared to what she discovered on the next night.

67

The last time Argentia had come to Frostwood, the forest's quiet had hidden great destruction. The demon Ter-at had sieged the elf city of Rime and left nothing in its wake but ruin and death.

Argentia was very mindful of this as the second day of her trek through the wood drew toward a close. She could hear the rushing of the Sylvastrym and anticipated she would likely reach her destination before dusk.

What happens then? When Ralak told her they needed a weapon to battle the demoness, some powerful internal voice had impelled her to return to Cafax's home to forge a new sword. She had trusted that instinct despite the fact that she had no idea how she would accomplish the task in a city that had been razed to rubble.

She was still pondering this when she passed through a final twist of trees and stopped cold in astonishment.

Before her, rising in alabaster splendor amid the silverleafs, was Rime.

"Impossible," Argentia breathed. She threw back her hood, turning her head every way, seeking for the source of what had to be an illusion. She had but to close her eyes and she could clearly see the corpses strewn like leaves torn down by an autumn storm, the buildings that were as black and blasted as her own tortured form—yet there was not even a hint of that devastation here. Every building, every delicately arched bridge, every softly spraying fountain rose in smooth, marble perfection. It took her breath away.

She moved forward as one in a dream, waiting for Rime to bleed away like a mirage. But it remained even after she had come to the side of a gazebo (she instinctively avoided the fountains and pools with their reflective waters) and pressed her cindered fingers to its rail, feeling the fine grain of the white ash that the elves crafted to miraculously mimic stone. *My God it is real....*

"Beautiful, is it not?"

The voice came from close behind her. For a moment Argentia, lost in her musings, thought the words had come from her husband, who had a penchant for sneaking up on her. She whirled, heart pounding, her over-awed mind half expecting to see Carfax's ghost hovering there.

"You!" It was not the ranger, but Argentia knew him: D'Lyrian, Prince of Falcontyr's Forest, where the elf court dwelt. "What happened here? Rime was ruined. The demon destroyed it. Burned it. I was here. I saw...."

"Tush," D'Lyrian said. The elf was slightly taller than the huntress. He was dressed in the browns and greens favored by his people, with long golden hair flowing past his shoulders in bright contrast to the walnut hue of his handsomely angular face. As with all elves, he possessed an air of reservation, of wisdom and sadness that came with ageless winters watching the world. "'Tis true, all you say," D'Lyrian agreed, his almond-shaped, golden eyes sparkling. "But evil never holds."

"How?" Argentia had first met D'Lyrian in the wake of the destruction of Rime. They had come into almost instant conflict and had parted with Argentia condemning D'Lyrian a coward for refusing to help against the demon. They met again under friendlier terms after the Battle of Hidden Vale, where D'Lyrian and his elves had in the end stood beside the dwarves of Stromness and the Unicorns of the Crown.

"We have rebuilt the city as a monument to Araland and our kin from Frostwood." D'Lyrian stepped back and bowed low, sweeping an arm toward the glittering white buildings, paths, and fountains behind him. "Welcome to Rime, Lady Firetress."

Argentia had been so amazed by all of this that she had completely forgotten her hood was down. D'Lyrian's words hit her like a slap. She reached for the hood. The elf caught her arm.

"Leave it," he said sternly. "Why should you hide?"

"You know nothing! Don't touch me! And don't call me Lady!" Argentia pulled free and yanked the hood viciously back into place. "What in the hell are you doing here, anyway?"

"I told you once before, this is an elf wood. 'Tis not I who trespass," D'Lyrian riposted.

"I'm not trespassing!" Argentia flared. "I'm here to—"

"I know why you are here," the elf said. He moved away, his soft, low-cuffed boots barely scuffing the earth, his gliding steps completely soundless, and seated himself on a low wall encircling a pool of crystalline water. "Come, please." Angrily, Argentia joined him. "Look," D'Lyrian said, spreading a hand over the water, which held the last light of the day.

Argentia looked. "I don't see anything."

"That is your failing." D'Lyrian inclined his hand toward the water, and then tilted it toward the huntress. "There, and there, I see Argentia Dasani. So do many others. But you must see yourself, Lady, else the rest means naught."

"I didn't come here for your lectures," Argentia snapped.

"Indeed not. You came to forge a weapon to slay a fiend." D'Lyrian said. "It might interest you to know that it passed this way yestermorn."

"What!"

"In a wagon heading west. The power of the wood weakened it, but 'twas strong enough to survive."

"Why the hell didn't you stop it?"

"'Tis not my affair," D'Lyrian said.

"You damned—"

"See?" D'Lyrian said, a sly smile playing over his lips. "You are not so different after all."

Argentia trembled with fury and sputtered something incoherent.

D'Lyrian raised a hand. "'Tis enough for one night." He pointed to a white cottage on the far side of the pool. "In that building you will find a chamber prepared. Rest. Sleep. We will begin at dawn—if you wish."

With that, the elf left her. Argentia watched him out of sight, glaring daggers at his back, but eventually, perhaps inevitably, she looked to the pool again. Her hand flashed down, slapping violently across the water, scattering the hooded image into a thousand shards.

68

"I'm ready," Argentia said.

D'Lyrian, seated once more beside the reflecting pool, looked up from his contemplation of a single white ash leaf. Argentia stood before him. Her hood hung over her shoulders, revealing the scarred hideousness of her face. The sack with the mithryl block dangled in one blackened hand. Her sandaled foot tapped impatiently.

For a long moment they simply stared at one another. "Mayhap," the elf murmured. He rose. "Very well. Follow."

The forge was nothing like what Argentia had encountered in Stromness or any city or village she had ever passed through. It was not in a hot, smoky, slag-reeking chamber, but in the open air of a glade nestled deep in the city. The furnace had been hewn into a giant white boulder. It was smooth and seamless as polished marble and carved with elvish runes. The anvil was black iron: the first use of that color Argentia had seen in Rime. Beside it was a white wooden bench with carefully arrayed tools: a hammer in a bucket of water, files, tongs, and burnishing stones. There was also a deep trough filled with ice and water, and a great whetstone in a wood-and-iron frame.

D'Lyrian went to the forge and prodded the banked coals, bringing the flames back to life. They were a pure, unwavering blue. Argentia unwrapped the mithryl block from the sack. It was a dull gray color, though she knew when it was truly worked it would outshine the brightest silver. She placed her scabrous palms on the block, trying to get a feel for the metal, to see the hidden sword within the bulky shape, and to remember all she knew of forging.

It had been more than fifteen years since the blademaster Toskan had instructed her in this art. At the time, Argentia had not seen the necessity for such lessons. She wanted training in the use of a sword, not in the making of a sword. But Toskan had insisted, telling her that the key to wielding a blade was to know it intimately, from its first forming to its final polish.

So she had learned to forge before she learned to fight. As she journeyed with Toskan and his sell-swords from village to village, city to city, she had managed to get in some practice in the smithies where the group had their weapons repaired, but most of her knowledge was theoretical, taken from Toskan's books and lectures or from watching others at work. She had never actually attempted to forge a sword. The katana she had carried until it had been lost on Elsmywr had been Toskan's dying bequest and all her other blades had been made for her.

Now she had to create a new weapon: one powerful enough to stop a demon. She was not sure she could. Worse, there was only one block of mithryl and time was pressing. There would be no second chance.

You will not fail, that same voice that had led her to Frostwood said in her mind. *You have never failed....*

I did. I failed against Mouradian....

Not so. You won your freedom. The wizard cheated. Lied....

That was a truth lost and forgotten. In the depths of her despair it had seemed unimportant, but now it reemerged. "I'll try," Argentia whispered, as she had in the alley.

No. You must do more than try. You must succeed. Your friend needs you....

"I know."

D'Lyrian, who was pouring a slick of water over the anvil, turned curiously toward her. "Nothing," she said. "Are you finished there?"

"The fire awaits," D'Lyrian said. He did not question whether she could manage this task, or offer any aid beyond one final piece of advice: "Trust yourself."

With that, the elf prince bowed and withdrew.

Argentia was left alone to face the forging.

69

Argentia set about her work methodically, trying to lose herself in her task, to focus solely on the demands of the crafting. She picked up the mithryl bar with the tongs and set it into the furnace. The blue fire licking at the metal stirred unwanted memories. Sweat poured off her as she watched

(her body)

the mithryl grow hot in

(the dragonfire)

the elven forge. By the time the bar was malleable, the huntress was also churning and volatile. Her cobalt eyes blazed as she clamped the ready metal to the soaked anvil, where it smoked and hissed like a cornered dragon.

She shrugged her way out of the cumbersome robe, letting it hang over the belt at her waist, freeing her arms to work. Seizing the hammer from the bucket of water, she struck the first blow. The white-hot metal gave with a spurt of sparks. She struck again, keeping her arm tucked tight to her side, her wrist firm, as Toskan had instructed so long ago.

The mithryl compressed beneath the force of the maul.

Inspired, Argentia hammered, and hammered, and hammered. Into each blow she poured all her anguish, all the torturing doubt and tormenting fear, all the self-loathing that had fettered her.

She was unaware of the bar beveling into a blade beneath her unrelenting attack. Of her voice screaming above the pure clash of metal on metal. Of the storm of red sparks. Of the ever-growing light.

Only hammered, and hammered, and hammered: every blow a catharsis.

D'Lyrian stood in the shadows at the edge of the grove.

He had lingered to watch Argentia about her task. She fascinated him. In many ways they could not have been more different: he a creature of cool reason and detachment, she a flame of instinct and emotion. Yet they both held true to honor and duty and were driven by their own particular understanding of right and righteousness.

It was duty, he knew, that had brought her here. It was a testament to her remarkable will that she had come so far—yet he was not sure she could find the courage to go on; she was only human, after all.

Still, he watched.

The mithryl bar steamed upon the anvil. The maul rose and fell, rose and fell. Sparks swarmed the forge like flying lanterns on a summer's eve. Screams of undiluted fury matched the crash of each blow.

D'Lyrian sensed a tremble in the air: a shift in the wind blowing through Frostwood. *Something is happening—*

For a moment there was only the hammersong, its cadence strong, sure, true.

And then there was light.

A glimmer at first—a flash like the sun striking off the dragon's tooth token that swung at Argentia's throat—but in instants it grew, and D'Lyrian realized his mistake.

The light was not a glance of sun off the token; it was *from* the token itself.

The elf prince threw a hand up, shielding his eyes as the eldritch glow pulsed brighter than an earth-fallen star, and Argentia's black silhouette burned in silver fire.

70

Argentia struck a final blow and came back to herself as if out of a fugue.

She had worked like a woman possessed, lost to time and place. Now she let the hammer fall away and looked on the child of her labor.

The block of mithryl was gone.

Upon the anvil lay her sword.

It was, of course, a katana: as sleek and deadly as she had seen in her mind's eye. *It's perfect!* she exulted, clenching a fist triumphantly. Her arm was aching as if she had just fought a horde of goblins, but she was thrilled with her accomplishment. Though much work remained to complete the blade, the most difficult part was behind her.

She glanced around. The sun was high overhead. Hours had passed while she forged away without pause. She shook her head. *No wonder I'm so exhausted—and hot....* Her hair was plastered to her back with sweat. *Ugh....*

She braced her hands on the edge of the trough and with a quick movement ducked her head and shoulders into the icy water. *Ahhhhh!* She came sweeping up, tossing her head back, spraying water everywhere from her sopping hair—

My hair.... Argentia froze. Water sluiced off her face, dripped onto the grass. Her heart hammered in her breast.

Slowly—very slowly—she peered over the trough again, daring to meet her reflection in the agitated surface.

Her knees buckled. She heard Ralak's voice as he sat with her in the *Reef Reaver's* cabin on the voyage back from Elsmywr: *Nothing can undo dragonfire....*

But something had.

71

Argentia regained consciousness as the evening sun was dropping away. She lay in a heap on the grass, where she had swooned after seeing her reflection. *What happened?*

She remembered.

Please God it wasn't a dream, she prayed as she opened her eyes. *Please God...* Full of terrified hope, she lunged up to re-confront her reflection in the trough. Her lips trembled. She clutched her throat, emotion choking her. Tears ran down her pale cheeks. *Oh Bright Lady— thank you! Oh thank you!*

She fell to her knees again, buried her face in her white hands, and sobbed for joy.

"Hail, Lady," D'Lyrian called.

He had kept vigil over the huntress from the edge of the grove, though there was nothing in Frostwood that would harm her. He waited until she had composed herself. When she was fully robed again and standing, he came forward.

She looked at him. In the fading light he could see the tears still standing in her eyes, brightening those cobalt gems. "What happened?" she whispered. She believed what she saw, but she could think of only one possible explanation, and even that defied what Ralak had told her. "Was it magic?" As she asked, she reached instinctively and enclosed the dragon's tooth token in her fist.

D'Lyrian smiled and nodded. "Of a sort and strength I have rarely witnessed." He had told her of what he had seen: of the light rising from the token like a plated sun, consuming her, purging her.

The elf's account confirmed what Argentia had intuited. The dragon's tooth token had come to her from Carfax, who had it himself from Catriana, his first love and an elf of this very wood. It had protected Argentia in the past, though never against such a grievous affliction.

Why now? she wondered. Why, after a moon and more of dormancy, had the magic of the token come forth now? Was the answer Frostwood itself? Had her return to the place of the token's making awakened some deeper strain of its power, greater even than dragonfire?

"Mayhap," D'Lyrian said when Argentia voiced these queries. "But 'tis more likely the magic was there all along, waiting."

"Waiting for what?"

D'Lyrian gestured at the trough just as he had at the pool on the previous night.

Argentia looked into the water. Saw herself.

Understood.

"For me," she whispered. The token had been waiting for her to find the strength to face and accept her fate. To stand and be true to who she was.

"'Tis a powerful gift, Lady," D'Lyrian said. "Keep it close."

A dragon had once told her the same thing. "Always," Argentia replied.

She tucked the token safely back into her robe and turned to the anvil, where the newly forged katana still rested in the clamp. She had lost time. Most of the day was gone. "Can you bring a light here?" she asked.

"I can, but I will not."

"Why? The sword—"

"The sword will wait. This night is for you," D'Lyrian said. "Take it."

She did.

72

Argentia returned to the quarters D'Lyrian had arranged for her. Last night they had been only a place to catch a few restless hours of sleep before her trial at the forge. Tonight she saw they were beautiful. Constructed completely of the pale woods of the forest, they boasted artfully scrolled mouldings, fluted columns supporting graceful archways between chambers, and light, airy spaces illumed by blown-glass lamps.

The room where she had slept had a table and chairs carved to resemble giant toadstools, and a sleigh bed piled deep with silks and pillows. The bed did not interest her right now. She crossed instead to the bath in the next room. The tub was porcelain; she knew the rare ceramic from her own childhood and her more recent expeditions to furnish her own estate. Its delicate beauty made it the perfect complement to the sparse, sylvan suite.

She heated water in a hearth—also white stone, like the forge. When the tub was full and steaming she washed with soaps that had been waiting on a shelf, then soaked herself, massaging her sore shoulder, rolling her neck to crack out a kink, letting the tension uncoil from every inch of her restored body. She wondered whose rooms these had been when Rime was vibrant with elves. *Carfax's? Cat's?*

Her eyes slipped closed and she dozed.

It was full night when she woke. Darkness lay over the forest, but moonlight played through the canopy and slanted in the ovular windows of her rooms. The water had grown cold around her. Shivering, she rose from the bath. Discovered she had no towel. Went dripping out into the bedchamber.

D'Lyrian had been busy while she slept.

There was a fresh set of towels stacked on a chair, and new clothes laid out on the bed. A tray of mushrooms and assorted greens and a crystal decanter of amber liquid waited on the table.

And there was a mirror.

Full-length, framed in silver, it hung on the wall opposite the bed. Argentia was certain it had not been there the night before. That was the one thing she had checked.

Snaring a fluffy towel, Argentia dried off but did not dress. She sampled the food: the mushrooms were tender and delicious, the greens spicy and biting, and the wine—if that was indeed what the decanter held—was smooth and almost as sweet as honey. She wandered idly around the cottage while she ate, admiring the elf craft, which paid meticulous attention to the smallest details. From the flowers etched into a table leg to the runes carved into the hearth, everything was immaculately worked by artisans who could easily afford to spend a week or a month or even a year perfecting the edge of a single petal.

Mostly what she did before finally surrendering herself to the bed was stand before the mirror.

It was not vanity as much as amazement. She had not forgotten what she looked like, but thirty-two winters tended to deaden appreciation. Now just being able to see herself instead of the fire-charred thing she had been was enough to make her rejoice.

She examined her body from every angle. Skin that had been scorched black was once more the creamy white, starkly contrasted by the rose-madder dusk of her nipples and the flaming tumble of her tresses down her back.

Everything was smooth to the touch now: smooth, and strong. From the firm, resilient curves of her high, full breasts and tight, round buttocks to the washboard plane of her abdomen and the play of hard muscles in her long limbs, her body exuded vitality and health. She had lost her scars: the deep punctures in her shoulder, back, and hips from sword, harpoon, and claws, plus the myriad other minor marks that innumerable adventures had left on her body. Even the livid M of Mouradian's branding been wiped away, and though her dragonfly tattoo was also gone, she counted it a small price indeed.

Best of all, however, was to be able to gaze in the glass and see the fine arches of her cheekbones, the slim straightness of her aristocratic nose, the skeptical cast of her brow, and the lush curves of her lips instead of the goblinoid mask that had brought so many tears to her cobalt eyes.

She had come full circle: from her first devastating glimpse of her tragedy in a mirror in a hidden grotto on Elsmywr to her jubilate witness of her recovery in a mirror in an elven chamber in Rime. Now, as then, she wept: this time with unbridled elation. She was giddy as a girl who had just stolen her first kiss from the handsomest boy in the village, and she could not help herself.

D'Lyrian said this night was mine, she thought. Hers it was, and she used and enjoyed the time well in relaxation. But never was she unmindful of what lay ahead of her—and even more what lay behind.

When she slept, it was with the dragon's tooth token embraced in her fist.

73

Dawn found Argentia at the forge.

D'Lyrian had left her elven clothes: soft, fitted gray pants, almost like the buckskins she favored; a green silk shirt; a mottled brown, gray, and gold vest; and low-cuffed brown boots. Even though the shirt had sleeves and the boots barely came over her ankles, she found the garments all vastly preferable to the clerical robe and sandals.

The elf was absent, but he had clearly been at the forge not long before Argentia arrived. The magic fire was already burning—she had not noticed yesterday how the blue flames that shot up within the white stones matched exactly the color of her eyes—and the anvil was covered with a white drapery. Beneath this she found her sword. She picked it up, marveling at the lightness and balance of the weapon. She remembered little of the forging process, but she had surpassed her expectations. *Or something did, at least....*

Argentia was not entirely convinced that some other spirit had not been at work yesterday, guiding her arm. She touched the dragon's tooth token—Carfax had smithed his own blade, magical Strafe, at the forges of the cyclopes—and wondered.

Setting the blade to the fire again, Argentia watched it absorb the heat. The mithryl moved through a parade of colors like the sun rising from dawn to noon. Once it was hardened, mithryl was nigh unbreakable, but in the magical fire of the elf forge it became as malleable as normal steel. Argentia lay the blade on the anvil again and began her final forging, using more delicate strokes of the hammer now, bringing the metal down to an edge, straightening the lines, crisping the bevels, knocking out the blemishes of the rough forging.

When she was satisfied with her work, she heated and air-cooled the blade three times. She remembered to use less heat in each cycle: a trick to reduce stresses in the metal that she had learned from one smith or another. By the time the third cycle was complete it was midmorning and she was hungry, so she went to find food.

Save the burbling of the Sylvastrym and the splashing of the fountains, Rime kept its customary silence. In her chamber, Argentia found fresh fruit in a bowl, but no other sign of D'Lyrian. *What could have happened to him?*

The mystery of the elf's disappearance was quickly forgotten once she was back at the forge. Argentia secured the sword in the vice, took a stone from the bench and scraped off the steely hammer scales littering the blade. She used a sen to refine the shape, and then set to the blade's edge with files. She could have used the whetstone and made quicker work of the process, but she took meticulous care of all her weapons and had always preferred the intimacy of hand tools.

Evening had drawn down over Frostwood by the time her edging of the blade was done. She thought she would have to find fresh ice, but the trough apparently was magical as well, for it looked like a miniature Sea of Sleet.

She stoked the forge, drawing the fire up full and bright. Seizing the blade with a pair of cast-iron tongs, she heated the weapon again, standing before the blasting furnace until she was soaked with sweat, her new clothes plastered to her. Even her hands were sweating within the cumbersome, hardened leather gloves she had donned for protection. But she endured, holding the blade in the blaze until it had gone from a dull red to a brilliant cherry and looked as if it was on fire from within.

Now.... With a single, smooth motion, Argentia pulled the blade from the fire and plunged it into the trough. Steam geysered up with a mighty FWOOSH! The entire trough burst into a violent roil. Argentia held the tongs tightly until all the agitation had left the tank, and then held her patience for another few minutes before finally drawing out the hardened blade. In the failing light, the water beading and streaming off the weapon made it appear forged of diamonds.

"Splendid."

Argentia nearly jumped out of her skin when D'Lyrian spoke from directly behind her. "Aeton's bolts! Where the hell have you been?" she demanded, more irked by the fact that he had caught her by surprise again than at his absence. He was an elf, quite capable of moving with utter stealth, but that was no excuse.

"About many tasks," D'Lyrian answered, that cryptic smile skittering over his lips. He glanced at the canopy. The trees were black shadow-shapes against the velvet blue of dusk. "You have done well, Lady," he said. "Let the blade be awhile. Come and dine."

Argentia shook her head. "I have to finish this."

"We shall return. I give you my word, the blade will be ready in time."

Argentia was famished—fruit and fungi were hardly her idea of meals—so she conceded and joined D'Lyrian in one of Rime's restored palaces. They arranged themselves on silk pillows before a low wooden table and dined on silver salmon and fiddlehead ferns, drank more of the golden mead, and finished with cups of esp.

"Why are you helping me?" Argentia asked. She did not mean it uncivilly, she merely wanted to know.

"Because I find you an endless source of fascination, Lady Firetress."

"Horseshit," Argentia muttered. "What sort of answer is that?"

It was apparently the only one she was going to get from the enigmatic elf, who merely inclined his head to her in a tiny bow and kept silent his motives.

They returned to the forge, D'Lyrian bearing a long wooden box under his arm. "What's in there?" Argentia asked.

"Temper your blade ere your curiosity." The elf set the box on the bench, drew forth several small orbs from his cloak and cast them into the air. They hovered and began to glow, throwing light down into the center of the grove, which had lingered in darkness after the moon hid behind a heavy bank of clouds.

While D'Lyrian tended the forge, Argentia rubbed down her blade with an oilcloth. Then she set it to the flame until the residual oils shone as dark blue stains on the mithryl. Another plunge into the icy trough and the weapon was tempered and ready for its final polishing.

With water stones and grit parchment, Argentia worked the length of the blade, rubbing back and forth with steady movements, buffing out the file scratches. It was slow, painstaking work, but by midnight she had the mithryl looking like a frozen moonbeam.

D'Lyrian opened his box and took out a collection of odd pieces that Argentia recognized immediately as the finishing touches for her sword. "When could you have had time to do this?" she asked, amazed and honored.

D'Lyrian spread his hands. "Now are the labors of my vanished hours revealed," he said with a laugh. "May they please."

They more than pleased. The guard was a circle of mithryl inlayed with elven runes. The fittings were silverleaf wood that wedded perfectly to the notches set in the tang. The grip was a piece of skin tanned from an albino dragonfish, the wrappings leather dyed a deep cardinal red.

Since it was considered ill Fortune for a smith to grip a weapon, Argentia let D'Lyrian drill the holes into the tang with a small awl that glimmered with elven magic as the diamond tip bored through the dwarven steel. He set the fittings, which he told her in elvish were called subuki, and fixed them in place with mithryl bolts. Argentia asked him where he had found his own supply of the dwarf-silver, which was almost unknown outside of the deepest mountain delves.

"From thy fire," D'Lyrian said. Argentia did not even bother asking just how he had extracted the excess metal from the forge, knowing the elf would merely smile and keep his secrets. Shaking her head, she rolled her eyes and watched him wrap the hilt.

He whisked a viscous glue from water and a glimmery flour that Argentia was sure was not found on any baker's shelves in any city in Teranor. Painting the glue on the fittings, D'Lyrian bonding the dragonfish skin tightly around the hilt. When it was secure, he wove the leather strips into a braid that left diamonds of the white skin as sets for her fingers.

Argentia marveled at the deft precision of his hands. In his movements and his falcon's focus he reminded her of Carfax. She stared up into the night. The moon was still veiled, but there were stars visible above the grove; her ranger might dwell among them, but so long as she had beat to her heart, he would always be far nearer to her than those celestial sentinels. *Always....*

Last was the kashira, which was welded carefully into place in a final hour of labor. The hilt's cap was itself a work of art—a mithryl circle embossed with a lion's head—and was easily Argentia's favorite part of the sword.

"This also." D'Lyrian drew forth a scabbard from the box. "White ash," he said. "A blessed wood." The scabbard had been hardened by elvish fire, stained and lacquered to a shiny black, and accented with a thin braid of the same red leather that wound about the sword's hilt.

"It's beautiful." Argentia said. "Thank you." By now it was very late, and her exertions in the past days had been many. Despite the esp flowing in her body, she was tired, but when she went to put the sword away, D'Lyrian stopped her.

"Do not sheath the weapon until you have tested its truth," the elf said.

"On what?"

D'Lyrian pointed. Argentia hesitated. The blade felt keen and strong, but what if she had misforged it? What if she struck and it shattered? How would she help Artelo then?

It won't. I know it won't.... Setting both hands around the hilt, she raised the blade above her head. The dragon's tooth token twinkled in the starshine.

With a cry, Argentia whirled and swept the katana down.

CRACK! Sparks leaped—

Thump...thump—

The whetstone fell in twain.

Straightening, Argentia wiped the stone dust away from the blade. The edge showed not the slightest evidence of the blow. She looked at D'Lyrian and grinned. "Not bad."

"No indeed." The elf nodded. "All that remains is the naming."

"Oh. But...what name?"

At that moment, the moon slipped free of the clouds and shone down upon Frostwood and the forge of Rime. The katana gleamed silver.

D'Lyrian extended his hand over the blade. "Lightbringer."

79

The elf prince left Argentia the next morning, but not before presenting three more gifts: a cloak of that strange elvish weave that was all colors and none; a pouch of esp, enchanted so that as long as one bean remained in the bag, it would replenish its store to fullness overnight; and a beautiful white horse. "He will bear you where you must go. When you have no more need, release him and he will find his way home."

"Thank you," Argentia said. "For everything."

"The greatest treasure you shall take from Rime is the courage of your heart," D'Lyrian said. "And it was with you ere your arrival. Do not forget that."

He jigged his own mount around to depart.

"Wait!" Argentia said. "Will I see you again?"

The elf turned back to her. "Who can say, Lady Firetress?" He laughed, but his eyes said yes.

Argentia had Rime to herself. She would not be here much longer, she knew. D'Lyrian had received word from a lark that a rider was in Frostwood and making for the elf city. It could only be Artelo. He would arrive by nightfall.

234

She spent the rest of the day practicing with Lightbringer, familiarizing herself with every nuance of the blade. It was lighter than her old katana, making her already formidable speed even faster.

As evening fell she went to the south part of the city, for that was where Artelo, coming from Byrtnoth, would enter. Not wanting him to pass through thinking the city was deserted, she made a small campfire near a fountain. The night air had a chill to it. She put on her cloak. Brewed a pot of esp. Waited, staring into the fire. The red flames no longer held any terror for her, but they did remind her that she had debts to pay.

She heard the approach of a horse. Thought of that night on the beach in Harrowgate. Of Artelo condemning her for abandoning him: *God damn you, Argentia! I thought you were my friend!*

It was time to prove she still was.

Interlude

"So."

Her telling complete, Argentia looked across the fire at Artelo. It had not been an easy story for her to recount, but she had told it true, hoping that Artelo would come to understand why she had turned from him in his need.

She was not sure he had.

"You don't look happy to see me," she said.

"No. I...am. It's...." Artelo, caught by surprise by Argentia's incisive observation, groped for the right words. "It's just a lot to try to take in at once."

Argentia rose. "You've got five minutes."

"What do you mean?" Artelo was on his feet as well, moving around the fire.

"That's how long I'm waiting before I start the hunt." It was past midnight, but the moon was up, the wood was full of silver light, and the esp was strong in her. She could easily ride until the next night, making up for some of the lost time before she reached the mountains beyond, where the unknown and likely treacherous terrain would slow her. "If you're coming with me, you have to trust me like you did before." She looked him in the eyes. "I won't fail you."

Artelo looked back. When Argentia had first lowered her hood to reveal herself, he had been stunned. With her red hair radiant in the firelight, her face once more unblemished and beautiful, it was difficult to conceive that the burned, half-dead thing that had struggled up the beach on Elsmywr and had fled from him down the beach at Harrowgate had ever existed at all. But it had, and the fact remained that whatever her form, Argentia had betrayed him.

Even after hearing her tale, with its intimate glimpses of her suffering, part of Artelo remained bitter, wishing she had fought her battle with herself after the battle to save Aura was won. But the rest of him understood. He was no stranger to disfiguring and crippling injury. He remembered how deeply he had to reach into himself to overcome the loss of his hand, and that was nothing compared to what Argentia had endured. He knew her tale had been not only an account, it had been an explanation: she could not have helped him until she helped herself.

It was easy to comprehend, harder to accept. He kept hearing her on the beach, refusing him aid in his most desperate hour. He struggled to grasp how deep her pain must have been at that moment for her to let it so overwhelm the good and honorable woman he had always known.

As he did, another memory rose: Argentia on their first journey together, after their devastating defeat by the vampyr, with their company scattered and broken, telling him everything was all right, promising they would still rescue Solsta.

The same cold fire that had been in Argentia's eyes that night was in them now, burning beneath the moon over Frostwood.

Artelo saw it, and he believed.

"I trust you," he said, extending his hand.

Argentia clasped his forearm, then pulled him forward and hugged him tightly.

"Let's go get your daughter."

PART V

The Hunt

75

Laeonus Castlebright was in love.

All his life the watchman had dreamed of something like this: a damsel in distress who would turn to him for protection. A villainous foe that he would defeat to set her free, just as in the stories of knights and monsters that had shaped his youth. So what if he was only a soldier and not a knight. Did honor come only with the Crown's dubbing? Was Sylyth's husband honorable?

Artelo Sterling had betrayed every ideal of chivalry that Laeonus knew. He had struck his wife, committed adultery, murdered his mother-in-law. He would have murdered Sylyth too, had she not been quick enough to escape. *And maybe even his own daughter,* Laeonus thought, clenching his teeth as he guided the wagon through the hills beyond Frostwood. *I hope he does come after us. I'll run him right through his coward heart....*

The last Laeonus had heard, the knight was a prisoner, but Sylyth was convinced Artelo was coming for her. He might have escaped, Laeonus allowed. Certainly killing his guards would be no deterrent. A man who had murdered a defenseless old woman was likely capable of anything.

Doesn't matter. Let him come. I won't let any more harm come to her. On my life I swear it....

He would do anything for Sylyth.

That had been true since their first kiss....

This can't be happening, Laeonus thought as they stood on the street in foggy Byrtnoth and Sylyth drew his head toward hers. There was a delicious moment of pausing, their lips a breath apart, hers waiting, his not quite daring to cross that last span: a gulf of fractions. Then she closed the distance, sealing their mouths together. He felt a mighty heat course through him, as if a sun had been born in his chest. The scent of her surrounded him, intoxicating. The taste of her lips was sweet berries gone soft and red with ripeness. Their curves were lush and hot, their press against his almost desperate.

Laeonus moaned. Never mind that all the tales said it was the woman who made the sighs; they were only tales. This was pleasure so potent it stole the strength from his legs even as it sprang up what was between them like a halberd at attention.

He drew her close, wanting to be against her, wanting to be inside her more than anything in the world. He paid no mind to the child pressed between them, to the sounds of the city around them. Knew only that he was kissing her and needed to go on kissing her.

But she pulled away. Her eyes, dark as the pits of the night, gleamed in the misty air. She licked her lips as if in satisfaction; her tongue was long and pink and articulate. The sight of it made him want her even more. He reached for her.

"Not here," she whispered urgently, stopping his mouth with two upraised fingers. "Please, I must get away from him. You have to get me out of here."

"Of course, but to where, Lady?"

"Out of the city. West. I have...family there. They can help me." Sylyth clutched the guard's shoulder, her eyes boring into his, working her magic. He was not completely hers yet, but he was close and she sensed that he would serve her well.

"I will help you," Laeonus said. "I swear it by Aeton."

She hissed at that name, but Laeonus did not notice. "We must go. Now. Swiftly." She did not know what had become of the knight, only that distance and speed were her greatest allies against him.

Laeonus shook his head. "We cannot leave the city until dawn," he said. "It's forbidden. But we can be gone with first light. I promise, no harm will come to you. They have your husband in custody. You're safe."

"We must go now!" Sylyth insisted.

"All right," Laeonus said, acquiescing to the desperation in her voice. "There's a way. A door I can sneak us out." It was a flagrant violation of the code of the Watch, but Laeonus sensed that his time in Byrtnoth was done. He had never felt for anyone as he did for this helpless, stranded woman. Whatever he had to do to

(have her)

help her, he would do.

"How far west?" he asked. "Will we need horses?"

"Ach—horses!" Sylyth spat. "I cannot ride. My wagon, I must have my wagon."

That complicated matters. He might have gotten them out the guard door, but there was no way to get horses or a wagon out save through the gates.

He tried to convince her that the city was safe, that they could take a room in an inn and leave in the morning, but she would hear nothing of it. "We must go now," she repeated. "Out of the city. You will return for the wagon."

And that was what they did.

Laeonus used his passkey to sneak Sylyth and Aura out the guard door on the south side of the city. They saw almost no one as they crossed the dark, wet streets to that exit, but Sylyth's head darted in alarm at every movement. Her paranoia was catching. Laeonus found his hand on his sword almost constantly as they moved through the mist and gloom of Byrtnoth in the aftermath of the storm.

There was a tense moment at the door when his key stuck. He jigged it furiously, hunched in the shadows, fearing that the Watch would come upon them. He had timed the move to the door from a hiding place across the street for the few minutes when the two wall patrols, which ranged in opposing circles, would be farthest from this spot—but he had not counted on this delay.

The doors were for evacuation purposes, to prevent crowds from clogging the gates in event of a fire or some other catastrophe. They were to remain closed and locked except in those dire circumstances, but all Watch Captains and Gate Wardens had keys. Some of the less scrupled among them would sneak out with women or assist smugglers and thieves making their escapes. It was a sad but true fact, Laeonus knew. He had prided himself on never using his key—until tonight.

Hurry up and open, damn you.... He jigged the key again. He could feel Sylyth (though he had not even known her name then) growing impatient beside him. He prayed the child would keep silent. If they were caught, he might be joining Sylyth's husband in the dungeons.

Open! With a final twist, the key found its way in and the door opened. Laeonus ushered Sylyth and the child out into the night. Locked the door behind them.

Keeping low, they ran hard. The dismal weather helped them, shrouding them in gloom and deadening the range of the watch fires. In a few minutes they passed beyond the lights of the city into darkness.

Laeonus risked his moonstone. Its magic would not last until dawn, but it would guide them to a place he knew not far from here: a grotto on the rolling banks of the Sylvastrym.

Once there, Sylyth set the still-sleeping Aura down on the carpet of dark moss. The chill and damp in the air were even heavier here, so Sylyth covered the child with her blanket.

She would not need it for what she intended next.

Naked, she turned to Laeonus. She could feel his desire. He would make an even more willing servant than the foolish wizardling who had summoned her. "How long before you can bring the wagon?" she asked.

"The gates open at dawn," Laeonus said, once he had recovered from the exquisite shock of seeing her standing nude as some nyad risen from the misting river.

Sylyth's strange, dark eyes gleamed in the glow of the moonstone. There was time enough. She knew she needed this one to last her a long time, but she was hungry, her feeding this night having been prematurely interrupted. *A taste, then....* "There are other things I must have," she said.

"Name them, Lady. If I may, I will bring them."

Food for the child, and water, she told him, and clothes for herself. "And one thing more."

"What, Lady?"

"You." She spread her arms toward him. "Come. Come to Sylyth...."

Laeonus came—and was lost.

76

Several hours later, as dawn crept shyly toward the rim of the world, Laeonus returned to Byrtnoth through the guard door and slipped unseen into the stables. Fortune was with him; the stablehands had not yet arrived.

Moving quickly, he took the horses from their stall and hitched them to the wagon in the correspondingly numbered bay. They were docile enough, so he looped the reins over a post and left them. The sound of hooves on the dark and mostly empty streets of the city would surely call attention, and Laeonus had other stops that were best made unnoticed.

On a corner not far from the Pink Tulip, he purchased the clothes off a whore's back in what was undoubtedly the strangest transaction of that harlot's long career. Food was more difficult. Laeonus lived in the Watch barracks, where meals were served in the mess hall. He had no stores to draw on, and even if he did, getting in and out of the barracks unnoticed was impossible.

So Laeonus took the liberty of opening the mercantile a few minutes early. He broke a window alongside the store's back door with a rock. The shattering glass sounded like a catapult ball smashing against a fortress wall. Every Watchman in the Tier surely had heard it.

Laeonus stood there in the alley, waiting to be caught. No one came. *Hurry up, fool,* he chided himself. *Waste any more time and you will be caught....*

He reached through the broken window and unlatched the door. The mercantile was dark and quiet. Laeonus risked his moonstone. The light would be visible through the store's windows but he had no choice. He found what he was looking for as quickly as he could. Took all that he could carry, leaving most of his coins on the counter to cover the goods and the repairs on the window.

He told himself he was not quite a thief.

The run back through the dissolving shadows to the stables was the most terrifying thing he had ever done. The city was beginning to stir. Lights were coming on here and there. Doors were opening. People were moving on the streets. Not many, but enough that Laeonus expected the broken mercantile window to be discovered at any moment and the Watch alarum to sound.

None of that happened. He made it to the stables. The bleary-eyed stableboys were there now, along with the few merchants or travelers of a mind to be out of the city as soon as the gates opened. Laeonus, his hood drawn low, his cloak close about him to conceal his uniform, hailed no one. He threw the sacks of food and empty waterskins—he would fill those in the grotto—and the whore's clothes into the wagon and mounted the driving board.

Now he just had to get out of the city.

Impatient, his heart racing, his breathing ragged, Laeonus waited for the dawn. When he heard the portcullis grinding up and the skree of the hinges as the gates swung wide, he geed the horses ahead. Timing was everything now.

He emerged from the stable third in the line for the gates. It was still mostly dark, but the braziers burning on either side of the city's doors made up for that, and the Watchmen had lanterns for a clearer view of anything or anyone they felt warranted a closer look.

Outbound travelers were rarely bothered—they stopped being the Watch's concern the moment they passed the city's gates—but Laeonus did not want to be recognized and have to answer any questions about where he was going in a wagon that certainly did not belong to him. Sylyth's husband might well escape the dungeons; the fewer leads he had if he did, the better.

That was why timing was everything. Laeonus knew from countless days working this shift that the Watchmen would be focused on the queue of incoming traffic: travelers on foot, on horseback, and in wagons who had waited out the night just beyond the city walls. This morning was no different. With plenty of arrivals to draw their attention, the gate guards—and Laeonus knew them to a man—let him pass along with the rest of the departing folk without much more than a glance in his direction.

Clear of the city, Laeonus felt a great weight lift, as if his soul had shrugged off the chains of fear in the same way that he doffed his armor at the end of a shift. He was leaving behind his home, his family, his vocation, everything he had known for twenty-three years, to follow this mysterious and distressed woman who had taken his heart and his virginity, and he was doing it without doubt or hesitation. *For love*, he thought. *For Sylyth....*

It was amazing how she consumed his thoughts. He had been gone only hours, and all he could think about was seeing her again, holding her, kissing her, burying himself to the root in her again, hearing her musical moans as she begged him to give her "More, yesssss, more!"

He made the horses go faster. When the city was out of view behind him, he turned off the road, crossing a field toward the river winding like a ghostly serpent through the twilight. When he reached the grotto, Sylyth—as if anticipating his need and desire—took him down upon the dark moss again, mounted him, and made those meaningless noises Laeonus found so empowering.

When it was over, the succubus dressed in the clothes Laeonus had brought, collected the child, who was shivering and irritable, and climbed into the wagon. She touched her belly. A gloating smile found her lips.

The spawn was fully formed within her now, awaiting only the magic of the shimmyr to draw it forth from her and implant it in the vessel, where it would complete its gestation.

77

Frostwood was nearly Sylyth's undoing.

They reached the wood a fortnight after leaving Byrtnoth. Sylyth felt the change the moment the wagon rolled into the cool shadows of the mystical forest. Frostwood was no longer home to the elves and their goodly magic—one of her own kind had seen to that, eradicating the entire forest of them—but she never would have imagined how their power had lingered.

By the end of their first day beneath the silvery canopy, Sylyth was too nauseous to rise, too weak even to take Laeonus to feed her powers. The keening

(singing, the singing of the elves)

in her head—a vile buzzing and thrumming that threatened to burst her eyes—had lamed her. She could only huddle weakly beneath her blanket, Aura and the slave and even the spawn forgotten in her misery.

Laeonus had displayed all the zealous concern of a lover. As Sylyth's condition worsened over the next two days, he grew frantic. When they came to the ghostly city, Laeonus insisted they stop. He would look for help while Sylyth rested in a place with a true bed, where she might be more comfortable.

The succubus, who had vomited black bile and was wracked with cramps, as if the forces of the forest were working to abort the monstrosity growing in her poisonous womb, was quite certain such a thing would have killed her. Mustering some last strength, she forced her magic upon Laeonus' mind again, ordering him to move the wagon as far from the city as he could, to go and go and not stop until the dreadful white buildings and paths and fountains were long vanished behind them.

She held on long enough to feel the wagon begin to roll forward once more. Then the darkness took her. There was no mercy in it. The keening and the pain followed her, hounding her toward madness. When she woke, she curled into a whimpering, fetal ball of misery, praying to her dark god that she might somehow endure this agony long enough to escape it.

Within her, the spawn did the same.

For Aura, Frostwood was a very different experience.

The wood flooded the child with good feelings. Until they crossed into the forest, sleep had continued to be Aura's refuge, freeing her from the need to face the things she could not understand. In sleep she did not have to eat the stale, nasty food that first the old woman, and now the man, and sometimes the Bad Lady made her eat, or shiver as the Bad Lady looked gloatingly at her with her ugly eyes.

In the forest, however, her spirits rose. She enjoyed the fresh pine smell blowing into the wagon on the breeze. When the man, fearing she would catch whatever Sylyth had caught and fall ill as well, took her out of the wagon to ride beside him on the driving board, she marveled at the many, many trees, and how white they were—like trees in the snow, but there was no snow here—and laughed at the white rabbits, silver larks, and ivory squirrels that it seemed had come forth from their wooded holes and hollows expressly to deliver a happiness she had all but forgotten.

These good feelings followed Aura to sleep. In her dreams the celestial woman came as she had come every night, but lingered longer to hold her and sing to her, whispering words

(Don't be scared,
'Cause Mama's here,
And I will always care for ye,
'Cause my babe I love ye so—
Now hush-a-bye, my little one,
My little one....)

as familiar as her heartbeat, and through the veil of stars before her face Aura knew her.

"Mama!"

The woman robed in light smiled and caressed Aura's cheek. As she faded into the insubstantial dust of dreams with the arrival of day, she let these last words echo: "Be strong now, love. Your Da's coming...."

78

The passage of Frostwood, all too brief for Aura, was still almost too long for Sylyth. But the succubus survived, gaining a little strength back with each mile that grew between her and the elf city.

She was weak and ravenous when, four days later, they broke clear of the western rim of the forest. The land rose steeply toward ragged, lonely Cragyntor, but for once Sylyth had a more pressing concern than the dark power at the Fel Tarn.

She called Laeonus to her. It was early in the day, but she could wait no longer. "I need you," she said when he had stopped the wagon and climbed into the back. She knelt and unfastened her blouse, cupping her breasts toward him like an offering. "Take me."

"Are you sure, Lady? You look so pale...." He was merely being solicitous: he was enfevered with lust for her; the week in the woods had been a hard abstinence.

Sylyth lunged forward, grabbed Laeonus, and hauled him down. "What about Aura?" he asked. The child was on the driving board, safely tethered but alone.

"Never mind the vessel," Sylyth hissed. She was afraid for her life. As they passed through Rime she had felt the spawn, deprived for three days already, begin feeding off her as it had not done since the earliest days of its formation. Its idiot hunger knew no bounds. If she did not provide for it, it would batten upon her womb until it destroyed her and itself. That risk had always been there, but to have it happen now, so close to the end....

"Inside me, fool!" She ripped at Laeonus' pants, her touch rough as she pinned him down and straddled him, not even bothering to remove her skimpy skirt. If Laeonus saw the demonic flickering of her visage as she bucked furiously atop him, he thought it but his imagination.

He lost himself in her, and Sylyth almost killed him.

Once she began copulating she could not stop. Out of control, she glutted herself, draining his seed, his spirit, his life. She would have taken him until his last gasp, leaving only a withered corpse, but Aura stopped her.

She had been left untended for hours while the wagon rocked and creaked in time with the frenzied lovers. At first Aura hadn't minded: the sun was warm, she could hear and see birds and other animals, and the memories of Frostwood held in her mind. But as time passed she grew bored and fidgety. She was hungry and she needed to relieve herself, but she could not unfasten the belt securing her to the driving board. Shadows came as the sun dipped behind the imposing mountains that rose to block out the sky before her. The day grew cold and no longer felt so friendly. She began to cry.

The noise pierced Sylyth's lust. She looked down at Laeonus, who was laboring for breath beneath her. Saw his drawn cheeks, his hollowed eyes, the lines of his veins and arteries visible through parchment flesh.

No! She was doing the very thing that would doom her for certain.

She spread a palm over Laeonus' face. He fell instantly into a deep sleep. Dismounting, Sylyth—looking every bit the ripe young woman who had entered Frostwood instead of the weakened, wasted thing that had ridden out—sprang from the wagon. She collected and attended Aura, who shied from her as she always did, but still took the food and water she was given.

The vessel would be healthy for the spawn, which was all that mattered.

Fearing she had done irreparable damage to her last source of nourishment, Sylyth let Laeonus sleep until dawn. They were still days from the Fel Tarn; she would need to feed again. *He is young*, she told herself. *He will recover....*

He did, though he woke with lines etched in his forehead and around his eyes that had not been there before, and a sallow cast to his skin. "I think I'm catching whatever took you ill, Lady," he said.

"You will be fine," Sylyth assured him as they started off again. She would use him carefully tonight, she thought as she lounged in the wagon, which bumped and stuttered over the rocky terrain. The watchman would serve his purpose, just as the wizardling had served his and the vessel would serve hers.

Sylyth let her ebony gaze wander to the child, who was playing with the toys in the wood-carver's wagon. She hated the girl's innocence, though perversely that was the very thing that made her necessary. Still, it would be a pleasure to watch that light die in her, corrupted and devoured by the spawn.

Aura felt Sylyth's evil gaze upon her, but did not turn. Instead she hunched her shoulders defensively and threw herself all the harder into her play, making a knight in oaken armor pummel a doll in a pinewood dress.

79

It was the worst kind of hunt.

The track was easy—it followed the Sylvastrym, and the wagon left ruts in the pine-needled earth that even Artelo could have held to—but time was against them.

It always seems to be, Argentia thought.

Day into night they went on, riding long after the moon had risen to turn the river to a stream of silver. It was often well after midnight when they set their camp. They ate swiftly, slept hard: three, perhaps four hours. Brewed esp for breakfast and were off again.

They emerged from Frostwood on the cusp of an evening. The mountains ahead had all but swallowed the light. Their crags lunged up at the red sky like the jagged teeth of some gargantuan beast's petrified remains. To the north, the frosted shank of the Gelidian Spur peeled away in a long arc that Argentia knew would eventually descend to the beaches of the Sea of Sleet. The Sylvastrym followed that path away to its hidden source.

To the south, the Dragon Mountains ruled, bending away in the opposite direction of the Gelidians. Between was this vale whose eastern portions contained the Hills of Dusk and Frostwood. At its western end stood their destination: Cragyntor.

It was a mighty horn. An anomaly of the shaping of the earth had left it part of neither the Gelidians nor the Dragon Mountains. Tall and grim, it rose in mighty solitude, blotting out the horizon with its great granite escarpments.

Tomorrow or the next day would bring them across the jumble of breakland that made the scruffy collar between wood and mountain. On those crusty slopes, the fate of Artelo's daughter would be decided.

"Why Aura?" Argentia asked.

The huntress and the knight were at camp. They had ridden as far after sunset as they dared. The ground was now too dangerous for the horses to go without light.

"It needs her to...hold its spawn," Artelo said. He did not look up to meet Argentia's eyes as he spoke.

Argentia shook her head. "Not what I meant. Why *your* daughter? Why not another? Any child would do, if what Ralak explained to me of this thing is true."

She already knew the answer to this question, but she asked it to get Artelo talking. He had been brooding since Frostwood and Argentia thought that might be a very bad sign, particularly since they were shortly to confront a demon.

She remembered all too well the power of a demon, particularly on the mind. Under Ter-at's influence, she had nearly killed Artelo, believing him a traitor. The last thing she wanted was to face the succubus only to find the knight who should have been her ally suddenly an enemy.

"If you can't talk about it, if you don't want to, I'll understand," Argentia said.

"Will you?" Artelo raised his head and looked at her: Argentia, perfect as he had ever known her, all her hurts healed, all her pain behind her, triumphant once more, while he was left bereft. He felt the rage in him again. "No. I think you should hear this. There was a wizard, Pandaros Krite...."

When the words came, they were a torrent. Artelo spoke of taking Pandaros into his home and how, in his absence, the wizard had released the succubus that had killed Brittyn and taken Aura. "I might have stopped him," he growled. "But I wasn't there!"

Argentia had expected this. It was the same accusation Artelo had leveled at her on the beach. Before she could respond, Artelo railed on. The floodgates had broken in him, and all the emotions he had checked for weeks exploded.

"What kind of madman would treat with such a monster? Why? I'd like to wring the truth out of his scrawny neck! Damned wizard! Did you know I saved his life? A wagon he was trying to fix fell on the idiot. I pulled him free. I pulled— God! Why didn't I leave him to die! Why—"

Argentia placed a hand on the knight's knee. "Artelo." He jerked away from her, tears coursing down his face. She persisted. "Artelo, listen to me. Krite's gone. You have to accept that. You'll never know why he did this, unless this fiend knows, and even if it does, it would only lie." She paused. "And laying blame doesn't change what's past. Blaming me or yourself or anyone, it doesn't do any good. I know that's hard to hear, but—"

"What do you know of it?" Artelo spat.

"Too much," Argentia snapped, her temper finally flaring. "*Much* too much. You're not the only one who's lost someone they loved." Her eyes flashed at him in the firelight and Artelo had a vivid memory of standing in the throne room in Castle Aventar, wounded and exhausted from battle, leaning on Solsta while Argentia held Carfax in her arms, her husband bleeding out upon the marble floor....

"Holding to the past won't help get Aura back," Argentia said, her voice quieting. "So let it go."

Artelo did not answer. Rage had wrapped about him, invisible as aether, tangible as stone. Only he could rip its cloak away.

So silence stood between them. Argentia sipped her esp, which was cold and bitter. She tossed the unfinished contents into the dark and wondered how much Artelo hated her. *Doesn't matter. Just get his daughter back. Let the rest fall where it will, but don't fail her....*

"Does it ever go away?"

Argentia, drawn out of her thoughts, looked quizzically at Artelo. In the flickering light, he seemed very young and tired, his storm of emotion spent. "What?" she asked.

"The pain. After Carfax, how did you...."

Argentia nodded slowly, sadly. "It's part of letting go." *The hardest part*, she thought, remembering the ranger's ashes scattering on the wind above Castle Aventar.

"But I miss her so much!" Artelo blurted.

Argentia took him in her arms. He resisted for a moment, then relaxed, slumping against her. "She's not gone," Argentia said. "Letting go doesn't mean forgetting. Not ever. You'll always have her here." She placed her hand over his thumping heart.

Artelo wiped at his eyes and nose. "Help me get my daughter back. No matter what happens to me, promise me you'll get Aura out."

"I promise," Argentia swore.

80

The next day, they found the wagon.

They had passed the morning in silence. Artelo was grim. He had been long awake after Argentia had dropped into a light sleep. He knew the huntress was right, that he needed to let go of his rage and hatred, but he was afraid. Those emotions were pure and strong in him. He had clung to them since this ordeal had been thrust upon him; they had brought him this far, and he would hold them to the end. Until Aura was safe and Brittyn avenged.

That was why he had made Argentia promise to get Aura out. No matter what anyone said, he held himself responsible for leaving his wife and daughter. His intentions might have been good, but his family had paid dearly for them. He could not undo it, but he could set it to balance. *A life for a life....*

Riding beside the knight, Argentia was also quiet. Hers was the focus of the hunt's end. She knew it was near; could taste it in the chilly morning air over this desolate stretch of undulating, rocky earth and sparse trees that reminded her of the Heaths. So it came as little surprise to her when, somewhat short of noon, they crested a rise and saw the wagon standing beside a jumble of boulders in the last declivity of the borderland between forest and mountain. The horses were nearby, trying to graze on the few tufts of yellow grass poking out of the broken stone.

The sight galvanized Artelo. "There!" He spurred his horse, sending it hard down the incline. Pebbles sprayed and dust rose in its wake as it tried to keep its ironed hooves steady on the friable slope.

"Wait!" Argentia shouted. She half feared Artelo would spill his mount and kill himself in the fall, but as she clipped her low boots to the white stallion and followed him down, what she was mostly looking for was the ambush. The wagon was the perfect setting—and Artelo was riding right at it.

Artelo skidded his horse to a halt, shouting for Aura as he leaped down and threw himself into the back of the wagon, vanishing behind the canvas.

An instant later, his cry rang out

Oh no! Heedless of the danger to herself, Argentia vaulted from her horse and sprang into the wagon, her hand on the hilt of her katana as she ducked through the canvas, narrowing her eyes to hasten her vision's transition from light to dark.

Artelo was on his knees.

There was no one else in the wagon.

"What happened? Are you all right?" Argentia looked around for evidence of a trap: a tripline rigged to a crossbow, something of that nature. She found nothing.

Artelo held up a small object that once had been clean and white, but now was soiled with wear and travel.

A child's bootie.

"She was here," he said weakly. "Right here."

Argentia put a comforting hand on Artelo's shoulder. "We'll find her," she said, looking around the wagon again. There was wooden clutter almost everywhere, but her eyes were quickly drawn to the dolls. She picked one up. "Take heart," she said. "If she was playing with these, she is likely well enough."

Artelo took the wooden knight from Argentia. He turned it over slowly in his hand. "Do you think...."

"That she was thinking of her father?" Argentia smiled. "I know she was."

They exited the wagon, which showed them something of how the trio—they had seen the signs of the third who was accompanying the succubus and Aura as they tracked the wagon through Frostwood—had subsisted on simple foods and water (Artelo grew furious when he thought of Aura forced to eat the cured meats and dried fruits that were the staples of travelers) but little else of note, save the rattan pallet whose sheet was enseamed with the residues of much sweat and sex. Argentia hustled Artelo out of the wagon before he could begin to wonder if his daughter had been present during the bouts that produced those stains.

The knight paced, cracking the knuckles of his remaining hand while the huntress searched the rest of the camp, examining footprints and the remnants of the fire. Finally, after what seemed an eternity to Artelo, but was in truth a matter of well-spent minutes, she called him to her.

"Less than a day ahead."

81

They set all the horses loose.

Cragyntor rose before them. The mounts would be no good on the mountain's broken paths. Artelo had argued that they leave them with the wagon, but Argentia, remembering what D'Lyrian had told her, shook her head.

"What about the return?" Artelo asked, looking at her as if she had gone mad.

"We won't need them." She drew Ralak's silver disc from her pack. "This will see us back to your home."

Artelo looked at the disc skeptically. "If it doesn't work?"

"Then we'll find another way. Rime's not that far. We can get there on foot."

The matter settled, she patted the elf horse on its snowy neck and bid it be off. The stallion whickered, calling the wagon horses and Artelo's mount after it, leading them back up the slope. Argentia watched until the white mare had vanished; it was the most beautiful horse she had ever seen.

"Let's go," Artelo said.

"Not yet." Argentia opened her pack again and took out the esp. The pouch was almost empty, but she thought there was enough for what she intended. With Artelo scowling all the while, she brewed all the remaining esp, leaving one bean in the pouch, as D'Lyrian had instructed. When the drink was ready, she filled two spare skins with it. "For the road," she said. They had made up a good amount of time in their run through Frostwood, but they were still behind, and there was Cragyntor to contend with. "I don't think we'll be stopping again until this is over."

For nigh three full days and nights they battled the mountain.

They went by sun. They went by torch and moon. They went almost without rest, spurred by desperation, sustained by the cold esp.

They did not catch the succubus.

Each night, they had seen the glow of a campfire on the cliffside above them, but Cragyntor had checked them. Though they grew closer and closer, they were unable to make up all the distance.

Indefatigable, they carried on. The wind cut with the edge of winter, making their lungs ache behind their ribs. Their hands and knees were bloodied by slips on the treacherous slopes. Their legs and backs were sore with strain as they picked their way up and up.

Still the mountain held against them.

For nigh three full days and nights they battled the mountain.

Evening, the third day.

The vale and the forest were small and far below. The gathering dusk brought a sense of impending doom.

Argentia pulled herself up onto a shelf. Stopped.

Artelo started to ask her what she was about but she silenced him with a raised hand and pointed. The knight followed her gesture.

A plume of smoke rose from the mountainside just a shelf above them.

They had found their quarry.

Artelo rushed forward. Argentia grabbed him. "The wizard," she whispered fiercely. "Summon Ralak."

"No. Aura's there." Artelo tried to pull away. Argentia held him fast.

"We'll need his magic, Artelo. Call him. Now."

Her gaze pinned him like a hawk on a rabbit. Her tone cut through his impulse to race on ahead to his daughter. He swung his pack off his shoulder. Pulled out the oculyr.

And was buried by a shape of shadow and fangs and burning red eyes.

82

"It comes!" Sylyth gasped.

In the dark recesses of a cave high on the western slope of Cragyntor, the succubus lay in the Fel Tarn. Though the black water was only inches deep, its malevolent force could not be fathomed. Sylyth was propped on her elbows in the chill murk. In the cleft between her wide-splayed legs, swollen labia surrounded a slit full of the writhing darkness of a storm-torn night.

Another contraction rocked her like a punch in her belly. Her whole body quivered with the pain, sending ripples through the oily water that lapped about her, drawing the spawn toward the moment of its birthing.

Sylyth had been laboring almost since she had entered the cave. The initial contraction had struck so suddenly and unexpectedly that it felled her beside the Tarn. Laeonus had rushed over, his aversion to the place—for there was about the cave of the Fel Tarn a palpable air of evil—no match for his love of his lady. "God! Sylyth, are you all right?"

"Keep your puny god," Sylyth snarled, black eyes blazing. Shocked, Laeonus tried to recoil, but the succubus wrenched him down. She had reached the end of her patience with his fawning servility, and her need for him was no longer so great. She was far from human habitation, but once she was delivered of the spawn, she would be able to control her hunger.

She pinned him, her jaws gaping, her teeth sprouting into vampyric fangs—

—and stopped, hearkening to the voice that had guided her this far. The voice of

(shadow, chaos, Bhael-ur)

the Fel Tarn.

Remember thy foes, it said.

Sylyth had seen the light following through the dead of night, when she pretended to sleep beside the drained Laeonus. Her enemies were coming, she knew, but she had set the defenses of Cragyntor against them.

And if they pass those? the voice asked.

Sylyth's fangs receded. She stroked a hand down Laeonus' trembling jaw. Kissed him, slow and lingering, funneling her magic into him, wiping away his memory of the last moments. When she felt his tongue slip forward into her mouth, twining against hers with ardent urgency, she knew she had her gull once more.

She broke the kiss. "Sylyth," Laeonus moaned. She drew his head up and whispered into his ear.

A few minutes later she watched him walk back to the mouth of the cave. He made a fire from their fardel and set himself resolutely beside it. He would remain there, her last line of defense, and would attend to nothing he heard or saw behind him.

A second contraction took her then, spiking through her as if someone had given her intestines a violent twist. When she recovered, she went to the vessel, the final piece remaining to be arranged.

Aura shrieked and shied from her. Sylyth seized her roughly. "*Som-na,*" she hissed, stunning her with magic. Aura went limp.

Sylyth laid Aura near the edge of the Tarn, where the ground sloped slightly down to contain the black water. She stripped the child's clothes, then her own. She felt a third contraction coming. Sensed it would be a strong one. Moving quickly, she took the medallion of summoning from about her neck and draped it over Aura's head, laying the tarnished gold on her pink stomach. The child flinched, her small hands twitching, but she did not wake.

Sylyth took a step backwards and surveyed her work. All was in readiness. *Now, Bhael-ur, let it be delivered....*

Sylyth slipped down into the

(shadowaether)

water of the Fel Tarn. As she did, the expected contraction struck her breathless. All else but the labor ceased to matter. Darkness suffused her. She heard the choirs of torment howling to Bhael-ur: a cacophony of praise for Sylyth, mother of the Gate-Breaker.

Lost to the world, she poured all her strength into this one act. Hours passed as minutes in pulses of exquisite numbness and excruciating pain. It would not be much longer now. The next thrust, or the one after. She was so close....

Her eyes rolled back in the afterthroes of her most recent push. She panted, waiting with perverse eagerness for the pain to blossom in her again, giving her release.

Outside the cave, where evening was falling fast toward moonless night, the slopes of Cragyntor echoed with sudden howling.

83

The dark-wolves of Cragyntor had crept upon Argentia and Artelo with perfect, magical stealth, slinking along the path from gloom to gloom, stirring no stones, giving no sign of their approach until their final lunging charge—when it was already too late.

"Ware!" Artelo had time to shout as the lead wolf buried him beneath its greasy bulk. He fell hard, skidding down the slope, the wolf clinging atop him, snarling and snapping. The oculyr flew from his hand, bounced on the stones, and rolled away.

Pain tore through Artelo's shoulder as fangs sank deep in his flesh. He screamed, struggling wildly, slapping at the shaggy head. Its pelt was oily, repulsive. He got a thumb into the beast's red eye. It yelped, releasing his shoulder.

Snick! Artelo's wristcap dagger sprang from its sheath. He thrust hard with his wounded arm, stabbing deep.

Argentia threw herself flat. A second wolf sailed over her, skidded for balance, and then flung itself down the slope toward Artelo.

Argentia scrambled to her feet as a chorus of awful howling erupted. *Where the hell did they come from?* She had heard absolutely nothing, had no hint or sign of the wolves' approach, no feeling of being stalked. Even now it was hard to make out how many were rushing at her. *Two? Four?* She saw shapes like bleeding shadows with eyes like flickering rubies, and—

Oh shit!

There was one right on top of her. It seemed to have materialized out of the very gloom. Argentia fell backward beneath the wolf, her hands grabbing its throat, trying to keep its head at bay. The dark-wolf was slick and slimy, as if it had been soaking in some unnatural liquid.

She could not hold it.

The wolf's jaws gaped. Fetid breath and hot saliva sprayed Argentia's face. She thrashed wildly, straining to the last. The wolf scraped at her with its paws, trying to pin her in place for a killing bite. "No!"

A silver-black shape blasted the dark-wolf off her.

Argentia rolled to her knees. At first she thought it was another of the wolves that had turned on its own, but it was no wolf at all.

It was Shadow.

She heard the wolf yelp in pain and fear as Shadow fell upon it without mercy, ending its life with a mighty crunch of his jaws.

"Shadow!"

Growling with bass fury, Shadow wheeled to face the trio of dark-wolves slinking down the slope. They regarded Shadow balefully with their ugly, garnet eyes, raised their hackles, and chilled the air with snarls of warning.

Shadow was undaunted. Born on the Nordic tundra, he was larger, stronger, faster, and had seen worse terrors than the dark-wolves of Cragyntor.

Argentia was still trying to figure out where Shadow had even come from when he sprang past her and brought the fight to the three wolves. She rushed after him, whipping Lightbringer free of its sheath.

Too late.

Shadow and the wolves went over the edge of the cliff in a tangle.

Argentia screamed for him. Racing to the edge, she saw the mass of bodies still sliding and tumbling away into darkness, dislodging a shower of rocks in their wake. "Shadow— NO!"

Artelo grabbed her from behind. In the fading light Argentia could see the blood soaking his shoulder. His sword was out, stained with the black blood of the second dark-wolf. "Aura," he said.

Argentia nodded. There was no time to worry about Shadow, no time to recover the oculyr and summon Ralak.

They were on their own against the succubus.

Grinning, Argentia started running up the last switchback toward the cave of the Fel Tarn. Artelo was right beside her. They crested the ledge. Saw the cave. The campfire.

The Watchman.

"Artelo Sterling," Laeonus Castlebright said. "So you've come to meet the Harvester. How I prayed for this."

Artelo stopped and stared. *God— What happened to him?* Though this was surely the Watchman who had helped him in Byrtnoth, he was barely recognizable. His youth had gone gaunt, wasted as if some leech had been feeding off him. His eyes burned with raw hatred.

Then, from the black depths of the cave, came a noise that made Artelo forget the Watchman entirely.

"Uhnnnnn! *Bhael-ur tan ivl eb! Tan ivl eb!* It comes!"

There was a ghastly ripping sound.

And a child's scream.

84

Artelo froze at his daughter's cry.

"Die pig!" Laeonus screamed, his sword heliographing the light from the fire as he charged, swinging savagely at Artelo's head.

Swift as a lioness, Argentia glided forward, Lightbringer sweeping across to intercept the Watchman's blade. The echo of the parry rang across Cragyntor. "Go!" she shouted to Artelo.

Artelo ducked safely past the combatants and bolted into the cave.

"Back away," Argentia said, using her sword for leverage to turn Laeonus aside, positioning herself between the Watchman and the cave. She could sense the essential youth in him beneath his haggard appearance. *He's not even as old as Artelo....* "I've no wish to kill you, but I will if I must."

"I've...no wish to kill you," Laeonus said slowly, like a man waking. A clearer light resurfaced in his eyes for an instant. Then it was gone. "But you leave me no choice!"

He made a quick feint to the left. Attacked high and right. Argentia parried easily, gaining an opening she could have struck through were she twenty times slower with her blade. She did not counter. "Come to your senses!" she shouted. "That thing you're defending—you don't even know what it is!"

"I'll never let him hurt her again!" Laeonus redoubled his efforts, his only goal to get past this woman so he could kill Artelo. But his every blow was blocked, some almost before he could begin them.

"It's not even human!" Argentia shouted, still trying to reason with the Watchman, to break whatever spell he was under. "It's a demon. A succubus!"

"Liar!"

In the cave, Artelo bellowed something Argentia could not quite catch, but the urgency of it spurred her. *Enough of this nonsense....*

Laeonus attacked again: the same predictable pattern they taught in the Cadetery. It was basic swordplay, no match at all for Argentia's gifts. This time she not only parried, she sent his sword flying. As Laeonus glanced reflexively after the spinning blade, Argentia quick-stepped forward and smashed her elbow into his chin. His head snapped back and he went down like a puppet with its strings clipped.

As the Watchman hit the ground, Argentia spun and rushed into the cave.

85

Sylyth completed her labor with a final push. She felt as if someone had torn her entrails out, but the heavy plop she heard as the spawn spilled free of her was the most gratifying sound in her long ages of existence.

The spawn lay in the water between Sylyth's twitching legs. It was a hideous gelatinous creature that looked like some demented artist's interpretation of an octopus: a dome of half-melted gray tallow over an array of splashing tentacles. It had its mother's dead black eyes set in its bulbous head, and those eyes were hungry.

"Take the vessel," Sylyth gasped, flapping a hand weakly toward the shore of the Fel Tarn. Once the spawn entered the vessel, nothing else mattered. Even if her enemies somehow recovered the child, the spawn would grow within the human girl, and when the time was ripe....

The spawn scuttled forward on its whiplike appendages. Behind it, an umbilicus of black slime stretched back into Sylyth's festering womb. From this cord the spawn drew the strength to negotiate the shallow slope beyond the edge of the Tarn. The air of this world was frigid and choking, but it could sense the vessel was near, and inside the vessel was all the warmth and life and food it would need.

It slurched its way toward Aura. It would nest within the vessel, growing as the child grew. Eight winters, or ten, or thirteen, or twenty it would lurk there, until it was strong enough. Then the vessel would be shed like a cocoon and the spawn would be freed to perform its great task of breaking the Gate and bringing the demons upon Acrevast again.

None of that mattered in these first dangerous moments. The spawn knew only that it was cold and weak unto death. It stretched out a tentacle. Hooked Aura's small, bare ankle, dragging her down the rough slope and into the shallows of the Tarn.

Aura, still trapped in her dark sleep, screamed as the black waters lapped against her skin.

The spawn reared, tentacles flailing, seeking an orifice through which to enter the vessel. The smallest hole would do. A mouth, an ear, a nostril. The spawn would find an anchor and its pulsing, malleable body would shrink and slither in like smoke sucked through a pipe.

There! A tentacle probed Aura's mouth, prying at her lips. Such warmth—

"In Aeton's name you will not touch her!" Artelo roared.

His blade flashed up as he charged across the cave, but he could not strike for fear of hitting Aura. He kicked out instead, lashing his boot forward with all his rage, punting the spawn off of Aura. It sailed through the air, smacked into the cave wall, and fell in a splattered, thrashing heap.

Sylyth felt the fragile umbilicus knitting her to the spawn snap like a bowstring drawn too taut. Shock and disbelief stunned her. In a matter of moments everything had gone wrong. She did not know how the dark-wolves and her guardian had failed, only that they had.

Then her mind was overwhelmed by the keening of the spawn: a noise of dying.

Demonlight blazing in her black eyes, Sylyth raised Brittyn's body out of the Fel Tarn. Her magic slammed Artelo, raping his will. His sword dropped from his numb hand. He knew that the thing rising before him, black liquid sluicing from every ripe curve of its naked body was not his wife, yet he stood helpless. Molten lust burned through him, evaporating anger like water cast on coals. His entire world honed to the throbbing ache between his legs. Eyes wide, pulse hammering in his head and chest and groin, he saw her reaching for him, and could not wait for her touch: to mount her and be buried deep in her. *Oh Brittyn....*

Sylyth's hands fastened on Artelo, her talons sinking deep as she slammed him to the stones. He felt no pain, only desire. She crouched above him, Brittyn in all her springtime beauty, soaked as if she had just stepped from a bath, her mouth opening to kiss him, white teeth gleaming, growing—

"Hey, bitch," Argentia said.

The succubus looked up in surprise.

Lightbringer blurred the air. Burning with the deep elf-fire of its forging, the katana sheared through flesh, sinew, and cartilage as easily as it had the whetstone in Rime.

Sent Sylyth's head flying into the Fel Tarn.

86

Laeonus Castlebright could not even find the voice to scream as Argentia closed the last distance to Sylyth, her katana blazing like a white-hot torch. The Watchman had recovered from Argentia's elbow, but had gotten no more than a few paces into the cave when the huntress struck the deathblow.

Laeonus fell to his knees again, his mouth frozen in a silent cry as Sylyth's head traced an arc that seemed to take forever to reach its apogee and splash into the Tarn. Her lifeless body toppled at the edge of the strange black water.

No, God, please no, Laeonus thought, shaking his head. *No— It can't be...*

Pouring like smoke from the gaping stump of Sylyth's neck was a nightmare of writhing tentacles.

Not good.... Argentia thought as the true essence of the succubus loomed above the Fel Tarn. She had killed the body Sylyth inhabited and thus released the fiend. Her brilliant sword would be no use against such a thing as this. "Out!" she shouted.

Artelo, still dazed from the succubus' attack, rolled to his knees. Sylyth's voice bludgeoned his mind, pleading irresistibly: *Give me the vessel! The vessel!*

Argentia slapped him across the face. "Come on!"

Snapped free from the last of Sylyth's spell, Artelo snatched Aura out of the foul shallows of the Fel Tarn and ran, hunching low to protect his daughter.

The spawn's keening filled Sylyth's being. It was dying and she could not save it, for she had no tangible form to bear the vessel to it. There would be no Gate-Breaker, no Dark Queen Sylyth.

But there could be punishment.

The succubus lashed her tentacles. Bolts of dark magic hurtled into the fleeing huntress and knight. They hit the ground hard, shadowaether coursing through their bodies like lightning. Argentia fumbled her sword. Artelo lost his hold on Aura, who tumbled out ahead of him. The medallion sailed loose from around her neck. Rolled toward the mouth of the cave.

Argentia saw it. Ralak's words flashed in her memory. *Have to get it....*

But Sylyth had seen the medallion too, and with it a last, desperate chance. She waved her tentacles, pummeling Laeonus with her magic, wresting his mind to her control again.

Laeonus snared the medallion and looped it over his head. "Sylyth!" he cried. "Take me."

The medallion blazed an ancient bronze light. The shadow-shape of the succubus was sucked across the cave.

Argentia heard the Watchman cry out. Saw him vanish into the onrushing tentacled darkness, and the darkness vanish into him. For a moment she was not sure what had happened.

Then Laeonus looked at her and she saw the fathomless hate in those unnatural black eyes. *Really not good....*

Smiling savagely with her borrowed mouth, Sylyth moved toward Aura—

Shadow skidded into the cave. Growling furiously, his hackles bristling like a lion's mane, he set himself between the succubus and the child.

The succubus stumbled back, screaming in fear. In that instant, her hold on Laeonus slipped. His eyes cleared. "Kill me!" he shouted. He could feel the demon's appalling dark madness choking his will. *So strong....* "End it!" he gasped.

"The medallion!" Argentia shouted. She was too far away to reach the succubus in time. "Artelo!"

Artelo lurched to his feet. Charged the succubus.

Argentia lunged, snared Lightbringer, and flipped the katana into the air. Her throw led the knight perfectly. He extended his hand without breaking stride and grabbed the katana's hilt just as the tip speared into the ground ahead of him.

Vaulting over Aura and Shadow, Artelo swung Lightbringer at Laeonus Castlebright's chest.

CRACK!

The medallion of summoning exploded in a thunderclap flash that shook the cave of the Fel Tarn.

87

Argentia felt something hot and damp on her cheek.

Wha— She opened her eyes. "Shadow...." Groaning, she sat up. Her ears were ringing. "Come here." She pulled Shadow close, hugging the big dog tightly.

She knew nothing of how Shadow had scented her in Aventar and run wild in the castle. Ralak, playing one of his semi-prescient hunches, magically attuned the dog's senses to Cragyntor and let him loose. Shadow had made the journey west almost without ceasing, holding to a course as the crow flew, undeterred by hills and streams. He had picked up Argentia's scent in Frostwood and chased even harder, finally finding her upon the slopes of the mountain, where he made hard battle against the things that looked like wolves but were not.

At present, this tale was the farthest thing from Argentia's mind. In the slowdown after the rush of battle, it was wonderful to just hold Shadow, to feel his steady heartbeat, his panting breaths.

She pressed her forehead to his, blue eyes peering into gray. "You know I had it all under control, right?"

Drawing back, she looked around. Saw that it was over.

"Artelo, get up," she said, crawling over and shaking the fallen knight's shoulder.

Artelo snorted in a breath and came to. "Aura—" He sat up sharply.

Despite the mayhem that had raged around her, Aura lay asleep. Her skin was scraped and dirty from her jouncing across the cave floor, but she seemed otherwise unharmed. Artelo quickly rounded up her clothes, dressed her, and wrapped her in his cloak. Though he spoke to her constantly, he could not make her wake.

While Artelo tended his daughter, Argentia recovered her katana. Lightbringer had survived its encounter with the medallion of summoning unscathed. Of the unfortunate Watchman there was no sign; the explosion had obliterated his body.

Argentia pitied him. Seduced and used by the succubus, he had still tried to fight the demoness in the end. She was sorry they had not been able to save him, but she would make certain his sacrifice was not in vain.

She went to finish the spawn. Found it was already dead. As she watched, it melted away until it was no more than a stain upon the stones. *Go to hell*, she thought with no little satisfaction.

Wiping Lightbringer carefully clean, Argentia slipped her katana into its scabbard. "Ready?" she asked Artelo. He nodded. She pulled a couple brands from the campfire Laeonus had made. Handed one to the knight. "Then let's get out of here."

88

Navigating by torchlight, Argentia, Artelo, and Shadow followed the path away from the cave and stopped at the place where they had battled the dark-wolves.

Artelo set Aura down and tried to revive her. "Aura..." She was breathing regularly and appeared no more than deeply asleep, but he could not awaken her. "What's wrong with her?" he asked nervously.

"I don't know," Argentia said. She was wondering what had happened to the bodies of the wolves. There was no sign of the corpses, and something about their disappearance boded ill. "Maybe Ralak—"

"I don't want any more of his help," Artelo said indignantly.

"Don't be a jackass. If Aura's under some kind of spell, you'll need his help."

Artelo shook his head. Argentia was not sure if he was refusing the help of the Archamagus or the possibility that his daughter was languishing in magical chains. "I just want to get out of here," he said. "Use the disc, if it even works."

"In a minute." Taking her torch, Argentia told Shadow to stay.

"Where are you going?" Artelo asked.

"I have to check something. As soon as I get back, we'll leave." Artelo scowled, but Argentia ignored it. Went down the path, wary of the shadows, searching for something lost in the darkness.

A few minutes later, as she was climbing back up the slope, she heard Shadow growling, and Artelo's voice: "Gen! Get up here—now!"

She sprinted the last distance. Artelo was on his feet, his torch thrown before him, Aura cradled in one arm, sword in hand. Shadow was beside him, his silver-dark body tensed, lupine ears flat.

Advancing steadily down the slope above them were dozens of ruby eyes.

It seemed whatever dark force inhabited the Fel Tarn was not content to let them leave Cragyntor alive.

As the wolves howled mockingly, Argentia reached into her pack and found Ralak's disc. "To me!" she shouted.

Artelo and Shadow wheeled toward her. The wolves surged forward like a dark tide.

Argentia flung the disc down. A column of light blazed up. "Go! Go!" she shouted.

Artelo jumped into the aethergate. It started to close the instant he touched it. Shadow plunged in as if chasing a rabbit down a hole. The last things Argentia saw as she dove after Shadow were the red eyes of the leaping wolves.

The light sucked her down into aether-struck oblivion.

89

An instant later they were back in the world.

Argentia rolled hard, feeling wood beneath her, trying to focus through the dizzy nausea of teleporting. She scrambled to her feet as the afterglare of the aethergate faded, fearing the wolves had followed them.

There was only darkness.

No wolves.... Gasping, Argentia dropped to her knees. Relief washed over her. With it came laughter. They had done it: beaten the succubus, rescued Artelo's daughter, escaped from Cragyntor....

Shadow barked. Argentia called him to her. Heard the clicking of his nails on a wooden floor as he padded over in the darkness. She draped her arm about his strong neck. "Artelo?"

A groan. Then: "Yeah."

"Got a light?

Another groan. Then: "Yeah. Just a minute." Footsteps in the dark. A thump and a scrape as he bumped something. "God damn it." A moment later the soft light of a lamp bloomed in the cottage.

The mate to Ralak's silver teleport disc lay on the floor, inert and dull, its magic spent. Argentia stood and looked around. The cottage was small, quaint, and neat. Artelo was lighting other lamps; Aura was still safely tucked against his bloodied shoulder. "Let me put her down," he said.

Argentia followed him into another room, where a child's bed stood low to the ground. Artelo pulled down the covers and laid Aura gently in the bed, then drew the blankets back up again. "Please wake up," he whispered. "Please, pumpkin. Wake up." With tears in his eyes, he kissed her forehead.

Aura stirred.

Woke.

She blinked sleepily, her mouth opening and closing. Her eyes focused on Artelo. "Da!" She struggled free from the covers and reached up to him. He fell forward, a shuddered gasp escaping him as he held her as tight and close as he could.

Argentia looked at Aura. This was her first chance to really see Artelo's daughter. She was beautiful, with blonde hair, bright gray eyes, and plump cheeks that dimpled when she smiled.

Argentia smiled as well. Then she quietly left the room.

With an effort, Artelo pulled himself together. Lifting up off the bed, he looked down at Aura, stroking her head. "You're home," he said. "You're safe, and Da'll never let anything happen to you again. I promise."

Aura nodded earnestly. "Bad Lady's gone, Da," she said. "Mama told me."

Artelo was speechless. He had not even begun to consider how he was going to explain to Aura that Brittyn was dead, and now this. It was happening too fast. He was not ready. Did not know what to say.

"Pumpkin, Mama's...gone away," he whispered, his voice breaking. He felt tears burning down his face, all the pain of his loss springing up in him again. "She's...."

Aura smiled. "Mama's with the light," she said. "I see her in my dweem."

Artelo's mouth trembled. He tried to hold his emotions in rein, but this was too much. "Oh. Oh, Aura...." He folded his daughter in his arms again and wept.

90

"How is she?" Argentia asked when Artelo emerged.

"Sleeping." As if on cue, he yawned himself. Though the prospect of facing his bed without Brittyn beside him left him feeling hollow, such an exhaustion had come over the knight that he thought he might manage to sleep.

"And how are you?"

He shrugged. Rubbed his bloodied shoulder. "I'll live," he answered. It was the only honest reply he could make. Argentia sensed that and nodded. The knight had a lot of healing to do, and the wounds he had taken in battle were likely the least of it.

"Good. You have much to live for." She moved to the door. "Remember that."

"You're leaving?" Artelo asked, surprised.

Argentia nodded. "I have some unfinished business. Sooner begun, sooner done."

Artelo knew from her tone and the cold light in her cobalt eyes that he would get no more from her on the subject.

"Keep this." Argentia pulled the oculyr from a fold in her elf cloak. It had rolled a goodly way down the path of Cragyntor and fetched up against a clutch of boulders, but its magical glass was not so much as chipped by the misadventure.

"Why?" Artelo asked. It was clearly what Argentia had gone looking for before the wolves attacked, but he did not understand her reason for leaving it now.

"I took it in case we needed to help Aura," she said.

"She's fine, thank Aeton."

"Yes, but someone still needs to tell Ralak what happened."

Artelo folded his arms. "You can do that," he huffed.

"I can. But you should." She set the oculyr on the table. "Shadow." The dog trotted up. Argentia opened the cottage door.

"Argentia." She turned back. "Thank you," Artelo said.

"Thank *you*," she said, still mindful that Artelo's words on the beach had helped spark her own recovery. "You're a true friend." She hugged him, careful of his injury. "If you ever have need, anytime, anywhere..."

"I will call," he said.

"Take care of yourself. Aura, too. She's a treasure."

"I know."

Argentia stepped out into the full and star-dusted dark. Artelo closed the door behind her, but her parting words drifted through to him anyway: "Get that shoulder fixed...."

91

Artelo sat at his table. He had finally cleaned and bound his shoulder. After checking on Aura and finding her sleeping peacefully, he had come to face this last task.

I don't want to....

Nonetheless, he knew Argentia was right. Sighing resolutely, he waved a hand over the oculyr.

The mist in the orb thickened, then cleared to reveal Ralak at his desk. The moment he saw Artelo, the Archamagus rose swiftly and thrust a hand out, calling his staff to him, ready to teleport.

"No need," Artelo said. "It's done."

Ralak furrowed his brow. "What do you mean? Why didn't you summon me?"

"We lost the oculyr for a while," Artelo said.

"You lost—" For one of the rare times since Artelo had known him, the Archamagus looked genuinely perplexed.

"Does it matter? I told you, it's over. All of it."

"Your daughter?"

"Safe."

Ralak nodded. "I am most glad. And the succubus?"

"Dead."

"And the medallion?"

"Destroyed."

"You are certain?"

Artelo nodded. Ralak exhaled a long breath.

He's more relieved about that than Aura, Artelo thought, the rage welling yet again in his heart. "That was all you cared about all along, wasn't it? Your precious medallion. I could have died. Argentia could have died. Aura could have died, so long as that damned thing was destroyed. Right?"

"You are talking nonsense, Sir Sterling," Ralak said irritably. "Where is Lady Dasani."

"Gone."

"Gone? Gone where?"

"I don't know. She just left. And unless you have any more questions for me, I'll be going too." His tone was biting, caustic.

Ralak was silent for moment. Then he said: "Listen to me. Whatever you may think, I—and certainly the Crown—prized *nothing* more highly than the safe return of your daughter." He saw Artelo's doubt and his eyes flashed. "Believe me or not, as you will, but we did all we could to aid in her rescue and we will do whatever else we may to help you now."

In the depths of his heart, Artelo did believe the Archamagus. But belief and acceptance were lands far apart for him. Someday, perhaps, when he had reconciled fully with himself, he would come to put his anger at Ralak and Solsta aside. Until then, he could see only one course.

"There is something," he said.

"Yes?"

"Leave us alone," Artelo said.

Before the Archamagus could reply, Artelo drove his wrist-cap down onto the oculyr. Even the magic of the glass could not withstand such a direct assault, and the sphere shattered on the table.

Artelo stared at the pieces for a moment. Then, sighing, he fetched the broom and dustpan and swept up, careful to gather every last shard lest Aura should cut herself in the morning.

92

Far to the west, the cave of the Fel Tarn stood in darkness.

The campfire had burned out. The survivors were gone. Only the body that had belonged to the succubus remained, and it was this headless shape that a dark wave rose over and dragged away from the edge of the pool where it had fallen.

The body floated on the surface for a time. Then, amid slow-bursting bubbles, it sank out of sight beneath black waters that were perhaps not so shallow as they appeared.

93

One month after leaving Artelo's cottage, Argentia was back in Harrowgate.

She did not intend to remain long. *Just long enough....*

Her first business was at the *Reef Reaver*.

Most of her crew had dispersed to the various dockside inns. That was fine. She was not looking to sail. She had ceded use of the vessel to the Crown; it was a pirate hunter now, though it had remained in port under Ralak's orders after its return from Elsmywr. Argentia spoke to the few men who chanced to be on board, took what she needed, and left Shadow.

Her affairs in Harrowgate this day were her own.

Her next stop was the Mast and Nest.

She opened the door to the inn where she had stayed during her short partnership with the Harvester's Gryphons. The majordomo, a thin man who reminded Argentia of Ikabod, handed a key to a young couple in line ahead of her and then turned to Argentia. "How may I help you, Lady?"

"You had a murder here. The Peregrine Suite, wasn't it?" All the rooms in the Mast and Nest were named for birds.

"Yes, Lady."

"Is it available?"

"It is." The majordomo could hardly believe he had heard correctly. The suite where the murder had taken place was the inn's finest, yet even after it was completely refurbished, it had stood empty. Those patrons the majordomo tried to place there recognized the name and flatly refused to enter. After several months of this, he had given up trying.

"I'd like to buy it."

The majordomo nodded. He did not believe in ghosts or haunts, so the idleness of the suite had been a source of personal and professional irritation. He was not about to let the opportunity to remedy that slip past. "For how many nights, Lady?"

"All of them."

"Pardon?"

"All of them," Argentia repeated. "I want to buy that suite. Name the price."

The majordomo was stunned. "I.... This is highly irregular. I will have to consult the owners."

"Do whatever you need to do."

Matters were quickly arranged. Argentia barely paid attention to the price; she had more wealth at her disposal than she could spend in eight lifetimes.

She paid the deposit with coin she had taken from the *Reef Reaver*, arranged for delivery of the balance on the next of her ships bound for Harrowgate, and took the keys.

Outside the door, she hesitated for a moment, memories rising: The sweep of her katana in the assassin's deadly hands. The spray of hot blood from Vartan's neck. The water in the tub where they had been making love turning hideously pink. Vartan's severed head bumping against her leg....

Enough.... She drew a deep breath. Went in.

There were no ghosts.

She had already avenged Vartan, but the thought of people using this suite as if nothing had happened offended her. A brave man had died here. She did not know what had happened to his body—she supposed the Gryphons had taken it, and wondered briefly if they blamed her for Vartan's death—so she would make these rooms a monument to him.

She crossed a suite that looked nothing like she remembered and entered the bath chamber. Stood before the tub. It was new as well, but she did not think that mattered. "Be at peace," she whispered.

She locked the room behind her. Left the Mast and Nest.

Threw the keys down the first sewer grate she passed.

There was still time to kill, so she went shopping. She knew the stores in Harrowgate well. Found everything she was looking for and carted the purchases to the *Reaver*.

On her way to find a place for dinner she passed a pawnshop. Glanced in the window.

No way...

There beside the clutter of used weapons, cheap jewelry, and dusty curios, were her beloved boots, presumed lost with the rest of her belongings from the Mast and Nest. She recognized them instantly, the battered black leather unmistakable to her: she knew every scrape, cut, and scuff on them. Paid and pulled them on right in the shop.

Her lucky boots. A good sign.

She ate alone. Purchased some information along with her dinner. Drank a mug of caf. Watched the sun set through the tavern window.

Went hunting.

Merec Quicksilver had always believed his name had determined his profession. He had been born to be a thief, he said, and he excelled at it. Harrowgate was the fourth major city in Teranor he had worked. No Watchman had ever come near to catching him, nor had any guildmaster's assassin been able to find and kill him for stealing on controlled streets.

His secret was his speed.

Merec never wasted any time when he took a pigeon. If they did not resist, he robbed them and vanished (he always had escape routes planned ahead of time—that was another of his tricks). If they resisted, he knifed them. No threats, just the flash of a blade.

After all, it was as easy to rob the dead as the living.

Tonight's pigeon was a fat noble who had chosen a poor shortcut through a shadowy alley near Harrowgate's famous brothel, the Mermaid's Tail. He was resisting.

Merec's knife flashed at the noble's ample gut—

A hand caught the thief's arm, spinning him around.

"Nice hat," a woman said. Yanking Merec's fedora down over his eyes, she punched him in the face. The thief went reeling into a heap of trash.

"He— He tried to k-kill me," the noble said, pointing at the thief.

"Stop blubbering and get out of here," the woman said, stepping from the shadows.

The noble stared at her, confused by her strange attire. "But—"

"Will you just get out!"

Yelping, the noble ran.

"You can't do that," Merec said, disbelief and anger in his voice as he rose from the trash, wiping at his bleeding nose. "No one does that to Merec Quicksilver."

He sprang for her, knife slashing. The woman slipped aside. They circled: silhouettes in the broken moonlight.

"I'm going to give you one chance," the woman said. "Surrender."

Merec laughed. The figure moving opposite him, a black scarf wrapped around her face and head, looked familiar but he could not place from where. The hilt of a sword poked past the curve of her hip; she made no move to draw it even as he menaced the air between them with his knife. "Who sent you?" he demanded.

"Lord Karsay."

"Never heard of him." Merec laughed again. The woman had caught him by surprise, but he knew he could take her. "What, he somebody got his purse snatched by Quicksilver?"

"Lord Erol Karsay," the woman said. "You robbed him, yes. After you killed him and his wife. I watched it happen."

Merec's eyes narrowed. "I remember you," he hissed.

"Do you?" Her voice was ice.

"Cut you up," the thief warned. "Cut you bad."

The woman beckoned with one hand.

Merec triple-feinted—left-right-left—and went straight in for her chest, thrusting the last distance like a fencer. It was his best attack: it had never failed him.

There was the familiar sound of a blade striking flesh.

Half of Merec's arm dropped to the ground.

The thief stared stupidly at the severed limb. The woman faced him, her katana poised beside her, dripping blood onto the alley.

"My arm…" Merec understood that she had struck him off her draw, but he could not fathom how. No one was that fast. *No one….* "You…."

The pain came, not only in the stump of his spurting elbow, but a strange fire in his chest. He clutched his remaining hand to his torso, where her reverse strike had unseamed him from shoulder to hip.

"Oh hell…." Merec crashed to his knees. "Who…are you?" he gasped as he toppled over.

The woman unwound the black scarf from her head. Dropped it on the dead thief.

"Argentia Dasani."

Epilogue

Dawn.

She stood once more before the sea. The last of the accounts weighted against her had been settled. The scales of duty were balanced again.

More importantly, the scales of her spirit were true once more.

Mouradian had stolen her form. He could not duplicate that which made her truly herself. That was why his army of simulcra had been ultimately ineffectual. No magic mirror could take her heart, her will, her conscience, just as no fire could burn them away.

She knew that now, wholly and completely. She had returned here only to make her final peace with it.

She bent her gaze across the gray water. Somewhere past the gilded horizon was the Emerald Island of Elsmywr. Mouradian's tower was a ruin now, blasted by dragonfire. Destroyed.

She remained.

"You lose, wizard," Argentia said.

Walked away.

Printed in the United States
By Bookmasters